I0766929

# THIS CITY IS EMPTY

Rovshan Abdullaoglu

BookLand
press

Published by BookLand Press Inc.
15 Allstate Parkway
Suite 600
Markham, Ontario L3R 5B4
Canada
www.booklandpress.com

Printed in Canada

Library and Archives Canada Cataloguing in Publication

Title: This city is empty / Rovshan Abdullaoglu.
Other titles: Bu şəhərdə kimsə yoxdur. English
Names: Abdullaoğlu, Rövşän, 1978- author.
Description: Translation of: Bu şəhərdə kimsə yoxdur. | Translated from
the Azerbaijani.
Identifiers: Canadiana 20240451112 | ISBN 9781772312515 (print)
Subjects: LCGFT: Novels.
Classification: LCC PL314.A33 B813 2024 | DDC 894/.3613—dc23

# Table of Contents

# THE GREEN BENCH: WHERE IT ALL BEGAN

*Many have to pay for actions that they were not brave enough to take.*

~ Wiesław Brudziński

"Hey, do you recognize him?" The tall, broad-shouldered boy with an athletic build turned to his friend who was walking down the road beside him.

"No, who is it?" his companion asked, scrutinizing a bearded man of medium height walking in front of them, dressed in a black jacket and baseball cap.

"You really don't recognize him? He's definitely someone you know. That's the legendary college quarterback Willie Owen."

"Willie Owen? The NCAA champ and MVP, 'Willie Atom'? No way. Willie Owen's in Houston?"

The friends, who were wearing bomber jackets, sped up to close the distance between them and the middle-aged man walking ahead of them. As they passed by, they glanced sideways to examine him.

"There's no way. That's not Willie Owen," his friend said.

"Yeah you're right. Willie Owen is a bigger, stronger guy and much better looking."

"Yeah. Can't you see this poor dude can barely drag himself along? There's no comparison," said his friend, shaking his head.

"But he really looks like Willie from behind."

His friend turned around. "Hey you! Con man!" He wadded up his hamburger wrapper and tossed it at the unknown man. "Guess who we took you for?"

The friends walked on, laughing, and the unknown man of medium height watched them go with a feeling of frustration. He walked on a bit farther, then meandered into a park on the right side of the road. He slowly approached a green bench and took a seat.

♦　♦　♦

One of the angels watching over everything from the heavens said to another, "Humans are so stupid that they knowingly let chances for glory slip through their fingers."

The other said, "Humans are creatures that can't take their eyes off doors that are closed to them and thus never notice the ones that are open."

"People want to live through their emotions, not their reason. And when living through their emotions becomes unbearable, they suffer."

"An understanding of others begins first of all with understanding yourself."

"What is man ignorant of, and what, more than anything, does he not believe in?"

"Probably the extent to which his power is unlimited."

"I really do not understand these people at all," said the first angel, appalled by the humans' behavior.

"To understand people, you have to be a human. There's no other way. And there's no way for one person to understand another, besides standing in his shoes. And to know himself, a person has to recognize who he is. Anyone who has lost his footing is doomed to loneliness and suffering throughout his life."

The first angel said, "But people aren't honest with themselves, so they shouldn't complain that they lack any understanding of themselves."

"People like to talk about happiness. But they don't realize that their greatest happiness is that they came into this world as human beings. They could have been created as an inanimate stone, an immobile tree, or an unaware animal."

Another angel chimed into the conversation, "Why do we want to change this man's thoughts and destiny? A person is a person, along with his mistakes, sins, and great deeds."

"That's a real pity. This person might never rise again after his fall. There are spiritual traumas from which it is very difficult to recover, and sometimes it can be impossible."

"Is that what our God meant when he said, 'Indeed, I will make upon the earth a successive authority'? Over these helpless people who are so weak and who surrender so quickly, who live meaningless lives and make war amongst themselves?[1]"

And at that moment God said, "Indeed, I know that which you do not know.[2]"

---

[1] Al-Bagarah, 30, The Quran

[2] The previous verse

# A MAN AGGRIEVED BY LIFE

*The biggest lesson I've learned is that if you have all the fresh water  you want  to drink and all the food you want to eat, you ought never to complain about anything.*

~ Eddie Rickenbacker

Willie Owen was melancholic by nature. Often sad, overly impressionable, solitary and shy, he was still very attentive to others, unable to offend or even raise his voice to anyone. The opinion of others meant a lot to him. Willie constantly needed the support of his family, often feeling guilty even for things that had nothing to do with him. He could not build relationships, which is why he had no friends despite the great desire to find someone to whom he could grow close. Trust did not come easily to him, but once it got a foothold, it soon became complete, like the trust of a child. The slightest injustice had such a profound effect on him that he did not dare let anyone near for fear of betrayal.

Several times Willie had been sent packing from a job because did not get along with his colleagues. He was in no way a troublemaker, but he always had difficulties interacting with people.

Willie was of average height with a round face and broad forehead. His small eyes were a bit puffy, like someone who had just woken up. He wore a beard and combed his hair back. His constantly pensive expression made his face look sad. Although he had put on a little extra weight, those added pounds could not completely hide his muscular frame. He had long arms like a basketball player's and thick wrists, which he had inherited from his father.

Willie had been an active rugby and football player at school. The teams he played for won high school and college championships, and the local papers frequently published articles about him. He had an athletic build typical for his chosen sport: a neck almost as wide as his head, large hips, and big calf muscles — all of which were mementos of his former days of glory.

In football Willie was famous for his flawlessly executed deep passes as well as his furious sprints down the field, both of which regularly scored touchdowns. At those moments, he was moving with such speed that it was easy for him to knock down any opponents in his way. His ability to cut left and right, and the way he could hit with his shoulder from a crouch and nimbly stay on his feet, made him fundamentally different from other players. From his blow, his opponent flew into the air and then fell onto his back amid the delighted screams of the public. Willie looked like he was jumping on a trampoline during the games. Several times he was voted MVP for his ability to carry the offense on both his high school and college teams.

But before Willie won these honors, he didn't play so well. His precise passes, explosive running, and ability to read the plays prompted the coaches to make Willie a quarterback. But he had felt more confident in the background and was badly affected by his new leading position. As before, he made his way to the opponent's end zone, but at the last moment, he'd look for a teammate and hand off the ball, giving up the chance to score a touchdown himself. Sometimes he'd get lost in the most decisive moment. Despite the coaches' attempts, Willie couldn't help himself. Once again, he became a running back.

Everything changed when Brendan came to see his son play. He did his best to support him and gradually even began to postpone appointments so as not to miss the games. His opinion meant the world to Willie. Now, it did not only matter to him that his team won, it also mattered that his contribution was visible. To Willie, his father was a hero. To attract his attention, he had to distinguish himself. Handing off the ball to another player at the crucial instant wouldn't do anymore. Now, he was making touchdowns himself, bringing his team points.

After that, a new era dawned in Willie's athletic career. He was switched from a running back to a quarterback again. Willie put all his tricky moves, running speed, and instinctive sense of opposing tacklers' intentions on display to lead the offensive attack.

He also possessed ideal physical qualities for the game: long arms, powerful muscles, and brawny legs. These were genetically-inherited qualities. His lack of height did not in any way prevent Willie from demonstrating his beautiful game. In many cases, once Willie got hold of the ball, he would knock down the opposing players one by one as he ran down the field. Not even opposing players with a height and weight advantage over him were an obstacle. Even when he had the chance to outrun his opponents, sometimes he preferred to bring them down. Willie did all this for his dad because Brendan really liked that maneuver.

"Son, you're doing great! You're destroying their defense like a bowling ball slamming into the pins! How did you send that big hulking number ninety-three flying? Not to mention ninety-six! God almighty! You caught him by the leg and tossed him over your shoulder like he was nothing but a little bird!" Brendan couldn't hide his delight. He tried to never miss a single one of his son's games.

Willie's high school team went undefeated and was ranked first in the state. At a stadium that seated ten thousand spectators, his teammates hoisted Willie onto their shoulders and circled the field. This sight filled Brendan with pride. Those were the most wonderful days of Willie's life. And at that moment, Willie had eyes only for his father. Holding the championship trophy aloft and looking for his father in the crowd, he wanted to say, "Dad, I did this all for you."

After graduation Willie was very happy to be recruited by his first-choice college. Willie did not put a lot of effort into his classwork and spent all his time training or practicing, thus helping his team win a lot of games in his first season. By his sophomore year they were runners-up in the NCAA national championship. And two years later their team won the NCAA championship in a stadium that seated almost one hundred thousand fans. Finally, Willie got drafted into the National Football League by the five-time Super Bowl champs the Dallas Cowboys.

Although every football player dreams of playing in the NFL, for some reason that even Willie himself did not understand, he turned down this opportunity. When asked about it, he simply said that he didn't want to. But of course, the answer was not so simple. Much later, Willie discovered the answer to this question for himself. But at that moment, only one thing was clear — he felt a profound emptiness inside of him. This was quite a distressing time in Willie's life because, right as he was about to receive his invitation to play in the NFL, his parents divorced. They hadn't been getting along very well, even when Willie was enjoying his greatest triumphs. The never-ending family squabbling, his mother's occasional departures from their home and then returns, plus his father's periodic absences at night had all begun to seem normal. Despite everything, Willie went on with his everyday life. He went to class, continued attending practice regularly, and often went out with friends.

But during those years, although Willie was in the middle of the family spats, he did not feel lonely or helpless. He knew that he had a family, and he knew that even if his parents never stopped arguing, they still loved him very much. At least that's what Willie thought. After the divorce, Willie's father moved to Houston, and living with his mother became unbearable. When Willie's father told him, "You're all grown up now, and you can handle things by yourself," that was the moment when he truly began to feel alone. Whatever his parents had been like, they had at least been there for him, but now he was left on his own.

This feeling of loneliness never left Willie, not at the festive family table, nor during a picnic with friends, nor even when holding a trophy and listening to the applause of fans. But now loneliness was swallowing Willie's whole life, like a stream of water destroying a dam.

In the end, Willie let slip the one big chance that could have changed his life. Our lives are not built on theories, but on our actions. In life it doesn't matter in the least what you are, what you think, what you want, what you're capable of, or that you're a "good person." What seems to matter in life is only what you're doing. Willie, like most people, lived his life as if he had no control over it. He was walking his narrow path, head down, and had no idea that he had so many different choices—to blame himself or others for his failures, to take responsibility or to avoid it. He didn't know that a change in attitude would change his decisions and his life.

Willie had seen his share of troubles in his life. The hardships he had endured had clouded Willie's already pessimistic philosophy of life and had snuffed out the fire in his belly.

Some time later, after his father moved to Houston, Willie's mother got married for the second time. She talked to Willie on the phone from time to time. Eventually even those calls stopped. But Willie kept waiting. He consoled himself by thinking *probably her new husband won't let her*. In time, his mother, like his father, faded into nothing more than a ghost from the bitter, painful pages of his childhood. By then Willie had grown used to solitude. He had no expectations of anyone because he didn't believe anyone even thought about him. His life experiences taught him to distrust others and reinforced his negative preconceptions of people.

After he graduated, Willie went to work for a while in Dallas. That was his hometown, where he had been born. He frequently moved to other cities for work. Then he went to Houston, the city his father had moved to when he had walked out on his family. But by the time he got to Houston, his father had already passed.

## SOMETIMES INSIDIOUS INTENT
## BEARS EXCELLENT FRUIT

*Bad intentions deprive us of grace.*

~ Ali ibn Abi Talib

Monroe Anderson was a famous banker and cotton merchant from Tennessee. The company, which he had founded with his half-brother, had, by and by, increased its turnover and joined the world trade. At that time, the state highly appreciated the enterprises that participated in social projects; they were given all sorts of concessions and tax breaks. Anderson decided to take advantage of this situation and created a charitable foundation with an initial budget of three hundred thousand dollars, named simply the Anderson Foundation. At the time of Monroe Anderson's death, the Foundation's budget had grown to nineteen million dollars.

Two years after Anderson's death, the state of Texas needed half a million dollars to build a cancer hospital and research center. The Anderson Foundation took on the expense. This is how the Anderson Medical Center was formed and gradually developed.

In 2011, the Sheikh Khalifa bin Zayed Al Nahyan Foundation donated a hundred and fifty million dollars to the Anderson Center, which led to a new stage in the development of the medical center.

It is the intentions of a person that are rewarded by fate. One's good intentions serve one well. Insidious intentions, on the other hand, will not allow one to use the fruits of one's work, even if they are excellent.

Looking through this prism at some events and their consequences, you feel the presence of a single goal and secret plan in the universe. It's as if we were fulfilling this plan despite ourselves. We're being directed toward hidden targets. Many things happen even if we don't want them to. But if you don't resist and instead become a voluntary participant of this plan, its benefits will affect you. As the wise men say: if you have a fortune and don't spend it on good deeds, then life will force the fortune out of your hands.

That's what happened to Anderson too. He was forced to create something that was of use to others, not to himself. This medical center, where thousands of lives were interwoven, was located in Houston, Texas, a rainy city where Willie had been thrown by the wind of change. This most densely populated area in the US contains many research centers, and one of them is our "city of angels" — the Anderson Cancer Center.

# WHY MD ANDERSON?

*Chance is perhaps the pseudonym of God when he does not want to sign.*

~ Anatole France

For about a year, Willie had held down a job as an orderly at the MD Anderson Cancer Center. Although he was making more money than in his previous work, he still felt somehow dissatisfied, though he didn't know exactly why. *The money's good, and the work's not diffi-cult. So why am I frustrated again? Why am I discontented?* he repeatedly asked himself.

During the year, he was offered jobs with better salaries and growth opportunities, but Willie did not accept any of them. Willie felt more comfortable at MD Anderson than anywhere else. The emptiness inside him was at least partially filled there. But he was still unhappy.

The human soul is not subject to material laws. Willie's inner world contained all the emotions and events he had ever experienced. His soul was like abandoned land. This deserted place once had contained houses and gardens; many wanderers had passed through these roads, many had stayed here for a while. All this had happened by and by. From the outside, you can only see fragments of all these events. But there was no time in Willie's inner self, like in all spiritual worlds. Everything that had ever happened was accumulating in one place, in one reality. Emotions and impressions that had gathered at different points in life were confusing him mentally. Willie's past cast a shadow over his present and future. He tried to make informed decisions, but his hidden feelings and impressions tended to play a crucial subconscious role. The experience might be forgotten, but not the conclusions, be they right or wrong. One who has suffered a severe accident will never forget the fear, horror, torment, despair, and hopelessness. If it was a car crash, this person will forever be afraid of getting into a car, afraid of both enclosed spaces and wide paths. Looking into your past, you can always see that only the most vivid impressions are preserved by memory. You remember the most joyful and sad events: there is failure, hatred, pain, helplessness, anxiety, loss, fear, disappointment—and these are all the opposing positive feelings. If you are very sensitive to the world around you, something new is built or grown in your soul every day. Sometimes it is a beautiful garden of happy emotions; sometimes an arid desert.

Willie's difficult condition was a bitter consequence of his past, with which he could not reconcile.

At MD Anderson, Willie was responsible for the general cleanliness of the rooms. Every morning, he checked them all, asked the patients how they were feeling, aired out the rooms, kept the windows, floors, and beds clean. When he entered the ward, he would usually focus entirely on his work. He rarely spoke to the doctors or hospital staff.

After finishing work each day, he changed his clothes as usual and quickly departed from the clinic. As was his custom, he went for a stroll after leaving the hospital. Stretching his legs a bit, he crossed the road and turned toward a nearby park. Willie always liked to sit and think there, seated on a wooden bench that had been painted green. The park was down a small hill to the right of the main road. To get there you had to zigzag down a stone staircase that was about three yards wide. The shadows of tall trees lay across these stone stairs, and that autumn, their golden leaves lay all around. The stairs led to a wide, open space carpeted with green grass. Benches were positioned around the perimeter.

He headed toward his bench. It was shielded by the broad trunks of tall trees, and for this reason, Willie did not at first notice the two young people sitting there. He wanted to turn around, but then he changed his mind and sat down on another bench a little farther away and leaned back.

# PEOPLE ARE RARELY ALONE
# BUT THEY ARE OFTEN LONELY

*Love is . . . the principal means of escape from the loneliness which afflicts most men and women throughout the greater part of their lives.*

~ Bertrand Russell

Sometimes you want to be alone. You just don't want anyone around. But during those moments, your thoughts can badger you like an uninvited guest.

*Our thoughts and dreams are all so ordinary and pointless.* Willie thought of himself and everyone else as consumers of these cheap thoughts. Everyone's lives, like those thoughts, became empty, pointless, and ordinary. *We destroy everything we touch, including our thoughts.*

*I am often visited by sad, pointless thoughts. And like always, I try to find some point to them. I also search for some kind of meaning in what's happening to me, around me, and in my life. Why should you look for meaning in life? Maybe the meaning of life is just to live a monotonous existence: to get up early in the morning, go to work, come home at night tired, and go to bed. And then do it all again the next day . . ."*

Willie glanced around indifferently. A mother and child were walking past him. The boy was dragging his feet, and she was practically jerking him along by the arm. "I already told you I'd buy it," said the mother, pulling her son along behind her without a backward glance as he dug his heels into the ground.

"But you always say that," said the sobbing child, clearly familiar with words he had already heard many times.

"A world filled with false promises, betrayals, and empty hopes!" Willie whispered, preoccupied. "People want what they want. That goes for this kid and his mother as well. But that power pulling her along and not letting her have what she wants — that's fate. The mother is pulling the child along and fate is pulling her along. As a result, no one ever gets what he wants. As human beings, our bodies grow, but the development of our hearts lags behind. In our souls, we're all children who, in spite of everything, stubbornly dig in our heels because we like something and want it. Like small children, we want everything in life to be exactly like we want it to be. And when life doesn't give us what we want, we feel anxious, our eyes fill with tears, and our hold on life feels insecure. We feel that each of our petty desires is big and important. But surprisingly enough, sometimes after we get what we want, we lose interest in it and cast it aside as something superfluous. It's as if we hadn't fought fiercely for our dreams right up until yesterday. Go figure yourself out!

"What is it that's troubling my heart? What is it that I even want? I don't know. I can't figure this out, no matter how hard I think . . . I just know that something is bothering me." With these thoughts in his mind, Willie raised his head and took a deep breath.

Willie's gaze was drawn to a small Christmas tree in the café at the end of the park, already festooned with colorful decorations. That was nothing surprising. The city's residents eagerly looked forward to the holiday season and started to gear up for it several months in advance. Thus, they could stretch out the festivities and have more time to enjoy them.

*Yes . . . Christmas is coming. But that holiday lost all its meaning for me ages ago. There's not a trace left of my childhood feelings. I used to get so excited waiting for Christmas. Just like that café owner, there was a time when we started getting ready several months beforehand. That's when my parents were around. Everything was so great.* A bitter smile appeared on Willie's face. His imagination took him back to the distant past. For an instant, he could feel all those bygone emotions again.

*But so many bad days and terrible nights, months, and years have washed away all those nice feelings. These awful years have distanced me from those cheerful days. Nothing could ever be like it was before. I don't believe in miracles anymore. For me, Santa Claus and all his presents just seem like a salesman dressed up in funny clothes ready to sell me something. But my God, it all meant so much to me back then. Now my values have changed.* At that moment, it was as though the earth had shifted under his feet, and the sky overhead had disappeared. And he was left in a void with nothing to steady himself. He felt utterly desolate on the inside, floating in the void. *I hate this feeling.* With these thoughts, he expressed his loathing of the all-too-familiar emotions washing over him once again.

*My life seems like it's frozen in place, as if everything is rooted to the spot and nothing can move. I can't feel anything. I'm numb and my brain has dried up. I exist, but at the same time it's like I'm not here . . . Time goes on, but I remain motionless, my life at a standstill. Even these thoughts come to me as if from out of nowhere, out of a void.*

*The void around me isn't so awful. It doesn't hurt me — there's air, and I can breathe. But when there's a void in my heart, it's unbearable. It's im-possible not to feel it."*

"I wanna be a kid again. I wanna only feel pain when I have to get a shot."

The words of one of the boys sitting on the next bench roused Willie from his imaginings, even if only for an instant. Sometimes out of the hundreds of words spoken around you, you hear the one thing you need, the one thing you want to hear. The human mind is quite amazing. Even if its thoughts are elsewhere, the mind is still taking in sounds and words. Some of these words can wake up a person and force him to listen. *Nah, I don't want to go back to the past,* Willie thought, not looking at the boys sitting on the bench.

*I don't care about the past or the present. Life plods along so dully that I can predict ahead of time everything that will happen, everything anyone will do, every word I will hear, and even every one of my feelings. I know what will happen at work, what will happen at home, what will be on TV. I even know in advance what I'll do on the weekend . . . The monotony is exhausting.*

*Summer has ended, and fall has come again. Another year is gone from my life. Winter is on its way . . . Life is moving at the speed of light. In the meantime, you don't even get a chance to notice how quickly you've grown old and how your children have grown up."*

It was as if autumn — with its cold breath and golden leaves — was saying to Willie: "The faster you can come to terms with this monoto-ny, the impermanence of life, and your loneliness, the faster you will find peace and tranquility."

*As human beings, we can get used to loneliness and monotony. We can become so accustomed to it that we see it all as happiness, as just part of nor-mal life. We even fear any changes that could destroy it and avoid people who might disrupt our habits. This is because we are afraid to lose something that has now become an integral part of us — our loneliness . . .*

*In Dallas there was a pastor I often listened to who said that after we die, our life in the Great Hereafter will be wonderful. Yeah, after we die . . . In the*

*Great Hereafter . . . If everything in my life on Earth is bad, how could everything be great after I die and I'm lying in the cold ground? Baron d'Holbach, I think, said that: "The expectation of celestial happiness, and the dread of future tortures, only served to prevent man from seeking after the means to render himself happy here below." We think so much about the world to come that we utterly forget about life on Earth. Dreaming about happiness after death, we forget to be happy in this world.*

These were Willie's daily reflections. On this day, as on all the others, he stood up, having resolved nothing, and drifted away with his unanswered questions. This was turning out to be a very depressing day for Willie. He felt more dejected than usual. He was as distressed as if he had lost someone dear to him. It felt like he was just about to hear some bad news. This feeling had remained with him throughout the day. As the day was drawing to an end, Willie still had not heard any bad news, which somewhat relaxed him. He looked at his watch. And then, reluctantly, he made his way to the bus stop next to the park, thinking that he was running a bit late this time. It was already getting dark. Five minutes later, he was staring at all the familiar places through the bus window, his gaze expressionless.

# AN ABNORMAL FAMILY,
# OR THAT'S HOW IT SHOULD BE

*The great thing in married life is patience. Love cannot last long.*

~ Anton Chekhov

An hour later, Willie halted in front of a house with a yard surrounded by a small, red-painted wooden fence. Dazzlingly beautiful flowers of different varieties were planted in the yard along the fence. Around each flowering bush, there were special colored stones. The freshly turned soil below the flowering bushes, in addition to the tidiness of the yard, with everything in its place, indicated that the lady of this house enjoyed her home. The neatly planted blossoms and carefully pruned branches showed a special fondness for flowers. The house had a big front porch with a dining table. Glasses sat on the table, along with a pitcher of lemonade and a covered cake dish. There was also a coffee mug inscribed with "World's Greatest Dad." Apparently, the family had purchased this as a present for their father's birthday—that's typically when such gifts are given. At least that's how it was done in Willie's family.

Willie was very fond of his home because he had been closely involved in its construction. Every time he came home, he remembered the effort it had taken to build it. He had shelled out a fair amount of money and still hadn't paid off the loan.

He rang the doorbell and had to wait a bit. By now he was used to that. So he just rang it once and waited patiently. Willy always knocked on the door, although he had his keys. Willie's family always argued about who should answer the door. After the usual delay, this time it was opened by his twelve-year-old daughter, Caitlin. *Yup, today it's Caitlin's turn,* thought Willie as he entered the house. "That's one thing I can't understand. If they take turns opening the door, why does it always take so long?" Willie muttered to himself.

Caitlin was a quiet girl with fair skin and long, straight blond hair. She had pale eyes and a freckled nose, just like her grandmother on her mother's side. She said hello to Willie and then immediately went to her room. Her friend was waiting for her on the phone. The girls had long been deliberating about what they were going to wear to the upcoming Christmas bash and how they would spend the holiday, as well as other details—they could not seem to get their fill of this topic even though Christmas was still far away.

As usual, Willie was greeted in the hallway by their black cat with white spots on her back. She charged at Willie's legs and began to rub against his pants. That was her way of saying welcome home. Like always, Willie's son, nine-year-old Kevin, was at the computer playing his favorite game. When Kevin started playing that game, he seemed disengaged from the world around him. There was no way to know if he was even aware that his father had come home. From the look on Kevin's face and the way he twisted his mouth from side to side, you could tell how anxious and stressed this game made him.

Willie's wife, Sarah, was sitting in front of the TV watching her favorite show, *The Anatomy of Desire*. A friend of Sarah's, who lived next door, was with them. The show depicted the high-pressure, stressful lives of people working in the medical industry. Sarah was watching TV while discussing the program with her friend.

"People working in the medical field really do have very challenging jobs," Sarah said.

Her friend, who had no idea what a stressful profession was really like, validated that observation by saying, "That's exactly why it's considered to be one of the most dangerous occupations."

"My heart starts pounding every time I watch them," Sarah said. "I didn't use to think about the medical profession that way, but after I started watching this show, my opinion of those people completely changed. We judge others superficially. When we really delve into their lives, we see that things aren't so easy and nothing's the way it looks from the outside."

"Yeah, the last time I went to go see the school nurse about my son John's immunizations, I baked her a cake to show my gratitude for all they do for our children. You wouldn't believe how happy she was."

Sarah nodded in agreement.

"Sometimes a person looks at things from the outside and not the inside," Willie thought. "For example, we look into a mirror to see ourselves. But there are times when we look at the mirror itself as an object. It stands to reason that instead of seeing ourselves in the reflection, we instead focus on the presence or absence of scratches on the mirror and look at its size and shape. This is an example of how we see something from the outside. Unfortunately, we all too often pay attention to lively, meaningful words and teachable moments, but not in a way that allows us to see ourselves or apply any of that to our own lives. We don't look at the meaning of the word, but at the word itself. Thus, what we hear and see has no effect on us.

"Sometimes we see ourselves as standing apart from the game of life and believe that admonitions or instructions apply not to us, but to others. And instead of using the footballs passed to us and the chances we are given to kick a field goal right through the goal posts, we observe these things impassively and then leave the game. We are faultless, while others have flaws. We don't make mistakes, but everyone else is guilty. We are good, yet others are bad."

As he listened to his wife's conversation, Willie didn't understand exactly what had prompted this train of thought.

Sarah was a thin, blonde woman with an elongated face. Her hair was cut short and parted in the middle. She was quiet and indolent, to some extent indifferent to events around her and not demonstrative. She wasn't easily upset and rarely flew off the handle. Although outwardly she seemed cold and unfeeling, that was not quite true. She analyzed everything and internalized all her anxiety. Others could be a little wary of her because her face was so impassive. Because of these aspects of her personality, she had few friends. But that didn't mean that Sarah was prone to loneliness.

Willie stepped into the living room. He walked over to stand behind the couch where they were sitting. This was how he let his wife know that he was home from work. Willie heartily disliked Sarah's favorite TV show. Although it was a very popular series about doctors and nurses, Willie never watched it. He liked to say he was allergic to it. He associated the show with feelings of scorn and indifference.

Willie and Sarah had been arguing for about a week now. After their last disagreement, Sarah had stopped speaking to him. Confronted with Sarah's coldness, Willie turned without a word to her and, as he had the day before, went into the small room he claimed for himself.

While the house was being built, Willie's biggest concern had been to make sure that there would be one room that would be his and his alone. He had never before had a room all to himself, and Willie had high hopes for this one. He thought he would find total peace there. But then he realized that when there are problems in a home, or when your spirit is uneasy, no room can protect you from that.

Willie lowered himself into a chair. Only now did he feel how tired he was. Willie could not remain unaffected by Sarah's coldness. *After a hard day at work, you come home, eat something, find a corner where you can put your feet up. The kids are playing all around, and your wife is hard at work . . . For some this is a source of relaxation and joy . . . but for others, it's lonely,* thought Willie.

Despite the fact that Willie's paycheck was paying for all the household expenses, his family seemed less than appreciative. They only thought about him when it was time to pay the bills. The children always went to Sarah with their questions and were only interested in her advice. Caitlin and Kevin cared more about what their grandmother and grandfather had to say than their father's opinion, and they even listened more attentively to their uncles than to their dad. They saw Willie as merely a source of income that left the house in the morning and returned at night. It was possible that in their hearts they truly loved him. But they didn't look up to him or view him as the head of the family. Caitlin was even embarrassed to introduce her father to her friends. When Kevin's friends told exaggerated stories about their own fathers' heroic feats, citing their dads' expertise at grilling steaks or other extraordinary gifts, Kevin chimed in with stories about his aunt's second husband or his maternal grandfather. He didn't see anything exceptional or praiseworthy about his own father.

After finding a lovely gift for someone's birthday, Willie would be valued, held dear, and showered with attention and care for a few days. But these expressions of love felt forced, and it was obvious that they were offered out of gratitude for the gift. Willie's own birthdays were never big events. Even their relatives wished him a happy birthday merely out of a sense of duty and not from their hearts. It was as though Willie were the cause of all the family's problems and hardships. And perhaps he was. Everyone held Willie responsible for the family's economic difficulties, and all their problems were pinned on him, from the children's poor attendance records at school to the malfunctioning of household appliances, and on it went. When one of the children got sick, Willie got blamed. The neighbors were also aware of the low esteem in which Willie was held by his family. Even they thought it acceptable to treat him rudely. Friends and relatives typically didn't invite Willie's family over to visit. And if they did, they would ask Sarah not to bring him.

"Sarah, bring the kids over here on Teddy's birthday."

"What about Willie? Isn't he invited too?"

"I don't know, Sarah. Whatever you think. You can ask him if you want . . . Whatever. But your husband never enjoys it when we get together. No offense, but if he comes, he's such a downer that no one will have any fun. I don't know. I mean, again, whatever you think. But it seems like it would be a lot better if you came without him."

But the strangest thing was that Willie didn't seem bothered by the situation. Maybe in his heart he felt troubled. But he had never once shown any unease. Occasionally, like a bear waking from hibernation, Willie would look up, take a painful glance at what was happening around him, and feel sad about his home life. Although everyone else thought Willie's life looked pretty miserable, he considered others to be in worse shape than he was.

Sometimes Willie was unable to restrain himself, and — as if he were trying to rectify matters or out of fear of loneliness — he would clutch Sarah tightly to him. He tried to find the warmth she used to show him and which he so needed. But Willie could find nothing there but the mingled aroma of perfume, cigarettes, and indifference. Then he would release her and regret his display of vulnerability. When Sarah said, "Willie, you're acting weird. What's up with you?" he chose his words with difficulty.

"It's nothing. I'm just depressed. It's stupid."

Whenever this happened, Willie looked on helplessly at the ever-widening gulf between him and his family. He felt powerless to fix the situation. After each of these unsuccessful attempts, Willie plunged once again back into hibernation to shield himself from a hopeless situation. Although these attempts to rouse himself from hibernation used to occur frequently, they had ground to a halt in recent years.

Willie's character was to blame for his fate, and Sarah's relatives were also partially answerable for it. They were intrusive and offered the family unasked-for advice. This included Sarah's parents, sisters, aunts, and even brothers-in-law. Even when her older sister's first husband ran into Sarah, he gave her advice about her household and explained to her how to create and sustain a harmonious family life.

Sarah didn't want to be rude, so she listened to everything everyone told her. She had a high opinion of everyone but Willie, and she carefully considered these points of view. In family matters, Sarah did not act on the basis of her own desires, but on the basis of all these conflicting viewpoints that had been drilled into her. She often felt sad about her husband's predicament, but she was unable to free herself from the hold the current situation had over her. Sarah had truly never wanted any of this to happen to Willie. But she was unable to withstand the united barrage.

Willie's physicality made people nervous upon initial acquaintance, and they kept him at arm's length. But that didn't last long. Soon their intimidation faded. They were like predators approaching a larger but meeker animal.

Willie thought this was unfair. He didn't want to be either the predator or the prey. But of course, Willie did nothing to invite empathy. He only thought to himself: *Why do you need people around you who don't have any respect for you? If that's how it is, it's much better to keep to yourself than to live life like a slave begging for love.*

It was lonely and cold on the inside. And an indifferent, treacherous world waited on the outside. He didn't feel at home anywhere.

# MORNING DAWNS AND
# IT ALL STARTS OVER AGAIN

*Feelings keep us alive.*

That morning, Willie left the house later than usual. Although the day before had been an ordinary one, he felt very tired, as though the muddled thoughts in his head were wearing him out. He remembered feeling this way back in the days when he used to go to practice. After an intense workout, his whole body would ache as if it were weighed down with bricks. That was probably why he had woken up late today. He had skipped breakfast, just downing a glass of milk instead, and rushed out of the house.

He had just made it to the bus stop when the bus pulled up. Willie hopped in. His short, involuntary jog and successful leap onto the bus had awakened some pleasant feelings in him. He had heard that physical activity performed with confidence can make a person feel confident and positive in their outlook. *If you want to be brave, pick up your step, look the world in the eye, and carry yourself like someone who is already brave!*

Willie, pleased with himself, sat down in an empty single seat. He chose it so that no one would sit next to him. "It's much more comfortable to sit alone," he always said.

The bus was following the same route, but Willie, who had indifferently gazed at these houses, bridges, parks, and restaurants before, now revived the memories associated with these places.

*I went to that restaurant for the first time with Sarah. Caitlin was still really little back then . . . And that's the bus stop I used to wait at when I had that other job . . . And there's the store where I always bought that cake Sarah likes. We had just started our family then . . . I haven't bought her that cake in a long time. If I hadn't seen that store, I wouldn't have remembered about Sarah's favorite dessert.*

A tall hotel could be seen in the distance. Willie knew that hotel well. There had been a time when Willie and Sarah had taken a picnic to the park near this hotel every Sunday. For a fleeting moment, it seemed to Willie that all of that had happened not to him, but to someone else.

# AN UNINVITED GUEST

*Marriage does not interfere with the happiness of those who are able to be happy, and the rest of it at least gives you an excuse to complain.*

~ Jean Rostand

Willie was born to an ordinary family. His parents were simple people. Willie's mother, Helen, had a bit of a gruff nature. She was constantly scolding her son and blamed him for all her problems.

"How can you be so stupid? You never understand anything, no matter how many times I explain it, and you can't seem to behave yourself!"

Willie never understood why he couldn't figure things out or how he was supposed to behave or what it was he had done wrong. Sometimes after he had done everything his mother had asked him to do, he still got in trouble. At first his mother's words had been very painful for Willie, and he spent nights quietly weeping in his room. But as he grew up, Willie's attitude toward her treatment of him changed. Her manner no longer bothered him. It had become a predictable part of his day. His mother considered Willie a bit slow and thought that he asked a lot of unnecessary questions, could not control himself, and occasionally laughed too much, while at other times he was too quiet. Everything he did irritated the young mother.

"Ernest Hemingway . . . who is that?" Willie asked, watching a TV show and wanting to know about the person under discussion.

Helen pretended that she hadn't heard him.

"Mom, I'm sitting right here. I asked you who this is."

"Who are you talking about?" Helen asked irritably.

"I'm asking about Ernest Hemingway."

"You've never heard of Hemingway? He's a world-famous writer. Other kids are reading Shakespeare, and you've never even heard of this genius."

"This is the first time I've ever heard of him. He committed suicide? How come?" Willie didn't see how his questions were pushing his mother to the edge or how she knitted her brows angrily each time he spoke. *How is it possible that the questions of her own child can annoy a mother?* Back then Willie didn't understand that.

"Enough already. Could you be quiet for just a few minutes? Shut up! I've had it!" Unable to control herself, Helen suddenly shrieked, infuriated by Willie's questions. He cringed and immediately fell silent.

As a child, Willie had never understood the real reason behind his mother's wrath. There was a time in his life when he had thought that maybe all mothers were like that. When he got older, he realized that was not the case. But even now there was something else he couldn't understand. Why were some mothers very affectionate and perceptive when it comes to their children, while his mother was so gruff and hateful toward him? Maybe his mother had just been trying hard to make him into someone exemplary, well-mannered, and well-read. Perhaps his mother had been only demanding the very best from him. For a while, Willie believed this and forced himself to do exactly as his mother wished. Over time, however, he realized that he had been mistaken. There was a different reason for her attitude. Once, Willie overheard what it was during an argument with his father. Helen acknowledged that Willie had been a surprise.

Back before they had really gotten to know one another, Helen and Brendan had become smitten. And after a while, Helen became pregnant with Willie. This had been an unwanted pregnancy and something Helen had felt completely unprepared for. For this reason, she had wanted to get rid of the baby. But Brendan, who was always afraid of problems and responsibilities, for once did not want to leave Helen on her own in such a situation, so he insisted that she go through with the pregnancy. Helen's family sided with Brendan in the matter. In the end, they decided to keep the child. But then everything changed, and the attachment between the two began to cool. Shortly before Willie's birth, they decided to get married and legitimize their relationship. Once Willie arrived, however, that relationship quickly fell apart. And to make matters worse, their frosty feelings for one another became even icier.

After the wedding, Brendan tried to improve things with Helen, but to no avail. After Helen got pregnant with Willie, she became pickier with Brendan. Now she saw faults in him that she had never noticed before.

"Your table manners are awful." "Brendan, you're talking too loud. You know how noise drives me crazy." "You're really full of yourself—no one likes you. And you're rude to me and never pay me any attention."

In addition to this friction, it seemed to Helen that Brendan possessed an unusually egg-shaped head, and she could barely see his neck under his long chin. Plus Brendan's shoulders, which she had initially seen as broad, now seemed very narrow.

In truth Brendan had quite a normal build. There was nothing in the least odd about his head or shoulders. Nor was his jaw particularly long. It was just that Helen's feelings had changed. She felt that she had been coerced into this marriage and saw Brendan as the main source of that coercion. Even when Willie was born, Helen was in no hurry to see her baby. While the nurses were describing Willie to her, Helen's head was occupied with quite different matters. Unlike Helen, Brendan had expected things to get better between the two of them once the baby was born. He also thought that killing a baby would bring tragedy to the family. Unlike Helen, Brendan did not blame his child for what had happened. What could a newborn baby possibly be guilty of anyway? If anyone were guilty, it was Helen and Brendan. A child can't choose what family he is born to, but parents can choose their own actions. And although Helen knew all this deep in her heart, she simply couldn't cope. She needed an object upon which to unload the anger, resentment, and bitterness that had built up in her heart. And because Brendan was at work all day, Willie was the best candidate she could find.

All this is not to say that Brendan was delighted with his new fatherhood. He kept his emotions to himself and usually wore a brooding look on his face. Brendan was having a hard time absorbing what had happened. But despite his distress, he thought it was wrong to blame Willie for what had occurred.

Helen, on the other hand, behaved very emotionally. She was unable to navigate this trial in her life. And yes, Willie was a trial in her life. Helen did not relate to Willie as a caring, affectionate mother—she very much saw him as a trial that she was unequal to and as the cause of her ruined life, something that had forced her to act against her will.

Human psychology is astounding. If a person is compelled to do something he would have done anyway on his own, he will refuse to do it. It's possible that even if this unexpected event had never happened to them, Helen and Brendan might have gotten married anyway. But because they were obliged to do so, this took a toll on their positive feelings for one another and prevented them from building a happy family. It was difficult for them, particularly for Helen, to accept a responsibility that they had not shouldered voluntarily. Once the human psyche is predisposed toward negativity, this can stifle every positive emotion in the heart. A person sees nothing but the negative aspects of what is happening. This is why a person tends to render judgments and act on the basis of his emotions. Once someone makes a wrong decision, he begins to act in accordance with that decision, up to the point that all is lost. This situation is similar to the plight of a compulsive gambler. He bets the people he loves, his dreams, and his feelings on a game—a game called fate—that he will eventually lose. And before it's all over with, as if all that hadn't been enough, he bets his own life.

Helen and Brendan didn't understand that much of what they disliked about their lives was actually good for them. It's essential to understand that the criteria for what is helpful or beneficial are not determined by what a person enjoys but by events that have occurred. Sometimes a doctor must prescribe a bitter-tasting medicine or painful injection for his patient in order to help heal him. It is not human desires that are considered, but what is wholesome and proper for them. So if that's the case, we must liken difficulties and painful events to a doctor's prescription for his patient. Willie did not enter Helen's and Brendan's family as a misfortune. Were it not for Willie, Helen would have started a family with a man who would have ruined her life, and Brendan would have moved to another state and faced a far worse future. Helen and Brendan were actually very compatible, and Willie was a gift of fate that should have united them into a wonderful family. But tragically, neither Helen nor Brendan was capable of realizing that. Willie, primarily for Helen, was a symbol of an unhappy life or, in other words, an uninvited guest.

# THERE IS ALWAYS HOPE, EVEN
# IN THE MOST HOPELESS SITUATIONS

It's all over.

~ The last words uttered by desperate people.

Despite the attitudes of his parents, Willie truly loved them. For him, the most important thing was that his family was there for him.

*There are so many children whose parents have gotten divorced and don't live together. But my parents are here with me. Sure, maybe there's some friction between them. But who cares! They're still here for me. If it weren't for me, they might have gone their separate ways long ago. And if they're still together, that means that they really love me,* thought Willie.

Sometimes Willie saw his mother sitting alone in a room and crying. He didn't know why. Once or twice when that happened, he wanted to go to her and comfort her, but she just gave him an infuriated look. Afterward, he decided to leave her alone when she got like that. It was possible that his mother was crying out of helplessness and hopelessness, out of her inability to express her feelings to her child. Helen loved him, but her rage and frustration prevented her from showing her feelings. What good is love that no one knows about? Maybe it shouldn't even be called love. In any case, deep in her heart, Helen was worried about what she had done to her son.

Willie, who could never quite relax around Helen, was happier when he was with his father. Brendan tried to not hold back on the love and affection he showed his son.

"It's easy for him," Helen said, noticing the easy affability between the two. "He's at work all day. He doesn't have the trouble of taking care of you. That's why he can be so affectionate."

Brendan pretended he hadn't heard her, and without stopping to get something to eat, he hoisted Willie up on his shoulders and went out into the yard. He could hear Helen say something before the door slammed shut. The closer they got to the front door, the louder Helen's voice got.

Willie felt more secure when he was around Brendan. The tension he endured all day long with his mother subsided as soon as he was with his father. Although Willie often heard his mother bad-mouth his dad, he never passed any of that along. It made Willie heartsick to hear her say those things. But he had to hear her out, or else his mother would get angry. But he only heard her insults — Willie never listened to them. During her outbursts, his thoughts were usually elsewhere.

At that time, Helen found a job. Her new life at work took her mind off things to a certain extent. Willie joined the school football team. Thanks to his genetic gifts, he was a natural athlete and soon thrived on the field, winning the attention of his classmates. This helped him gain some self-confidence, despite being picked on at home. At that point Brendan changed jobs. He was now working at a distant location and could only come home once or twice a month.

"These are just temporary difficulties," Brendan said. "Once things ease up a bit, I'll come back to get you."

It does seem that every hardship is followed by some relief. There is hope in any hopeless situation, no question. The relationship between Brendan and Helen eventually stabilized somewhat. And this stability pleased one member of the family most of all. That was Willie. Willie's grades rose, and even his relationships with his classmates and teachers sorted themselves out. The boy didn't understand the real reason behind these developments. This was a small, positive change in the family, but it was a big one in Willie's eyes. And this seemingly insignificant change prompted big transformations in his life.

In the meantime, Brendan wanted another child. "If we had another child, he could help anchor Willie. Besides, Willie's no longer a child; he's a big kid. If he needs to, he can look after his brother."

"I don't want another child," Helen said. "I've got enough on my hands with Willie. And besides, how do you know it would be a boy?"

"They run in our family. The first few children are always boys," Brendan said with a smile. "If it's a girl, then you can name her, and if it's a boy, I will, okay?" Brendan pretended to give her a stern look.

Brendan thought that if he and Helen decided they both wanted another baby, then that child would greatly improve their relationship.

Both he and Helen had made a lot of mistakes in their marriage. Brendan was somehow sure that this new baby would bring joy to their family. He believed that Helen would provide the baby with the love in her heart that she kept hidden and did not offer to Willie, the uninvited guest. All because this would be a wanted child. Then Helen would feel like a mother. And at that point, who knew, maybe she would also find some genuine love for Willie.

# THERE IS NO PLACE FOR ME IN THIS HOUSE

*Sometimes we look at past events as if they were ghosts.*
*Only later do we realize that this apparition was the reality.*

After some time, Helen began to suffer from nausea, weakness, and headaches. This was exactly how Helen had figured out she was pregnant the first time. Brendan was wildly happy. On the days when he was gone, he often called Helen to find out how she was doing. He tried to please his wife with various gifts.

"How is it that now you're here every week when you used to only make it once a month?" Helen asked Brendan, giving him an appraising once-over.

"I turned my work over to someone else for a little while. But I'm only here for a few hours and have to go back tonight."

Even with Helen working, the family was barely bringing in enough money to cover the essentials. Brendan promised that after the baby was born, they would move into a new and more spacious home. But Helen knew that they would be stuck in their tiny two-room apartment for a long time.

Once, Brendan was happier than usual when he came home. That was because Helen was supposed to go for a checkup that day.

"What's the news? How do you feel?"

"We were wrong. All I had was a cold."

"But we thought . . ." Helen shook her head.

Although Brendan was devastated, he tried to pull himself together. "It's all right," he said. "It's not the end of the world."

Brendan quickly forgot that incident. And so several years passed, and Willie's family stayed the same. Despite how much Brendan and Helen wanted a baby, she kept miscarrying in the second month. The doctors didn't know why. "It's odd how the fetus was developing normally, but then it suddenly stopped growing," the doctor said.

Brendan even took Helen to the best physicians in the city. For someone who originally hadn't wanted a baby, Helen now ached for a second child. Brendan saw this in her face each time she exhibited the signs of pregnancy and went to the doctor. People are far more likely to covet and yearn for things that are difficult or even impossible to obtain. They only realize how much they need something once it is lost. And now Helen even dreamed of the baby. She was sure it would be a girl. But she kept this premonition to herself because she knew how much Brendan wanted a boy.

Once Brendan bought a present for Helen and Willie while on his way home from work. He climbed the stairs to his house in a very pensive mood. He was still one floor below their apartment when a girl came out of the shadows and took Brendan by the hand. She had fair skin and big eyes, round cheeks, long eyelashes, and long curly hair. She was wearing a white dress that highlighted the features of her face even more. The red shoes on her feet matched the belt on her dress.

Holding on to Brendan's hand, the girl began the arduous ascent up the steep stairs. As the little girl climbed higher, she began to huff and puff, as children do when they suddenly wear themselves out. The girl was climbing the stairs, always putting her right foot on the next step. In this way, she reached the doors of Brendan's apartment. Brendan was enchanted by this lovely child. Despite the fact that he had only known her for the time it took them to climb a few steps, he felt a powerful kinship with her. He kept his eyes fixed on her. He looked her over from top to toe and studied the features of her face. The girl held two of Brendan's fingers tightly squeezed against her plump, white palm, and Brendan could feel the softness and warmth of her hand.

When they reached the door, Brendan went down on one knee and gazed into her big, dark eyes. Those eyes fascinated him. Brendan stared at her silently for a moment, and then said, "What's your name, little one?"

The girl smiled but was slightly taken aback. "My name is Thea," she said. "I'm Thea, a gift from God."

"What a sweet, pretty girl you are. Where do you live?"

"Nowhere. I have no home."

Brendan was a bit surprised. "Who do you belong to?" For a second, Brendan thought the child was lost.

"Daddy, what's wrong? Why don't you recognize me? It's me, your daughter," said little Thea, ducking her head and beginning to look fretful the way children do when their feelings are hurt.

Brendan was struck dumb. *Of course children speak without thinking. They'll call any man they see 'Daddy.'*

"Are you coming to visit us, sweet girl?"

"No, I'm not coming to visit you." The little girl shook her head and tightened her lips, offended. "You don't have any room in this house, and it would be too crowded with me there. And you don't even want a girl; you're wishing for a boy." She started down the stairs.

Brendan froze in place. He was so shocked, he didn't have the strength to go after the child. But after he had collected himself, he wanted to run after her. "I can't let her go off on her own! Should I go see where she's gone? Who is that girl?" These questions raced through his head. But he felt so physically drained that no matter how he tried, he couldn't run after her. Feeling desolate, he sat down on the stairs. He looked at the steps the girl had run down. Even the sound of her little shoes had died away.

Brendan finally managed to drag himself inside. His whole body was covered in sweat. He walked over to the couch and sat down wearily, as if he were recovering from an illness. Noticing Brendan's odd behavior, Helen approached him with a look of concern. Wiping away the sweat from his forehead, she asked, "What happened to you? Do you feel sick?"

Brendan looked into her eyes and said, "Helen, did you get an abortion? I remember there were some signs . . . but then you said that we had been mistaken. Answer me! Tell me the truth!" Brendan felt his eyes fill with tears. As he spoke, his speech faltered, and his lips trembled.

"Brendan, forgive me. It's all my fault. You know . . . How can I explain it? Things weren't easy for us then. When I found out I was pregnant, I went into shock. And the doctor thought this one might be a girl. You so wanted a boy. And we weren't making much money, and you know how small our apartment is. I decided that now wasn't the right time for a baby. There's hardly enough room for us here as it is, and it would be an even tighter squeeze with a baby . . ."

Brendan buried his face in his hands and began to sob. Then, without a word, he left the house. He didn't come home for a while.

# EVERYBODY GETS JUST ONE CHANCE AT LIFE

*I've noticed that everyone who is for abortion has already been born.*

~ Ronald Reagan

It hadn't been such an easy thing for Helen to do. She had gone to the doctor to have her abortion on several different occasions, but at the last minute, she would waver and return home. Helen thought that while the child was still as tiny as a pinpoint, it would be easier to get rid of. Over the course of that short time, she had become strongly attached to this living being, this "pinpoint." This mother, who was still uncertain of whether she would keep the child or not, had already named her future baby Thea. She thought she was carrying a girl. She gave her that name so the girl would bring happiness to their family.

Helen saw how hard Brendan was working to support his family, yet their financial situation was difficult. And she didn't want to burden him with added responsibility. Helen knew that Brendan would find a second job to support the child and would work longer hours than before, and yet, cutting out of work, he would sneak off home to visit them on the sly. Each of these trips home would cost extra money. *How long can that go on?* Although the relationship between Helen and Brendan had really turned a corner, Helen wasn't ready to have another of Brendan's children under these conditions. At the same time, she was worried that she might hate and despise this baby as she had Willie. She was continuously tormented by hundreds of burdensome thoughts. On one hand was her desire to keep the child, but on the other was a recurring worry and sense of fear that resulted in great stress.

Finally Helen decided to have the abortion. On the way there, she talked to her baby. "Forgive me, Thea. I have no choice. It will be better this way for everyone . . ."

"Maybe for everyone. But certainly not for me."

"You're still so little. You haven't even been born yet. You're an invisible pinpoint."

"Yes, right now I'm a pinpoint, a single cluster. But you can be sure that this pinpoint wants to live as much as you do."

"I am in no way ready to have you. Once I made a mistake, and I don't want to repeat it ever again. I'm still young. I'll have another chance to be a mother."

"You'll have another chance to be a mother, but I won't get another chance to be born. You'll have other children, Mommy, but they won't be me; they'll be Susan, Robert, and Katherine . . . But there won't be any Thea, because everybody gets just one chance at life. And without ever being born, I have to say good-bye to this world.

"And you don't even know me very well yet. What's the hurry? Wait a bit. Give me a chance to win your love. Don't kill me after you've given me life! After all, you were the one who gave me this life . . ."

"Thea, later on it may be too late." Helen dissolved into tears. "This is just the wrong time for a baby! We're barely making it as it is. There's hardly enough room for us now, and it would be an even tighter squeeze with a baby."

"I won't take up much room in your house. If you want, I'll sit in a corner all day and not bother you. I won't eat or drink much, only what you don't need, so I won't be a burden on you.

"Mommy, it's just been two months, but I already love you so much. And you love me too, I can feel it. I can really feel it. I'm closer to you than you are to yourself. I wake up to the beating of your heart. I know what you eat and drink, and I even know your worries. I'm inside of you. I'm a little fragment of you. If I don't feel these things, who will? I'm going to miss my brother, Willie, and my father, Brendan. Please, Mommy, don't take them away from me or me from them."

Helen, silently shedding tears, listened to the little voice of the still-unborn, living being coming from inside her. Each protestation unsettled her even more. So she decided not to speak. She no longer knew what to say or how to explain her predicament to the child.

"Mommy, if you keep me, when I grow up, I'll take care of you. I'll help my dad and brother. I'll go to school like other kids my age. You'll iron my clothes and brush my hair. When I come home from school, I'll give you a kiss and a hug. I promise never to upset you — I'll be a good girl. When you get sick, I'll look after you. Even if my daddy and brother forget your birthday, I'll never forget it, and I'll remind them. I'll buy you presents and be the first one to wish you a happy birthday.

"Mommy, I'll grow up to be a doctor, you know. But I'll never perform abortions. Because I truly understand what they mean.

"Mommy, you know what? I'll have black eyes just like yours. Nothing but my nose will look like my dad's. My face, skin, hair, and hands are all like yours. We'll be a lot alike, Mommy . . . I won't look like my father very much . . . Can you hear me?" Thea spoke like a child resorting to flattery to get what it wants. She was trying to win her mother over.

"Mommy, don't do it! Maybe to the doctor I'm a meaningless pinpoint, but I know you can't look at me that way. To you I'm Thea, a gift from God. That's what you named me yourself. I want to be born. You know, Mom, it's so dark in here, but I can feel you every moment. I want to see you so badly! Don't you want to see me? Why are you so quiet, Mommy? Why don't you say something? Talk to me! Pretty please? Mommy, talk to me! You're so quiet, and it scares me . . .

"Mommy . . . Mommy, you haven't changed your mind, have you?" Helen did not say a word. After a short pause, Thea spoke up again. "Mommy, whatever happens, I love you very much. You're my mommy. I'm grateful to you for giving me life, even if only for two months."

Helen, holding her head in both hands, sat down on the floor and started shrieking. The woman who was next on the list looked at her and said, "She seems to be in pretty bad shape. I can wait a bit; let her go ahead." Helen didn't know whether to be thankful or angry at her. The nurses led her into the surgery.

Because it was a minor procedure, Helen was to be released that evening. But until then, she lay down in a recovery room to rest a bit. The doctor's voice was coming as if from the bottom of a well: "Shortly before, the embryo stopped developing. It's rare for a normally developing embryo to suddenly stop growing, but it is possible. I guess you're just a rare case."

"She couldn't bear . . . my indifference and heartlessness. I abandoned her."

"I'm sorry, what did you say? Who couldn't bear what?" the doctor said.

"Thea . . . Thea couldn't bear it . . ."

"Ah, I see. You've been through some stress. Every woman who has an abortion gets an attack of nerves, especially the first time. When you get home, make sure you get some rest. And tell your husband that he has to really pamper you."

The whole way home, Thea's last words echoed in Helen's ears: "Whatever happens, I love you."

She tried to forget those words, as well as everything else that had happened. To forget once and for all everything that had anything to do with Thea. But she didn't realize that those last words would be etched in her memory in capital letters for the rest of her life. And nothing but death would have the power to erase them.

# HUMAN LIFE BEGINS AT CONCEPTION

*We kill our children and believe that afterward life will be easier.*
*It won't! Spilled blood cannot ease anything.*

Brendan thought that happiness had left their home along with their dead child. After ridding herself of two-month-old Thea, Helen found that, for some reason, she could not keep any of their subsequent babies in her womb for more than two months. Everything came back to where it had started. Sometimes the mistakes we've made turn our life into such a vicious circle. No matter how we try, we keep finding ourselves back at the starting point and having to begin again. Brendan hoped that his life with Helen would return to normal. It had seemed as though things were working out. But now they were all back to square one. Brendan was still trying to make allowances for Helen's sharp tongue while trying to overlook her blunders. But he could neither forgive nor forget her most recent transgression. Perhaps the offense that Helen had committed had brought out resentment and anger toward his wife that had been building unseen in Brendan's heart for years.

So far the family had held it together thanks to Brendan's stamina and industry, but now he found it hard to focus on anything. His thoughts were muddled. Brendan, who had once rescued his son from death under more difficult circumstances, had been unable to rescue his daughter at a time when things between him and Helen had been amicable. Brendan felt that everything had been looking up. And for this reason, no matter how he tried, he could not understand why Helen had acted as she had, and he could not excuse what she had done. All of Brendan's efforts to move things in the right direction had been rendered null and void by her act. Now Brendan believed that he had toiled in vain and that Helen had played him for a fool.

After Helen's confession, Brendan became withdrawn and despondent. He rarely laughed or spoke to his wife and paid her no attention. Any trifle could spark an argument between them. He had previously been eager to talk about things that had happened at work, but now he spoke not a word. After this earthquake, he couldn't even manage his relationship with Willie. Brendan treated him like a stranger. Willie's efforts to cheer up his father were futile.

Brendan came home only rarely. Walking past Helen without looking her in the eye, he went to see Willie and then left again, not staying the night. Helen blamed herself and tried, at first, to be extra nice to her husband, but eventually she became quite surly toward him. Brendan's indifferent attitude once again awakened feelings of rage in Helen, as it had in the early days of their marriage.

*I've had enough! How much can anyone take? I made one mistake, and now it's the end of the world? It hasn't been so easy for me, either, all this time. My conscience has been tormenting me!*

*He doesn't come home for months at a time and you don't know where he is. And when he does come home, he doesn't talk to anyone . . .*

Helen knew that Brendan was neither vindictive nor stubborn. She had been sure that he would make a concession, as always, so she never did anything to make peace. But now Helen was nervous because Brendan hadn't been home in months. She could not accept that it was different this time. Brendan's stubbornness was making her irate. Neither of them wanted to understand the other's point of view.

They both knew that things couldn't go on that way for long. A year later, the couple went to a lawyer to ask for a divorce.

They wept for their unborn child without once remembering Willie, who was right there with them and needed their time and attention all the more. Sometimes we weep for those we have lost and forget to value those who are right here with us.

# CHURCH, THAT IS SEPARATION

*Sometimes happiness is a chance to see, just for
a moment, a person you had missed terribly.*

Willie missed his father terribly. Helen used a variety of pretexts
to pick a fight with Brendan every time they were together. These
quarrels drained Willie dry. The incessant squabbling meant that Willie could not spend time with his father. Willie would keep one eye on
the clock as the arguments dragged on. He knew his father's time was
limited. Because he hadn't seen him in so long, Willie prayed to God
that the fighting would soon be over, so he could spend more time
with his dad.

Helen nagged Brendan in part because she didn't want to lose
him completely. These explosions of anger were her only remaining
way to communicate with him. She was trying to find an opportunity
to open her heart to him. She was waiting for Brendan to recognize
this, so they could rebuild their relationship.

Whenever Brendan was leaving, Willie accompanied him to the
front gate. He would watch him walk away until he had disappeared
from view. At that moment, Willie felt a great emptiness open in his
heart. He thought about the next time his father would come home.
But there was no way to know when Brendan would visit again. This
uncertainty only added to Willie's sadness.

As Brendan was leaving, Willie would envision a particular day
of the week in his mind. He thought that that would make his father
come home on precisely that day. And when his father did not return

on the day Willie had imagined, Willie simply chose another day, ultimately changing the day he had in mind several times as he anticipated his father's reappearance. This was how Willie comforted himself and calmed his anxieties while he waited for his dad. When Brendan did not show up on the day he was supposed to, Willie was a bundle of nerves, and his mind was in a whirl. He couldn't get anything done all day long, and he felt very weak. All that night he would think about his father. He found a thousand excuses for him. And when dawn broke, he was still awake, tossing and turning in his bed. Brendan had no idea what his son went through when he didn't come home.

Once Willie wanted to tell his father about how anxiously he waited for him, about his bargain with God, and about how he fantasized about certain days in his mind. Maybe once his father found out how much Willie missed him, he would visit more often. He thought that once his father realized all this, he would begin to stroke his hair as he was leaving and ask him, "Willie, what day are you envisioning this time?"

"The second," Willie would answer happily.

"Ha. The second? That's tomorrow."

Then Brendan would understand how much Willie loved him, and that, like all children, he wanted to see his father every day. Maybe then he would take his son along with him. And they would take Helen with them as well. Willie thought that his own words and wishes meant so much to his father that he even had the ability to reunite his parents. And that if he asked, his parents would go with him to a new city they had never seen before and start a new life there.

On one occasion, Willie struck a deal with God that if his father would come home on the day he was supposed to, Willie would go to church, but if not, Willie wouldn't . . . So after that he didn't go to church anymore. At first, it was because he didn't feel God had kept his end of the bargain, but later it was because of the anger that had flared up in his heart toward the church. Whenever he saw a church, he thought of his father. In his mind, the church was a symbol of his father's absence and of the broken pact.

Willie kept silent.

"Do you know why your dad almost never comes home? He doesn't want to see us because he has a new family. The neighbors saw him with another woman.

"Your father thinks everything's my fault. He told our neighbor John Lewis that I alone was the problem. As though I were a bad wife from the beginning. Can you believe that? Men are always like that! But then, who am I talking to? You're one of them. I get it. You'll take his side."

Helen sat down in a chair in front of the window with her hands trembling. In the still voice of someone exhausted and on her last breath, she said, "Look at me. Do you see what sort of state I'm in? I devoted all of my youth, all of my life, to the two of you."

"I love you so much, Mom. I know how you feel." Willie hung his head.

"I don't know, Willie. I don't know anything anymore. I don't even want to think about anything. I've lost faith in everyone. I feel so alone. I've never been in such a hopeless situation." After a moment of silence, she sighed heavily. "Oh, you don't understand what I'm saying."

Willie was no longer a child. He understood perfectly. Although he blamed his father for some things, he felt that most of the fault lay with his mother. But he also pitied Helen. There was so much he wanted to say to her. But he had never mustered the courage to tell her what was in his heart.

Helen even held Brendan responsible for her problems at work. He was to blame for everything. How was it possible that his father was the source of her problems at work or that it was his fault she had forgotten to turn off the oven when leaving the house? Willie thought his mother's criticism was inappropriate and ridiculous.

Willie felt like he was suffocating at home, especially when his father was very late coming to visit him. Helen liked the idea of Brendan coming to the house despite the fact that they were now divorced, although she did all she could not to show it. Helen became cross whenever Brendan was very delayed. She could not reconcile herself to their divorce. Helen didn't understand what she wanted. She was trapped in the vortex of her emotions. There was much she would not admit. It was as if there were some force preventing her from sharing what was inside her with Brendan and Willie. Brendan had always been right there for Helen. For this reason, she thought that she was indifferent to him and didn't love him, that their marriage had been a mistake. But now that she was certain she had lost him, she realized that she was feeling different emotions toward him.

*Maybe I've loved him all my life. Maybe he has always been someone special to me.* But Helen had always been afraid to admit this, and even now she was hesitant to do so, remaining unsure.

*What would happen if I confessed my feelings? If things hadn't started out this way for us from the very beginning, if I hadn't been so stubborn and had been able to lay aside my scorn that was so uncalled-for, been more understanding, admitted my mistakes, and included him in some decisions and asked his advice . . . Could things have been different?*

Helen wanted to go back in time but could not—she had no power to stop the clock. She wanted to change her life and resurrect her family's dashed hopes, lost happiness, and serenity. But she didn't know how to do it. And time was not standing still. Helen was floundering, falling into an abyss.

Willie devoted all his love to his father. His father was his hero. Even in his saddest, most difficult moments, thoughts of his father lifted his spirits and gave him strength.

Brendan liked the idea that his son played a rough sport like football. And this was a big incentive for Willie to keep training. Willie initially went out for sports so he'd have somewhere to spend his free time, but then, seeing what a big deal it was for his dad, he started getting serious about his training. He wanted his father to be pleased every time he helped win a game. It wasn't the game that really mattered to Willie; it was his father. He shared each victory, each word of praise from his coaches with his father.

When Willie tried out for the football team, Helen grumbled that he was going to end up breaking his neck or his back and spend the rest of his life in a wheelchair. None of that meant anything to Willie. He just wanted to make his dad happy.

Whenever Willie talked to his father about football, his dad—a big football fan—gave him tips. Most of Brendan's advice about how to be a better player was, in fact, misguided. But Willie didn't really care. What mattered to him was being with his dad and feeling his affection and attention. Brendan's advice might have been flawed, but it was his way of paying attention to his son. Willie kept his eyes on his dad's face, nodding and listening as raptly as if Brendan were the head football coach. Every word Brendan uttered sounded fresh and interesting to him. Willie periodically nodded, as a sign of acknowledgement and attention. And Brendan, seeing his son's interest, got even more excited and wanted to offer even more advice.

Willie tried to devote a lot of time to the sport since his father was interested in it. Now Willie was playing an important role in the life of the university for his beautiful game.

Football helped Willie cope with his longing for his father. This was the time in his life when Willie gained national fame on his college team. His talent was different from that of anyone else on the team. The coaches claimed he was destined for the pros.

When Brendan and Willie met up, his dad told him stories about work and what was happening at his job and about a guy there named Tom, who was a great cook. He also told some jokes he'd heard from Jimmy, the warehouse loader, and about his crazy misadventures. In his imagination, Willie became friends with his dad's work buddies too even though they'd never actually met in person.

His life from one encounter to the next was nothing but a void to fill now.

## YOU LOOK INTO HIS EYES, AND YOUR GAZE SAYS: "I'VE REALLY MISSED YOU"

*When a father hates the mother of his children,*
*it affects his feelings toward his children as well.*

Gradually, Brendan was becoming a stranger. Brendan used to be happier with Willie; he liked spending time with him at home. But now, the anger seemed to take over his entire being, eradicating all pleasant feelings, happy memories, and even fatherly love. Willie no longer received the same warmth from him. Brendan's eyes seemed to belong to another person.

♦　　♦　　♦

Imagine that you've been desperately waiting for someone for a long time. You're so excited, you feel your heart is about to beat out of your chest. But when that person arrives, you see no emotion of any kind reflected in his face. Then all your joy evaporates. Although previously your heart was aching with longing for him, now it aches because of his coldness and indifference toward you. And he says nothing but, "Hey, Willie. How's it going?" and then starts talking about something else before you have a chance to answer. Looking into his eyes, you say to yourself, *I've missed you so much. Every day I wait for you. Even at school, you're all I think about. So how exactly do you think it's going?*

At first Willie didn't believe that his father would remarry. He didn't take his mother's words seriously or attach any meaning to them. Nor did he want to listen to the neighbors' gossip. But soon an event erased all his hopes.

The team bus left the highway and rumbled through the wide streets of Houston. None of Willie's teammates had ever played in such a large stadium, and Willie had trained extra hard for this playoff matchup. When the bus rolled to a stop at a traffic light, Willie turned his head to look out the window, and his mouth dropped open. There was Willie's father, Brendan, strolling with a woman who held the hand of a little boy. They looked so happy. His father occasionally said something to the woman, and she answered him with a smile. Walking on a bit, Brendan rumpled the child's hair and took his hand. It seemed like the bus was never going to move, subjecting Willie to mental torture by forcing him to watch this distressing scene. Willie gazed at his father and his new family that had replaced Willie in Brendan's heart and hijacked all his love. Willie had been waiting for him every day, counting the hours until his arrival, but all the while Brendan . . . Now it was obvious why his father came home so rarely. He no longer had any time or love for Willie. His father's new family had so much of what Willie's family needed.

Willie was deeply shaken. All his hopes had been turned on their head, and everything that he held dear had been lost in an instant. As they arrived at the stadium, he could still see in his mind the scene he had just witnessed and the child's happy face.

During the playoff game, Willie still couldn't pull himself together. "Willie, number forty-six is coming right at you," his coach said. "Knock him down, knock him down!" Willie looked over at the sideline. "Don't stand there like that!"

Willie allowed the players who were running toward him at full speed to knock him off his feet without attempting to dodge. He was opening himself up to dangerous hits. He seemed to be punishing himself. "What's going on with you!" his coach yelled. "Why are you playing like this? You're standing right in front of the other team's guy. It's like you're doing this on purpose." The coaches paced the sidelines. Willie was mercilessly punishing himself for all the lies he had been told for so long, for the deception, betrayal, and loneliness, and because he had been cast aside.

Willie suffered more injuries in that game than in any other. The coach debated at halftime whether to pull him out or not and finally did after Willie took a blow to the head early in the second half. Although he got back on his feet quickly, indicating that he could keep playing, his coach insisted that he leave the game. Willie took two or three steps, then lost his balance and fell to the ground. The medics rushed onto the field to help him. He had a serious injury that sent him to the hospital for a while. That was his last game.

Willie was disappointed in his father, but he didn't entirely understand his feelings toward him. His insides felt empty and numb. He couldn't rouse himself to anger and couldn't endure any other emotions. Despite all that had happened, Willie still waited for his dad. His eyes sought him out whenever visitors stopped by his hospital room. But Brendan didn't come. His father visited Willie and his mother after he had already been discharged. Willie didn't say anything to him about his injury. And he adamantly told his mother not to mention it.

Willie didn't tell anyone — not his mother nor anyone else — what he had seen that day from the bus. What could he say to his mother? That she was right that his father didn't love them and had found someone else to take their place? That he didn't need them anymore?

Willie could not renounce his father. He was very upset about what he had seen, but Brendan was still his dad. He had accepted his father taking a job in a different city, the family living separately. But he couldn't accept the lack of attention his father paid to him.

Brendan truly had changed a lot recently. He had become moody and hard to please.

"How's everything at school?" In the park, they were sitting next to each other. The questions were mechanical. Brendan's thoughts seemed elsewhere. Willie could have predicted what he was going to ask. He answered with silence.

"How's practice? Are you still going?"

Willie said nothing.

"Listen to your mother. Lately she's been looking really tired. I've never seen her like that."

*If only you knew what was in our hearts, our state of mind, how hard it is for us to wait for you.* These words swirled through Willie's head. He wanted to say, "Dad, please, no more. Just go back home. We can't take it anymore; just leave!"

"Yeah, you look good, Willie," Brendan said, stepping to one side and looking at him, trying to lighten the tense mood. "A real man now."

"If you say so, Dad . . . if you say so." *You probably know how I'm doing.* How could a father not sense the emotional state of his own flesh and blood, his own child whom he had watched grow up before his own eyes? But this time Willie kept these thoughts to himself.

"Maybe you need something?" Brendan said.

Willie was utterly crestfallen. He couldn't speak and was having a hard time keeping his cool. He had no idea how to explain to his father how he felt. Willie was convinced that his father had no interest in his life. Brendan's indifferent attitude was a signal that he was throwing in the towel.

"You know, Willie, I'd like to give you some advice. This is something all really successful people do. You know what it is? You should write yourself a letter. Address it to the Willie of ten or fifteen years in the future. They say that a letter like that will help a person accomplish whatever he writes about. If a person tries to live up to everything that's written in the letter, his life will follow suit. I read about this in some scientific journal. And after a certain amount of time has passed, you're supposed to open the letter on the appointed day and read it. Then you can judge whether you've reached the goals you wrote about. And you could even let someone who's close to you read the letter, and let that person decide if that's the life you have, if you've achieved those goals. It would be best if that person were your own father. I mean, who could be closer to you than your father? Who can you trust more than your father?"

Willie listened to him as if his father were talking about someone else. He didn't understand what these words were supposed to mean. He couldn't understand why his dad was saying all this. His father's words seemed insincere. Willie didn't believe what his father said about the letter written to his future self. Those dry, meaningless words felt like a lie. Willie didn't need a letter written for some future date. He needed a father who would be at his side as he stepped confidently into the future and who would be a tower of strength for him during times of darkness. He did not want to write his heartfelt words and plans on a piece of paper; he wanted to talk about these things with his father, with someone who was close to him, someone of his own flesh and blood.

*Yes, he is looking for something to fill his place; he's trying to comfort me. What is he saying? This is ridiculous; doesn't he understand!*

Brendan looked at his watch and raised his eyebrows. "Yeah, Willie, I gotta get going," he said. "Was there something you wanted to tell me?" Willie stood motionless, staring at the ground with his head bowed. His father got up from the green bench where they had been sitting and gingerly ran his fingers through his son's hair. "See ya, Willie," he said and slowly walked away.

*If only I could yank out my heart and hand it to you, then it wouldn't be so agonizing waiting for you to show up.*

Although he guessed that Brendan wouldn't be back, Willie still waited for him. *He's really busy and works far away. Clearly his new family is taking up a lot of his time.* Willie tried to find solace by convincing himself of this. His dad wouldn't be able to stay away from him for too long. After all, he was his only child. His father would never abandon him. Then Willie remembered the boy he had seen walking alongside his father. *Well, even if I'm not the only one, I'm his eldest son.* There was a place for every child. His dad loved him; he was sure of it.

Willie often went down to the creek where he and his father used to spend time together. Sitting there, he looked at the tall reeds that grew all around. A little ruined wooden bridge stretched halfway across the creek from one bank. As he watched a flock of birds take to the air, Willie remembered the days he had spent here with his father and what his dad had said to him. He had replayed those words so many times in his head that he now knew them by heart and could not possibly forget them.

Willie continued to bargain with God about when his dad would return. But after two years, he had grown tired of this. A feeling of rage toward his father had arisen inside him.

He had completely given up going to practice. He no longer had an incentive to motivate him. His wrath toward his father infected everything he associated with him: football, the creek, the bank they used to sit on. Now Willie had decided to destroy everything that reminded him of his dad. He burned his uniform, the awards he was given for winning the playoffs, and his souvenir footballs commemorating certain games. By setting fire to these, he emptied his heart forever of every warm feeling and happy memory.

A lot had changed in those two years. Helen was far more on edge. And now Willie, who had always held his peace no matter what his mother said, no longer tolerated her unjust treatment. So they often clashed. In light of this, Helen decided to live on her own for a while, without Willie. She sent him to stay with her sister. Some time passed. With his uncle's help, Willie found a job. Once he was earning a little money, he rented an apartment, and his relationship with his aunt gradually grew more distant.

Helen came to visit Willie occasionally at first, but eventually she stopped coming by.

But despite all this, Willie loved his parents. Even though he felt like a third wheel within his family, and even though his parents often argued and he got angry at them, Willie still loved them and tried to understand and excuse their behavior. Willie forgave them for all the mistakes they had made with him over the years and tried to be understanding about everything except for the fact that they had abandoned him. They both said, "You're a grown-up now," and considered him to be on his own. But no matter how much Willie had grown up, there was still a child inside him who needed the affection of a father and mother, who wanted to sit at the dinner table with his parents in the evening, and who ached to feel that they were at his side. Willie was baffled that Brendan and Helen could not understand such a simple truth.

*They should know this. These are normal feelings that all children have for their parents.*

*He's the reason I'm so unhappy, I'm all alone at night, and my friends make fun of me . . .* After Brendan walked out on him, Willie was already holding his father responsible even for things his dad had nothing to do with. Whether he had a fight with a friend, failed a test, had a spat with the neighbors, got on the bus without his backpack, or even if he got sick, it was all his dad's fault. Willie had better insight into his mother now. He felt bad that he had judged her so harshly when she had criticized his father.

Everything seemed to Willie to have collapsed in the blink of an eye. But to be honest, their family and happiness had been shattered long ago. Only a dry, empty husk remained. Willie just didn't want to see it. He tried to convince himself that everything was fine. He was looking for happiness. And he wanted to find it within his family, not elsewhere.

# A STOLEN SMILE

*If people do not love one another, they will certainly hate one another.*

~ Mozi

After the last time Willie saw his father, there was no more news of him. He only heard about his dad's death from lung cancer many years later.

Willie's mother remarried. Sometimes she called to talk to Willie on the phone. But then even that stopped. On the rare occasions when she did call, sometimes he wouldn't pick up. But deep in his heart, he longed for his mom to call. It had been a long time since his mother had come to see him.

"I shouldn't have refused to answer when she called the last time. What if she's mad at me now? What if something's happened to her? What if she's sick?"

With these questions really bothering him, Willie couldn't help it—he had to call her. But no one picked up. He waited until that evening and then dialed her number again. This time a middle-aged man answered. Willie immediately hung up, and he began to kick himself for having called his mother. Nevertheless, the next day he decided to go see her. If Helen offered him just one kind word, Willie would hug her and would forget all his grievances.

The next day, Willie went to the address his aunt had given him. He found his mother's house and watched it from the outside for a while. It was already getting dark. The yellow, soft light seeping from the window drew Willie. Without quite knowing what he was doing, he approached the house. He was not planning to go in. He did not know what he was going to do. As he got closer, Willie sneaked a glance through the window. His mother was standing next to the Christmas tree in the corner of the room, smiling, a box in her hands. The boy next to her was taking decorations from the box and putting them on the tree. Sometimes he'd show Helen a piece and ask her something. In response, she'd point her finger at an empty branch. Sometimes, she'd ruffle the boy's dark-blond hair fondly.

Helen turned around to call the boy sitting at the table. He reluctantly got up, took the box from her and started helping his little brother. Willie looked at his mother's smiling face in amazement. She said something, left the room, and soon came back, her hands full. She started setting the table. A small middle-aged man with a streak of gray in his hair came in and took the place at the head of the table. The family had gathered for dinner.

For the second time in his life, another person's happiness caused him more pain than his own unhappiness. He decided that the love he had lost had been stolen from him by others. That day riding the team bus to the playoffs, it was his father who had made him feel that way. And now—his mother.

Willie looked at Helen as if she were no longer his mom. Without thinking, he sat down on the ground and hugged his knees. He buried his face to muffle his sobs. Bitterness gripped his heart. He wanted to stand but could not—it was as if his legs would not support him. Why should he go on living? He felt drained. He sat frozen like that for some time.

He felt a need to go home but was unable to tear his gaze from the ground. *Hmm . . . Home . . . What home?* Home was a place where people were eagerly waiting for you. But he had no one to wait for him.

Willie went back home. The whole way there he was racked with feelings of shame, disappointment, and rage. He truly loved his mother and, for many years, had endured her insults and rudeness to win her love. Willie always took the first step. And this time, he had swallowed hard, and ignoring the rancor in his own heart, he had gone to throw himself at his mother's feet. He had gone there with the hope of a fresh start. He had wanted to give her a chance to apologize and himself a chance to forgive.

The whole way back Willie was fixated on one idea: If everything was supposed to end like this, if they were just going to cast him aside, then why did his parents even have him? If people weren't going to provide their children with love and were going to walk out on them in the end, then why do they even need children? If he'd never been born, he wouldn't have had to feel so much pain. *What an enormous injustice!*

# NO ONE CAN BE HAPPY WHO
# ROBS ANOTHER OF HAPPINESS

*Most of the misfortunes in our journey are*
*a fair consequence of our mistakes.*

This time Helen wanted to avoid the mistakes she had made with her first family. Her husband was a stern man, very different from Brendan. He had none of Brendan's sensitivity or gallantry. And although Helen did everything in her power to win them over, the children didn't like her. They saw her as a stranger who had taken their mother's place. Helen understood this. But at the same time, she wanted to give them the love that she couldn't give Willie and thus earn redemption. Helen blamed herself for the fact that Willie could not find the happiness he deserved. She had left him without a father and destroyed that gift they had been given from God. As she tried to save her troubled second family in any way she could, Helen punished herself for the mistakes she had made in her previous marriage.

Helen often remembered the days she had spent with Willie and Brendan. Although she had no contact with Brendan — they were both busy with their new families — Helen could not forget him. She was deeply sorry for everything she had done. Sometimes she dialed Willie's number and listened to his voice. And she often went to his workplace but hesitated to approach him and merely watched him from a distance.

Once she saw him in a fight with some other guys outside the big company where he worked. They kicked and punched Willie and then left him lying on the pavement. Helen felt as if a knife was stabbing her in the heart, to the point of feeling physical pain in her chest. She wanted to run to Willie to hug and kiss him and ask where it hurt, but she couldn't move. For the first time, Helen realized that Willie was not a stranger to her, but someone precious. Her head was spinning, and she didn't know what to do. So much pain was built up inside her that she couldn't even cry. Instead of running toward Willie, she ran away from him. She ran until she fell and struck her head against the ground. As she lay there, Helen pressed her head against her knees and began to sob as if blows were raining down upon her. A police officer approached and asked, "Is there a problem, ma'am?" Clasping her hand, he helped her to her feet. But Helen could not pull herself together.

Willie did not know any of this. His mother would take the truth with her to her grave. And Willie was doomed to live with pain and fear in his heart for a long time.

Helen's rage had kept her estranged from Willie. And by the time she was sorry for what she had done, it was too late. There was a huge gulf between them, and Helen was unable to cross it. She was too ashamed to approach her son. Ashamed and afraid. How could she not be ashamed when Willie had been abandoned at a time when he really needed his mother? And so Helen reproached and punished herself for what she had done and avoided her child. Helen was afraid that Willie would rebuff and belittle her. That would have been un-bearable. She still pictured Willie as a quiet boy who listened to his mother's criticism with a bowed head. It frightened her to picture him quite the opposite. What's more, Helen's new husband didn't want to see Willie in his house.

"My kids are enough for us," he said, "and they wouldn't get along with Willie. And what do we need with three boys? Our house isn't big, and it's cramped just with us here. There's no room for Willie in this house."

These words were so familiar to Helen. She knew that human deeds always have repercussions, and what goes around, comes around. Life was like hitting a tennis ball against a wall, and life bounced Helen's actions right back at her.

Helen found the separation from her son to be unbearable. Her heart overflowed with love for him—love that had built up over the years and which she had never shared with her son. Despite her best efforts, she was never able to give that love to someone else's children. That love didn't belong to them, but to another. The rudeness of her husband's children always made her think of sweet Willie as a little boy, forever enduring her own rudeness with a bowed head as if he were guilty of something, silently listening to her undeserved reprimands. Her stepchildren weren't like that. Helen didn't have the right to yell at them. Neither they nor their father would stand for that. Nor did Helen want to aggravate an already stressful situation by being brusque with them.

Willie had changed a lot during this time as well. He had grown up and toughened up while also becoming more withdrawn. His life experiences also affected his friendships. It became harder for Willie to build relationships with his peers. Helen was aware of this and throughout those years kept an eye on her son from afar.

Willie had asked God to keep his parents together. But Helen and Brendan prevented God from answering Willie's prayer. Now it was Helen who was praying for something. Helen asked God to bring back Willie and the old days. But she was asking for the impossible. She felt ashamed to request anything from God because it was she who had ruined the happiness the Almighty had granted her. But over time, her sense of shame gave way to a sense of need. The mother felt the need to be loved by her son although she had deprived him of love.

The first time the conversation turned to the possibility of her second family moving to a distant state, Helen became alarmed. To stay closer to Willie, she used a variety of arguments to convince her husband not to move. It was a great comfort to Helen to be able to see Willie, even if only from afar. She didn't think she could survive losing him again. Once, when making her customary visit to Willie's workplace, she was unable to find him. She went back several more times to look for him. Then she learned that Willie had moved, but no one knew exactly where. Nor did her sister know anything about it. He had cut ties with all his old friends. Helen asked everyone he knew, as well as her sister and Willie's work buddies, to let her know as soon as they heard anything about him. Hoping her son would return, she went to every place he might be but couldn't find him. She no longer feared approaching her son, no longer wanted to run away from him. She wanted to find him, hold him tight, and ask forgiveness for the years that had been lost. She was no longer concerned about what Willie might say or even about her husband's opinion.

Discussions about the need to move to another state came up once again, and since her husband was so insistent, she agreed without too many objections even though the move made it less likely that she would ever find her son. She didn't want to tell her husband she was looking for Willie until she had found him. Helen still waited for her son even after moving to a new state. Deep in her heart, she clung to the hope that he would return.

# EVEN THE VERY OLD STILL
# HAVE HOPES AND DREAMS

*One's fate in extreme old age depends upon
the way one's youth has been spent.*

~ Stendhal

Human beings are extraordinary. They can experience different, conflicting emotions at the same instant. They can both rejoice and grieve for the same reason. Sometimes they may want to do something while simultaneously not wanting to. Sometimes they can be so weary that they are certain they are indifferent to their fate yet also want to do something to change it. Despite that indifference, in the depths of a person's soul lies excitement and interest in his own destiny.

Helen's stepsons, Benjamin and Jonathan, had wanted to move her to a nursing home once their father had become bedridden from illness. But it was awkward for them to just come out and say so.

"Today's nursing homes are nothing like they used to be," Benjamin said. "It's too bad that, in this country, people still think only heartless, ungrateful children send their parents to nursing homes just to get them out of their hair. Isn't that so, Jonathan?"

Jonathan was sitting at the table quietly, looking at his plate and poking his food with his fork. "What? Oh. Yeah, yeah," he said as if wakened from sleep. Seeing the pleading expression on his brother's face, he said, "You got it, Bro. It's just the media that promotes that silly idea. Today's nursing homes offer everything anyone needs. They're more like hotels. I wouldn't mind living in one myself."

"You know, we shouldn't even call them nursing homes," Benjamin said. "They aren't nursing homes. I'd say a resort for seniors. Yeah, yeah, a resort." Benjamin corrected their words.

"Jonathan, you know what? I've already told my children that when I get old, you won't have to tell me to go; I'll go myself. I'd rather live there than sit around all day staring at the four walls. What could be better than meeting new friends, being with people your own age, and getting to know them? You wouldn't even notice the passage of time. Most of these resorts are beautifully landscaped—tall trees, green grass, and flowers everywhere you look. What could be better than that? They're a tonic for the soul. But at home there are four walls and a TV.

"Modern resorts have all the amenities. They offer daily medical exams, delicious food, morning strolls, invigorating leisure activities, group movie nights—" Seeing how well informed they were, Helen realized that they had already done quite a bit of research.

"Everything comes down to money nowadays," Jonathan said. "It's true that the state-subsidized homes might not be so great. But it's a whole different story with the private ones."

Helen listened to all of this and silently considered what they were saying. She was unconcerned for her future and knew that she had no choice in the matter anyway, but with every word, she sank further into despair. She didn't think there was any difference at all between a senior resort and a nursing home or between a state-funded nursing home and a private one. No one could live a normal life there, no matter how comfortable it was. They would sit inside one of them like a prisoner sentenced to death, waiting for the end to come. *What are you saying? No, I'll die in such a place. All my life I have been accustomed to freedom, and now in these last days of life . . . How?*

"I don't want to go anywhere and leave your father; he needs my help," Helen said in a loud, agitated voice. "And when Benjamin and his wife have work to do, I also watch his children. No, no . . . I don't want to go anywhere." Helen was trying to keep her voice from trembling.

Silence reigned. Then Benjamin said, "Helen, why do you take everything so personally? No one's sending you to a senior resort! And anyway, we hardly ever leave the children with you, they're usually with their mom."

"I know. You're right, Benjamin." Helen played the last ace in her hand and said, "But your father needs my help. If I leave, he'll feel lonely."

The doctor had told Benjamin that his father would only live another two years. Benjamin and Jonathan wanted to send their stepmother to a nursing home and move their father in with one of them. They had hatched a plan to sell his house. Some days later, Helen happened to overhear Benjamin telling his brother, "We can't keep Helen with us. She's not blood. After Father's death, it will be difficult to get her out of the house." His words burned their way deep into her heart, and her entire body trembled. Helen felt sick to her stomach and went into the bathroom to vomit. After closing the door, she turned on the faucet to drown out the sound of her sobs. Pressing a hand to her mouth, she began to cry bitterly. As her tears flowed, she thought of Willie and Brendan. The days she had spent with them now seemed so sweet. She would have allowed herself to really howl if she had been certain she wouldn't be overheard. And she would have cried until her eyes wept blood out of grief for how she had ruined her own life as well as the lives of others.

Afterward, Helen was cool to Benjamin. When he asked what was wrong, she claimed to be tired. But after a while, Helen noticed Benjamin's solicitude, and her heart began to soften.

*Perhaps Benjamin spoke without thinking. He couldn't possibly do that to me. I've been a true mother to him. If they want to sell the house, let them sell it. I can move in with them as well. I'll look after their children and help his wife around the house. Their wives aren't often home anyway. And the children are just left here or there, or else they hire a babysitter. They could really use my help. I don't think they would ever do that to me,* thought Helen. She was like a child, quickly offended and quickly appeased. But in the end, Helen sensed that she had been defeated by her stepchildren and had no choice but to reconcile herself to her situation. Her feelings of hopelessness affected her behavior, and now she did her best to please her stepsons.

After her husband died, the house, which already felt alien to her, now felt even more alien. Helen felt lonely and unwanted in addition to guilty for having lived such an ignominious life.

Talk of a nursing home began again, and although initially Benjamin had talked about a private home, he later changed his mind.

"There's no difference between state-subsidized and private homes," he said. "Private homes are just a gambit to extort money. In the end, they all provide the same services. The cash we would have spent on a private home we could give directly to Helen as spending money. It would amount to quite a lot."

"Absolutely," Jonathan said. "Plus, we'll visit her all the time. And we'll bring the kids, so Helen doesn't miss them."

The days in a nursing home passed so slowly. Benjamin and Jonathan came to visit Helen only twice during the years. And they called her on the phone a couple of times. The first time they came to see her, Helen was overjoyed. Although she was only their stepmother, she was really happy to see Benjamin and Jonathan. "Well despite everything, they haven't forgotten about me or about what I did for them and all my efforts . . . I raised both of them as if they were my own children. I gave them the love I didn't give Willie." Helen reassured herself.

But as Benjamin was leaving, he handed her some documents to sign regarding the sale of the house, and Helen became quite upset. As they were preparing to leave, Helen could no longer hold back her tears and began to cry in front of them.

"Helen, please don't," Benjamin said. "You're like a mother to us. We love you very much. Don't cry. We'll come see you all the time."

"See, you've only been here a few months, and we've already come to visit you," Jonathan added to Benjamin's words of comfort.

They thought Helen was crying because they were leaving. But in truth, she was crying because of the faithlessness and treachery of life.

The second time, they came at Helen's request. Helen called them and told them that they needed to stop by because of something urgent. She thought they would give her the runaround unless she phrased it that way. This was the most difficult period of Helen's life. She waited for them for a long time. Helen wore her prettiest dress in honor of their visit. She had carefully combed her hair and borrowed some perfume and nice shoes from her roommate. Her spirits were high on the day they were to arrive. One of the staff members at the home said, "Helen, you look lovely today!" And indeed, this was a day that Helen wanted to look good for her guests. Despite her aching back, she wanted to appear young and cheerful.

It's fascinating how people, until middle age, want to be seen as grown-ups and, after middle age, want to prove to everyone that they're still young. Helen was surprised by her own behavior. *Sometimes, to escape reality, you don't even want to look in a mirror. But the aches in your back and your joints, as well as the wrinkles and frailty associated with old age, never stop reminding you, every day, of your advancing years. Is this really life? No, this isn't life, it's the end, just the end . . . Yes, Helen, the train is slowly pulling up to its last station . . ."*

*Maybe it all comes down to care and love. A woman is young as long as she is loved . . . That's what they say. I wonder, if I didn't know my own age, how old would I guess that I was? Perhaps that age should be considered my real age. A person's as old as she feels. It all depends on what's going on inside,* Helen reflected, as she climbed the stairs to her room. *Actually, in their hearts, everyone's the same age. They all want to feel young. After all, the heart never grows old. We women, completely forget about our age after we turn forty. In fact, we want to forget it. We only remember other people's ages. Ahhh, you go from youth to old age so quickly. It all seems like yesterday. And the interval between yesterday and today is just one time falling asleep and one time waking up. You fall asleep and wake up one time and you're young, one more time and you're old. And eventually you fall asleep and never wake up again. When I was a child, I wanted to be happy, and in my youth, I wanted a nicer, cushier life. But now I don't want any of that. I only want to live with my family, with the people I love. I so badly need just one kind word from them, some affection. How I crave just a little bit of attention . . .* mused Helen, heartsick.

A member of the staff called up to her, "Helen, Helen! You have some visitors. Your sons, Helen!"

"I'm coming, I'm coming! Tell them I'm coming," Helen said, starting down the stairs with uncharacteristic agility.

# THE UNLIVED PAST

*No one wants to die. Even people who want to go to heaven don't want to die to get there. And yet death is the destination we all share. No one has ever escaped it. And that is as it should be because death is very likely the single best invention of life.*

~ Steve Jobs

When Helen saw the boys in the waiting room, she felt like a little girl seeing her parents after a long absence. Smiling, she handed out some cookies she had bought for them.

They chatted a bit about this and that, then Helen told them that she was very unhappy there. She wanted to return to a familiar environment. Nice as it might be there, she felt as though she were in prison. Swallowing the pride of her youth and begging like a child, she asked them to let her leave with them. Benjamin and Jonathan looked at one another.

"Please get me out of here," Helen said. "I can't stay here. I swear I won't be a burden to you. I won't take up much room in your house." These words, so familiar to her, which had marked the beginning of her life's destruction, had come roaring back. As she uttered them, Helen could not help thinking of her own past. She faltered a bit, and then, making an effort to swallow the lump in her throat, she said, "I loved you as if you were my own children. I always took care of you and your father. And I can still work. I'm not that old. Look at my legs — I can still use them! And my hands are just as strong as they ever were." Helen no longer knew what she needed to say to persuade them to release her. She was so eager to leave that she would agree to anything to convince them.

"Helen, we'll take you home." For some reason Jonathan, who always spoke second, had now taken the reins of the conversation from

Benjamin. "But it can't be done in one day. Give us a little time. We have to get a room ready for you, talk to the nursing home director, and deal with the paperwork. Don't worry, it's all going to be fine. We'll do it the way you want."

Helen never saw them again. After their visit, she phoned them a few times. At first, they answered some of her calls but then stopped even doing that. Helen, crushed and disillusioned, decided not to pester them any further. She had already reconciled herself to her situation.

Near the end of her life, she experienced severe pain in her legs and back. She could no longer walk. Old age and brooding had turned her beautiful hair completely gray. Wrinkles creased her formerly smooth skin. Her elegant fingers, like those of a pianist, had become rough and shriveled, relinquishing their graceful beauty over the course of her arduous journey through life.

She sat in her wheelchair at the window or on her balcony all day. She spoke to no one, sitting quietly off to one side. She always seemed to be lost in thought, but no one knew about what. And perhaps she was not thinking of anything in particular. She brooded without thinking. Sometimes people just stopped in their tracks, not thinking about anything, as if their thoughts had ground to a halt. If they were asked what they were thinking about, they couldn't answer, because they don't know what's going on inside their own heads. They're not contemplating anything. This empty-headedness is due to the lack of meaning in their lives. People like that can't find their footing.

Helen's life now consisted only of memories of the past because she found her past a far more pleasant place. But in her imagination, the past was not as it had been but as she wanted it to have been.

It was snowing in Dallas. The snow lay down carefully in front of the windows and the door.

The naked trees were being covered with a white blanket. The smoke from the chimney was warm and cozy.

This was the house with the yard where they had settled after marriage. It had witnessed the happiest days of their lives together. They never left it.

The doorbell rang. Today, Brendan came home early from work. He pressed the bell, hoping Helen would open the door. But the house remained quiet. Brendan took the keys out of his pocket, opened the door, and went in. Thea ran toward her father, hugged him by the legs, then climbed into his arms. Helen was happiest of all about

Brendan's arrival. Busy preparing dinner in the kitchen, she warmly greeted him from there.

Brendan leaned against the kitchen door and watched her.

Soon, the dinner was ready. Helen set the table, and little Thea tried her best to help her. A dress the color of a snowy winter night fitted in perfectly with her puffy cheeks and large black eyes. "Sweetheart, where's Willie?" Brendan looked at his watch in concern.

"Did you forget he has a game today? He told you about it," Helen said to her husband.

The doorbell rang.

"Willie, Willie! My brother's home!" Thea ran to open the door. She couldn't quite reach the doorknob, so she started pounding on the door with her little fists, trying to make it open faster.

As soon as Helen opened the door, Willie burst in, smiling and cheerful. It seemed as though his team had played well again, as usual.

"How was the game, sweetie?" Helen asked, kissing him.

"Like always, Mom," Willie said, walking into the kitchen. "I'm so hungry I could eat a horse!"

Brendan joined the family conversation. "Uh-huh. Playing sports has turned you into a bottomless pit. You'll eat us out of house and home!"

A few minutes later, they all sat down to eat. Brendan sat next to Helen. He put his hand around Helen's neck and whispered something in her ear, looking at the kids. Helen smiled. Willie noticed the joy in his mother's eyes and smiled back at her.

"I love you so much! Merry Christmas, Mom! I'm so glad you're here with us. It's thanks to you that we have such a loving family. Thank you for your endless love and sleepless nights, for loving us and feeding us and bringing me and Thea into this world. Just—thank you for everything you've done for us. All I asked Santa for was that our family be together. And my wish has come true." Willie came over and wiped her tears away. Thea rushed into Brendan's arms. Together, they hugged their mother.

"Mommy, Mommy, don't cry." Thea wiped away her mother's tears with her soft little hands. "It's okay. We love you so much. Why are you crying?"

Brendan was also moved, but tried to hide it. "Okay, that's enough. Or Santa Claus is gonna turn around and leave; he'll think he came on the wrong day." It was Christmas Eve. A tall, decorated tree stood in the middle of the living room. They had trimmed it right after

Thanksgiving to make the holidays even more fun for the children. Christmas was Thea's and Willie's favorite holiday, and they had been getting ready for months. Helen knew all they could think of was Santa delivering their presents tonight.

"Helen, what is loneliness?" asked a secret voice from the depths of her heart.

*Loneliness . . . Loneliness is when all your dreams are only imaginary and will never come true. Loneliness is when you're only happy in your daydreams. Loneliness is feeling helpless. Loneliness is crying, regretting the life you've lived that was given to you by God as a gift, but which you ended up ruining. Loneliness is growing old without any loved ones who will bring you a glass of water so you can take your medicine before you go to bed. Loneliness is dreaming while sitting in front of a balcony and looking through the window into the courtyard of this nursing home. Loneliness is the desire to go back in time to relive one's life. Loneliness is constantly waiting for something, but you don't know what it is, and waiting for someone but knowing that person won't come. It's when you stand up and leave, without saying a word to anyone. You think that your absence will be unbearable for everyone, especially the ones you love, but then you realize that no one particularly cares or has even noticed that you've gone. And everyone gets along just fine without you. Whether you're there or not is quite unimportant. You thought you were important to them and they would suffer without you. But in fact, you have vastly exaggerated your significance to them. No one cares how you live your life, and they haven't for a long time. You have no place in their lives. And the most upsetting thing is that you have no one to whom you can offer a place in your own life.*

Although all this took place in Helen's imagination, she thought that she had never been so close to the truth.

On one ordinary day, Helen — waiting for her son at the window, daydreaming and gazing at the spruce in the yard — simply closed her eyes upon this wearisome world. At the time, Willie was sitting on a bench in a park near MD Anderson Hospital in Houston, feeling very depressed. He spent the entire day of his mother's death with a sense of foreboding about bad news. Since Willie's name was not listed as one of the elderly Helen's family members, he was not informed of her death in time. The nursing home staff searched for Helen's sons, but it was her stepsons who got the notification, not Willie.

Willie didn't know anything about it. Not that his mother had searched for him, had wanted his forgiveness, or that she had lived a tormented life. Nor did Helen ever learn what had happened to Willie, or that he would have forgiven his mother. Helen had dreamed of that for so long. She prayed to God for that every night. She desperately prayed that Willie might forgive her . . . That prayer of Helen's would have been answered. But even if Willie had forgiven her, her life and past would not. That was the worst part. But to Helen, who had surrendered to fate before her death, this was not the main thing.

Helen's one prayer went unanswered. She prayed that she might see her own son, Willie, who was now a grown man, before she died. She wanted to gaze into his small, perceptive eyes one last time. With all her heart, she wanted to smooth his hair with her wrinkled hands as she had never done before. She wanted to say the words to him that she had never said: "I love you, and I am terribly sorry. Please forgive me, son." But her wishes were not granted. Because some chances are only offered once in a lifetime.

# HE WAS ONE OF THE "ANGELS"

*With the last breath of hope, dreams come true.*

Willie suddenly roused himself and looked out the bus window. Any farther and he would have missed his stop.

Fifteen minutes later, as he did every morning, he entered the MD Anderson Hospital service entrance to go to work. He walked quickly to the elevator. He looked at the red numbers on the digital readout above it.

*Five . . . four . . . three . . .* As the numbers appeared on the display, he silently kept track of them. He often did that. He counted the stairs he climbed, the number of trees he passed, and the number of cars parked in the lot. This was an unconscious habit. Sometimes he would realize that his head had been spinning all day long with these meaningless calculations. He had asked a therapist about this but was told that it was just a nervous quirk.

Finally, "1" lit up. Willie followed other hospital employees into the elevator. *Yet another pointless day. This day has just begun, and already I don't see the point of it,* he thought to himself.

Willie walked into the staff room and changed into his uniform. The night nurse gave him the information about the latest patients to arrive and important updates.

One of the new arrivals was Wisam, a young, twenty-two-year-old guy of Arab background. He and his family had moved to Texas from Lebanon four years earlier. Wisam had been brought to the hospital with a diagnosis of lung cancer. He was a very skinny guy with big sunken eyes. The skin all over his body had turned a yellow-ish color. Because of chemotherapy, he had lost all his hair. Wisam had a constant hacking cough, and his voice was hoarse and weak. He was often dizzy, and his bones ached terribly.

Willie had seen many patients like this. None of them held any particular significance for him. Not because he was indifferent to their tragic plight, but because he was used to such cases, and it was all part of his job. Willie saw him as just another patient that he needed to attend to and clean up after.

Despite the fact that Willie had worked at the hospital for only a brief time, he could make a guess, based on the patients' diagnoses, which ones had the best chance to survive. Lung cancer was one of the worst diagnoses. In private, the staff half-jokingly referred to the cancer patients as "angels" because they often didn't live long. Wisam was one of these "angels." When the nurse gave Wisam's medical information to Willie, his first thought was that the young man wouldn't be there for long.

Willie put on his gloves as usual and began inspecting the rooms. He went from one room to the next, working step by step, starting with the highest priority tasks. He'd become so used to his routine that he didn't even notice the sick or their faces, tortured from the strain of their illness.

He saw Wisam for the first time when he went into room seven-teen. With a sideways glance toward the bed, Willie saw the patient was sleeping. Wisam had taken Mrs. Simpson's place.

She had been seventy years old. Although she had many children and relatives, she suffered from loneliness. During the three weeks she was there, her children only came to see her three times. The first time was when she was admitted to the hospital; the second, when she had an operation; and the third time was when she died. During his time at the hospital, Willie had often witnessed people lonely and for-gotten, even if they had a large family and many relatives and friends. Perhaps Mrs. Simpson's children felt that, although they weren't of-ten with their mother, at least they were with her at the most crucial moments. Deep in their hearts they probably thought that by putting their mother in this expensive hospital and sending her everything she wanted, that they were fulfilling all their obligations to her. After all, someone had to go to work to pay those big hospital bills. And some people might feel that made sense, but that logic didn't comfort the heart of an elderly mother who was facing death, nor did it lessen her loneliness and longing for her children.

For Mrs. Simpson, none of the days she spent in the hospital were any less significant than the day of her surgery. She wanted to see her children every day. How to explain to an elderly woman that, for her children, there was a huge difference between ordinary days and the day of the surgery? One day was very important to them, while the others were not. An elderly mother would be more frightened and worried by being treated badly by her children than by the pain from her stomach cancer.

When Willie had left work the day before, the old woman's condition had deteriorated, and it was quite likely that she wouldn't survive until the next day. And so he wasn't surprised to hear of her death. Something Mrs. Simpson often used to say to console herself echoed in his head and tugged at his heart. "Soon I'll die, and all this pain will end. I've long taken comfort in that." Mrs. Simpson frequently used this expression when she grew tired of waiting for her children. The first day she got to the hospital, she wanted the bed closest to the door. She saw that as a lucky omen and hoped that she wouldn't be there long. But after a while, she said that she wanted to move to the bed next to the window.

There were moments in life when Willie was confronted by events that he wanted to forget, to erase from his memory. But as luck would have it, those were the ones he could never forget. He wanted to erase from memory some extremely distressing and sad incidents that he witnessed some patients experiencing. Once, Mrs. Simpson's sister came to see her. During that conversation, Mrs. Simpson had accidentally discovered that a contractor was working on the house she shared with the family of one of her sons. The contractor was there to incorporate her bedroom into the newly expanded living room. When she heard this, she didn't know what to say and sat, frozen in silence, for a long time. Willie thought words failed a person at such moments.

Finally, Mrs. Simpson spoke. "And . . . and whose idea was this? After all, I'm still alive. I'm alive . . . And when I come home, where will I sleep? Or are they thinking that I won't come home? Who did this?"

"I don't know," her sister said, but she did. However, she didn't want to name the person who had come up with the idea and thus further wound her dying sister. For Mrs. Simpson, finding out whose idea it had been was more important than finding out that her bedroom walls were being knocked down. She could not have borne it if she had discovered that it had been her own child's notion.

"Probably Emily wanted to do it," Mrs. Simpson had said, rapidly blinking eyes that looked dull in her wrinkled face. "Clearly it was her decision. She always fantasized about getting me out of the house."

Remembering this, Willie's heart beat faster, and he felt even more cheerless.

Wisam's room was designed to accommodate four patients. Usually these rooms were filled with elderly people, but recently they had been occupied by young guests. Willie looked at each new arrival as an ordinary case, but they all had their own painful life story. Each was unique and multifaceted. But at the same time, all the patients were experiencing similar emotions. Willie thought this was because they all shared a common misfortune. Suffering gave them similar facial expressions.

Patients who came here were not usually inclined to chat. They felt dispirited and overwhelmed by their unrelenting disease and resigned themselves to waiting for the end.

Willie went to open the window to let in some air. When he pulled open the curtain, the sun hit him right in the eye. "I'm already sick of this heat," he said quietly.

"Some people dream of feeling this heat."

Willie was startled to hear the hoarse voice of someone speaking with a pleasant accent. Turning, he saw the newly-arrived patient looking at him with large, smiling eyes. Those eyes looked too big for his emaciated body. The eyes were the only part of the young man's body that did not look wan and haggard. They were a celestial color. These were the smiling eyes, filled with faith, of a man who had not surrendered to his disease or to the hardships and difficulties of life. This was the first time Willie had ever seen a terminally ill person whose eyes retained a smile despite how little time he had left. After hearing the young man, Willie became so flustered that he left the room without a word.

From his first day of work at MD Anderson Hospital, Willie was hoping for a miracle of some sort — to see changes. The strange presentiment that had been preventing him from leaving the Anderson clinic now suddenly intensified.

*I've noticed that the patients who end up in this room are always destined for something surprising. This room is home to some very complex lives,* Willie mused, thinking of the patients lying there.

What's more, it seemed to him that his past and future were linked to this very room, room seventeen. His very own past and future.

# TIME DOES NOT HEAL, IT ONLY
# TEACHES ONE TO LIVE WITH PAIN

*You'll never understand pain until you've burned your own fingers.*

Willie had been working at MD Anderson for more than a year now. But still no one valued his work or showed any interest in him as a person. No one ever even thanked him for what he did. Everyone considered his efforts to simply be his job duties, for which he received a paycheck. He was invisible to those around him. Most of the staff saw Willie as a boring man with a boring life.

Everyone prefers chatty, smiling, sociable types. They're referred to as "the heart of the company," and everyone is fond of them. The leading roles in movies and novels are usually brave, scrappy, strong, romantic, beautiful, and very interesting people with extraordinary abilities. Everyone loves them. Even people who are nothing like them. But Willie was an introverted man who shunned society and friendship and, in general, any kind of extended interaction. So he was not popular, and no one felt an affinity for him.

No one knew what was going on inside Willie's life or head. There were times when he felt more pensive and downcast than ever, and he wouldn't utter a single word. Sometimes after work he would walk around for hours out in the cold, all alone, just thinking. He would sit in the same park or roam the deserted streets, hatless, with his coat undone. He often left the house at midnight and didn't come back until almost dawn. Sometimes he would go back to work the next day without having returned home. Not even his wife, Sarah, could break through Willie's protective shell and find the path to his heart and inner world.

Willie's behavior hinted at timidity and caution and seemed rooted in fear. Dr. Stevens, noticing Willie's demeanor, said, "People like that are statistically more likely to kill themselves, and all the red flags for suicide are evident in Willie's behavior. Yes, I think things will end badly for Willie."

People can adapt to conditions that they first viewed as intolerable, and Willie had spent years getting used to this life-in-a-cave that he was now living. He had learned how to be alone, living an isolated existence even when surrounded by other people. Of course anyone who gets used to a life like that is no longer really living. Willie was just dragging himself along, counting down the days he had left while bearing up under all his baggage. He continued to haul that baggage around, even when his heart was broken with grief and the walls were closing in on him.

People are always looking for someone who is simpatico, a friend with whom to share life's joys and sorrows, someone to whom they can open their hearts and get advice when they need it. That search can take a while. Sometimes, despite combing the whole world, even a single person who will listen and be a friend cannot be found. The world is filled with people, but they are only interested in themselves. No one worries about someone else's boring life—it's not interesting. People only pay attention to their own lives. Everyone wants to read their own opus and write their own novel.

Floundering in the ocean of life, Willie became inured by loneliness. And for fifteen years, he did not share his feelings or concerns with anyone. After living this way for so long, Willie felt emotionally numb. Nothing could make him happy anymore, and nothing could upset him.

Willie had lost his faith in people. This was the result of the psychological trauma he had suffered at the hands of his parents. But for Willie to understand why he had erected such high iron walls to keep others out, he had to first break the ice in his heart. Willie did not want to relive the betrayal and the agonizingly painful feelings that he had experienced in the past. That was why he didn't let anyone get close to his heart. Willie's past seemed to have ripped out his soul, leaving only a lifeless body behind. Willie had lived with his wife, Sarah, for many years, and he was surrounded by good people at work, but he had never during those years uttered a word about his past or about his feelings. He had buried his past deep within his heart and never considered letting anyone in. After the blows life had dealt him, Willie was destined for a lonely fate.

# IT'S A MAN'S WORLD

The second time Willie went into room seventeen, Wisam asked, "Are you Willie?"

Startled, Willie raised his head to look at Wisam and said, "Yes, I'm Willie. You're our new arrival, Wisam."

Then quickly, Willie turned to his daily tasks. Wisam watched everything he did, as if to form his own impression of this person with whom he was going to spend his last days. And Willie kept busy with his work, as if unaware of Wisam. At times their eyes met. Then Wisam would smile amiably and nod his head with satisfaction. This situation made Willie feel awkward. Shyly, he would again drop his head and continue to work. An onlooker would have thought that it was Willie's first day on the job. He seemed lost and fumbled around, dropping things.

And so the days passed. Whenever Willie stopped by room seventeen, Wisam would smile at him and say, "Welcome." Wisam greeted everyone warmly, not just Willie. But Willie comported himself differently from the other staff, and this drew Wisam's attention. Wisam understood that when a person has retreated into a shell, there are reasons why he has ended up that way. He sensed that Willie needed help and that he could not escape his predicament on his own. Although Wisam was in a difficult situation himself, he forgot about his own suffering upon seeing another's troubles. He wanted to help this stranger he felt so drawn to. But he didn't know how. And so to figure out what to do, Wisam tried to strike up a friendship with him. Willie sensed that Wisam wanted to get to know him. This was the first time in his life that a stranger had made a determined effort to make his acquaintance. No matter how Willie tried to distance himself, Wisam did not take offense and remained good-humored. When Willie was working in his room or they encountered one another in the hallway, Wisam talked to him, attempting to draw him into conversation on various topics. But whenever Wisam asked him a question, Willie became flustered. He sensed that Wisam wanted admittance into his inner world that he kept off-limits.

Wisam observed Willie's relationships with the other hospital staff. He noticed that his coworkers sometimes expected Willie to take up their slack.

"Hey, Willie, something's come up, and I have to run. Take over here, okay?"

"Willie, could you do this? I'll be right back."

"Willie, they told me that you're supposed to hand over the medicines. Come on, hurry up!"

All these extra tasks meant that Willie was forced to carry an additional load. And the doctors at times scolded Willie for every minor lapse. Dr. Stevens seemed to seek out opportunities to speak harshly to him. He enjoyed the feeling of power this gave him. Everyone felt entitled to say these things to Willie. But no one ever said a word to Willie's coworkers. In fact, people made an extra effort to be charming to them. That those employees would never tolerate an unwarranted reprimand seemed to be common knowledge.

Wisam was very worried about this ambiguous attitude. When he asked the people who treated Willie unfairly why they did so, they justified their behavior in some astonishing ways.

"Oh, you know, Wisam, that's how you have to deal with people like Willie, or else they get out of hand. Actually, they're grateful when you give them something to do. They like to be ordered around—that's just the way they are. They're sort of masochistic. If they didn't like it, they'd definitely say something."

"Everything we say to him is for his own good. We point out his mistakes so he can clean up his act. Otherwise, we wouldn't say a word, as it brings no benefit to us."

"Willie's used to it."

"The most horrifying member of any social group is the doormat. You really have to be careful with them."

Wisam didn't even want to think about how these words could be used to justify insulting behavior and dumping your work on someone else. To the extent that he could, Wisam tried to defend Willie when he saw it happening. But Willie seemed indifferent to it all. It was as if he didn't notice Wisam's efforts on his behalf.

Once Wisam saw Willie carrying a record album.

"Can I take a look?"

Wordlessly Willie handed it to him. An African-American musician was pictured on the cover. And the song titles from the album were listed in the photo. "James Brown . . . Oh yeah, the famous Mr. Dynamite . . ." Wisam sighed.

Willie, who usually preferred to hold his tongue when interacting with patients, felt compelled to speak up when Wisam referred to the most popular nickname for this musician who had once been one of Willie's favorites.

"You know who he is?" Willie asked quietly. *How could some guy from Lebanon, a Muslim Arabic country, know about the Godfather of Soul?*

"My father liked him."

Now Willie was even more astonished and wondered why an Arab Muslim would like a mid-twentieth-century American R&B singer. "You like him too?"

"He sings from his heart," Wisam said. "I think James Brown was one of the few artists of his era to reach such creative heights. His voice had an unusual timbre, and his performance style was quite distinctive. Plus his stage energy — that's what really stands out about James Brown." Wisam's comments amazed Willie even more.

"My father used to listen to him at home in Lebanon. There are three of his songs that I really like: 'I Feel Good,' 'It's a Man's World,' and also —"

"Let me guess. 'Try Me!' Am I right?" Willie said, smiling. "Anyone who likes 'I Feel Good' has to like that one too."

"You got it." Wisam started laughing. He liked seeing Willie get excited about a conversation.

"And what about 'Out of Sight'?" asked Willie, with growing interest in the discussion.

"I don't remember that one. I might have heard it, but the name doesn't sound familiar," Wisam said. "I haven't listened to all of his songs, only a few."

While he was chatting with Wisam, Willie felt that his original assumptions might have been wrong. He was getting to know someone from a country that he had thought was completely cut off from the rest of the world.

"First impressions are usually wrong," Wisam said, as if he could read Willie's thoughts by looking at his face. "Spending time with a person — that's the way to get to know them. Where I'm from, they say that the best way to get to know a person is to take a trip with him. Of course, that's just an expression. To really get to know someone, you have to be with him during the most difficult moments of his life. Hardships pull aside the curtain and expose a person's true face."

That was the day that Wisam and Willie had their first good conversation. Candid and open communication will open the path to someone's heart. If people communicate in a sincere manner, then in their hearts they will want to draw closer. It's natural to be guarded and leery of strangers. But Willie was an extreme example. Wisam continually tried to engage Willie in meaningful conversation, attempting to get to know him by asking all sorts of questions about his children, his relatives, and other concerns.

At one point, Willie got sick. When Wisam heard about this, he asked a nurse for Willie's phone number and called him.

"Hello! Have I reached Willie's house?"

"Yes."

How's he doing? You're probably Caitlin, aren't you?"

"No, this is Sarah."

"Really? I thought you were Willie's daughter."

"Does my voice sound so young?"

"Yes, ma'am, it does."

Sarah was very pleased by this. "Who was that, Willie? I think he knew who I was. He was just being a gentleman." Sarah's words made Willie smile.

After that episode, although their relationship was still not entirely candid and open, Willie became a bit more sociable and friendly toward Wisam. During this time, Wisam's condition improved slightly. It was not difficult for him to get around the hospital. When he went out into the hallway, he and Willie would sit in the chairs intended for the patients' relatives and chat a bit. Sometimes they would go get a cup of coffee in the hospital cafeteria. During these conversations they usually discussed topics they were both familiar with, such as the hospital, other patients, and the nursing staff. Neither Willie nor Wisam shared any stories about their pasts. Willie was frustrated by his relationships with his friends and family. Wisam sensed that from his guarded answers to Wisam's questions. Wisam suspected that Willie always felt out of place, unconnected, and in the way, particularly in his own home.

Each day, Wisam and Willie's friendship grew, relegating their patient-staff relationship to the back seat. Wisam saw how Willie now sought him out, no longer avoiding him. There were times when Willie would give Wisam the cold shoulder again, acting like he didn't know him, but Wisam took no offense and continued to chat with him amiably as if nothing had happened. Wisam thought that Willie was confused about his feelings and exhausted by painful memories of his past and the spiritual trauma he had endured. Wisam didn't think that Willie had any goals or meaningful activities in his life. His emotional state was the result of everything that had built up inside him.

"Yes, Willie. All of that would knock anyone off his feet." Sometimes Wisam would look at Willie and—guessing his mood—say something like that. Willie would smile shyly at Wisam, having no idea what he was talking about. "But how long will it go on that way?" Not even Willie was able to answer that question.

Once, when the two were quietly drinking coffee in the cafeteria, Wisam said, "Willie, why are you hiding yourself from me? Because the more you try to hide, the more you expose yourself. No matter how you try to conceal your feelings, your eyes give you away. Everything's written all over your face."

Willie was taken aback by this sudden question.

After a few moments of silence, he suddenly started talking. "I feel strange around you. You're the one with whom I want to share all my thoughts first, but also, it's as if I don't even need to speak. It seems to me that my heart is completely open to you. And you see all the wounds in my soul and touch them with a glance. Even if I wanted to, I wouldn't be able to hide from you. Each time I talk to you, painful emotions awaken in my heart, and my life becomes more difficult. Yet I find talking to you to be very comforting. I don't know, maybe I'm suffering because you've opened the wounds in my heart that I've been hiding from everyone. And then you heal them. My heart melts. My senses come alive. It's as though my tears return, and having cried, I want to free my heart. Before I met you I was used to feeling shut down. My emotions and my life were identical. Now everything is changing because of you.

"Now with you around, my feelings and thoughts are growing more muddled every day. There are deep scars in my heart caused by sorrow, betrayal, loneliness. Do you think that makes me feel bad? No! It bothered me in the beginning. But I got used to it over time. But now the sorrow and grief are tormenting me and causing me pain. They say that time heals, but over the years I've come to realize that time is no doctor. It only teaches you how to live with pain and sorrow.

"I've never in my life been so afraid of anything as of allowing myself to dream. I've watched all my beautiful dreams be destroyed. Wisam, I'm afraid to be happy. I'm terrified to feel joy or hope for the future. I don't feel like I deserve anything from that future. Perhaps I'm afraid that I won't be able to seize hold of it. Working in this hospital I've seen when people are sick, they are surrounded by others who value them, but when I get sick, no one cares. Even my immediate family only pretends to care about me. I think that they want to nurse me back to health quickly, so I can get right back to work and keep earning money. They don't want to have to endure my presence at home. Every time I get sick, I think about this . . .

"But when you phoned . . . You called when I was sick. I haven't been so pleased about a phone call in a long time. You don't even know me. But you took an interest in me, and you were so respectful toward me. Maybe that phone call was no big deal to you, but it made me really happy anyway. Only my heart has known how awful I feel. My heart is the only thing that has stayed near me every single instant."

Willie sipped his coffee. After a brief silence, he said, "All these years, without even knowing it, I've been trying to protect my inner world from everyone else. I saw them as alien beings. And naturally others sensed that and distanced themselves from me. I kept retreating further inward, but I couldn't stop it. I stopped hoping that I would ever find someone to whom I could open my soul, but then you came along. Wisam, I had absolutely no strength left to tackle life.

"I take the most joy in solitude. Even when I'm around people, I'm still lonely. But I feel most at ease when there's no one around me. At first, I thought I was probably losing my mind or that I would eventually kill myself. But gradually you get used to things, you know?

"Now I can always find a place to hide away. Usually I just hole up in a park near here. I go to that park every day, sometimes sitting there for hours, especially when I'm particularly low. But no haven can replace the lake that was next to our house in Dallas that I often visited with my father. Back then I thought that my dad loved solitude, just like me. In fact, we went to that lake so we could hide away together. I felt supported, but also lonely.

"Sometimes, when I was by myself, I imagined I was an explorer, a rich man who traveled around the world with a house by the sea on a very distant island. It's odd that even in my dreams I was always alone, always . . ."

Wisam mulled over everything Willie was saying, analyzing every word.

"People can get used to lengthy bouts of solitude. Then they begin to grow accustomed to anyone who wants to interrupt that solitude. People like that can start to see themselves as strong. They think they can withstand suffering and loneliness. Every time the sun comes up and they are alone again, they exclaim, 'I'm strong—I can bear it all!' But having reassured themselves, they whisper, 'I'm already tired.' Yes, Willie, I heard your whisper, not your exclamation. I saw the loneliness you've gotten used to, as well as what your heart wants from within that solitude."

*People naturally tend to judge others by their appearance,* Willie thought. *But no one tries to uncover the treasure that lies hidden underneath that appearance or the years of secrets that are concealed there. Even the simplest, most unhappy man can have big secrets in his life. I wonder why we don't more thoroughly analyze people when we express our opinions of them. After all, don't we check out the shoes they're wearing, right down to the brand, quality, and material? I wonder why we never want to stop to think, but rush to express our opinions? No, Wisam's completely different from all those people. He's not like that. He's wormed his way inside of me and read my heart.*

"Willie, no matter how painful and cruel life can be, no matter whether a person is lonely and defenseless, there's always someone who will save him from that loneliness. You just need to find that person. Often God himself will send someone at just the right moment," said Wisam, looking into Willie's eyes.

"You might be surrounded by wonderful people," Wisam said, "but if they already have someone they are closer to than you, you feel lonely.

"You're focusing your gaze too far away and not looking right around yourself. And that's making you lonely. It's possible that in your family or at work there are people who would like to be your friend. It's even possible that one of those people is sitting across from you right now, drinking coffee." Wisam smiled. "Willie, feelings are like flowers. If you don't look after them and take care of them, they will wilt. You need to share your feelings with others and not hold back on your love for people but give it to them in full. Then you'll see how a beautiful world can emerge within you. If you suppress your feelings, then after a while, they die."

Willie realized that he had been too candid. He paused for a second, then changed the subject. "I'll be honest, I didn't realize you could speak English so well." Wisam smiled. "When they first told me that they had put someone from Lebanon in that room, I thought I would find a patient who could only say hello and good-bye."

"I took private English lessons in high school," Wisam said. "My parents felt it was important that I know English."

# HE CREATES NOTHING BUT BEAUTY

*If a problem is fixable, then there is no need to worry.*
*If it's not fixable, then there is no help in worrying.*

~ The fourteenth Dalai Lama

Wisam did not know since when he caught this disease. For a long time, he complained of coughing and chest pains. The doctors misdiagnosed him. He was treated sometimes for bronchitis, sometimes for allergies. Eventually one doctor referred him to the oncology center. After an exam, they determined that he had been suffering from cancer for several years. "If you had gone to an experienced doctor immediately, this disease could easily have been cured in its early stages. If you had gone to an oncologist right from the start, you wouldn't be in this condition now," his roommates and acquaintances often told him.

Willie pondered that as well sometimes. "Lung cancer is mostly caused by smoking and living in big, industrial cities with a lot of air pollution. And since Wisam didn't smoke, probably it was moving to Houston that made him sick. And given the frequency of oncological diseases in this city, my theory is probably correct. So if Wisam had moved to a different city, he probably wouldn't have contracted this illness."

But Wisam had a different philosophy of life to explain events.

"If you flip through the pages of your life, pay attention to acquaintances and events. Compare them; you'll notice their strong connections and wisdom," he said to Willie. "My coming here, your getting this job, meeting me, the creation of the MD Anderson Foundation—there's more here than meets the eye. We believe that from the very beginning, the Creator has preordained every event that occurs on Earth, including illnesses and even death. Everything that happens to every person has been specifically selected and devised for that individual. During this selection process, all of a person's abilities, skills, and strengths are taken into account in considering that person's future life and, most importantly, his welfare. For this reason, in every case there is much that is beneficial and wise. All these things help that person to thrive materially and spiritually. This divine preordination is intended to encourage that person to progress, not regress. It is not merely the imposition of hardships for the sake of suffering. Therefore, no one should be distressed because of something that has happened to him or because he has been deprived of something. He shouldn't grumble about his misfortune and tribulations. Our sacred book says, "No misfortune ever befalls on Earth, nor on yourselves but We have inscribed it in the Book before We make it manifest. Surely that is easy for God."

"Yes," Willie said, "but what about human freedom and determinism?[3]"

"Of course man is free," Wisam said. "He makes his own choices without being coerced. We have free will to manage our own affairs and to conduct ourselves. But what happens is not dependent upon us but is, of necessity, preordained. Willie, you were born to some family in Dallas, and I, to one in Lebanon. Later, I came to Houston and contracted this disease, and our will played no part in any of that. The events that occur have meaning, Willie. Look around you! Look at the beauty, the order in nature, at the give and take. You can see the same thing in outer space. The movements and shapes of the planet and stars — there are laws in the heavens and on Earth. It's all under the control of a precise and meaningful system. We're part of that natural world. How is it possible that throughout the universe there is order, meaning, and beauty, but in human beings, which are one part of that, and in their lives, all of that is absent? There is beauty everywhere, but that part of the natural world that includes people is filthy and chaotic. I don't know, Willie; something doesn't add up. I don't think it works like that. There's something here we don't understand.

"The whole universe has a single source. The heavens, Earth, planets, and all living beings all come from a single source of creation. This single source is the Creator, the source of wisdom, justice, compassion, and beauty. Since everything comes from Him, those things

---

[3] This is a scientific and philosophical doctrine positing the dependence of all events on shared, objective laws and including a causal link, meaning that everything that occurs is a consequence of causes and effects.

must reflect in themselves the same beauty found in Him. The Creator is excellent, and therefore His creation must be excellent.

"You know, Willie, that's the only way the Lord can create. He Himself consists of excellence, so all His works are endowed with the same qualities. God is excellent, His creations are excellent, and as a result, life is also excellent, Willie."

"You're a pretty good talker," Willie said with an ironic laugh. "You sound just like a philosopher." His smile could not conceal his inner displeasure. "Every day we bear witness to the error of your words. This is MD Anderson, where each day we encounter hundreds of sick people who are doomed to die. Many of them are as young as you are. Just go out into the streets. Have you seen the people sleeping in gutters, tunnels, and under bridges? Everywhere in the world we see wars, squalor, and adversity. What's excellent about that? How can this be explained in relation to the infinite love and infinite wisdom of your Creator?"

"Willie, nothing you've said is proof that there is no Creator. Even adversity, wars, and the awful stuff we do can't serve as proof of the Creator's injustice or the absence of wisdom in what's going on. Looking at the nightmares that you've listed, I'm even more convinced of the existence of a Creator. I'm convinced that these horrors are perpetuated by evil people like us, not by the Creator. I'm convinced that there must be a Lord who will punish these tyrants. There must be someone who will give those sinners who destroy and disfigure the beauty He has created the punishment they deserve.

"Willie, everything you've mentioned is like a shadow. In the natural world, when the sun's rays fall upon an object on Earth's surface, they produce a shadow. A shadow is the absence of light. Shadows are the natural result. God didn't create shadows as a separate thing. All adversity consists of the absence of compassion, and diseases are the absence of health. War, many diseases, and most of our unhappiness result from poor life choices. That's not what God wanted, nor what he created. We and our own actions are to blame. Which of the murders, crimes, and wars that go on in the world are God responsible for?

"Sometimes you can see that many of the problems people face are just an echo of their own irresponsibility and inaction. Often people who are destitute have made some regrettable life choices."

"The Bible says the same thing," interjected the patient lying across from Wisam while being attended to by a nurse. "It seems that all sacred books promote the same ideology."

"All these words are beautiful," said the nurse, "but if you don't believe, then as they say, your life won't work out. That's what my grandmother told me when I was just a kid. She was a Baptist. And sure enough, as soon as I run into problems, that's where I start casting blame, starting with my fate. Well, good for you Wisam. You believe in all that stuff. You Muslims have a very powerful ideology. That's why you don't become demoralized although you have so many political and economic problems."

Wisam truly did believe all this, with all his being. This was why he was friendly with everyone, always joking and laughing, without showing anyone how he was suffering. He just went on with his life. He always spoke with hope and talked only about the good days. Seeing him this way, Willie at times forgot that Wisam was living out the very last days of his life.

# A MAN WHO CRACKS A JOKE FROM HIS COFFIN



*Know from where you came, where you are going, and before whom you are destined to give a judgment and accounting.*

~ The Torah

"How do you feel today, John Brown?" Dr. Stevens said to Wisam upon entering his room one day. "Do you want to know who John Brown[4] was?"

"I'd love for you to tell me, Doctor."

"John Brown was a leader in the abolitionist movement who launched a revolution against the system of slavery. He was an odd one, like you."

"And how was he odd, Doctor?"

"Even when John Brown was being taken to the gallows, he was quite calm. They seated him on his own coffin in the back of a wagon, but he still bantered with the onlookers." Dr. Stevens smiled and glanced at the others in the room. But neither the patients nor the medical staff of the cancer center seemed to find his humor at all funny.

"Don't misinterpret what I'm saying," he said. "John Brown was a very courageous and freedom-loving man. He wasn't afraid of death because he was fighting for a just cause. Yes, yes . . . Despite the wild commotion of those who were accompanying him to the scaffold, he remarked calmly, glancing around, 'This is a beautiful country; I have not cast my eyes over it before—that is, in this direction.'"

---

[4] In the mid-nineteenth century, John Brown was one of the first to begin an armed struggle against American slaveholders. He resorted to terrorist methods and violent opposition to abolish slavery. Brown and his group were unusually ruthlessness in their attacks. In the end, he was arrested by the US government and executed for inciting a slave rebellion and committing murder.

"Dr. Stevens, what you said didn't bother me," Wisam said. "Actually, you're sort of right. However, if I, like Mr. Brown, had been a crusader for the sake of millions of people deprived of all their rights by the slave system of the the United States[5], perhaps I would be happier today. And yet, I don't think it's right to use terror and violent opposition to achieve one's goals like John Brown did. When it comes to stuff like that, I agree more with Gandhi's[6] views, and I think his technique of *Satyagraha* is more effective."

Wisam was naturally a quiet, good-natured man, but at the same time, he had a quick wit and was not shy about expressing his opinions. Dr. Stevens immediately understood what Wisam was hinting at, although it was clear from the doctor's face that he was unfamiliar with the term "Satyagraha." He didn't say a word but suddenly developed an interest in the condition of the next patient.

Willie and the nurses in the room were overcome with laughter. "Some people seem to have a special gift for driving others crazy just with their presence," said one of the nurses in a quiet voice with her head lowered, so she could express her annoyance out of Dr. Stevens's earshot.

After Dr. Stevens left the room, one patient who was lying by the window and leaning on his pillow said: "I'd love to march up to that Stevens and ask him if being so thickheaded has caused him any problems in life."

After the nurses left the room, Wisam's smiling expression turned serious. Lifting his eyes upward, he said, "Under these circumstances, Willie, I'm actually trying to conduct myself like Burayr and Habib ibn Madhahir."

Willie looked at him questioningly.

"Burayr and Habib were faithful followers of the Prophet's grandson and successor, Husayn. Husayn and his followers rebelled against a cruel tyrant of that time who was brutally violating the rights of his people. As a result, they were all tragically killed in a region of the desert known as Karbala. Before that bloody day, the ruler, Yazid, surrounded Husayn's forces in Karbala and deprived them of water

---

[5] John Brown spent a month and a half in prison before being executed. A few days before he was hanged, he wrote to his family: "I go joyfully on behalf of Millions that 'have no rights' that this 'great & glorious,' 'this Christian Republic,' is bound to respect."

[6] Mahatma Gandhi is considered the spiritual leader of all the people of India. Mahatma Gandhi, who was well-educated and broad-minded, considered it the highest honor to be allowed to defend the oppressed. He felt it was wrong to resort to violence in any form, even to thwart tyranny and injustice.

for eight days in the blazing heat. And then he mercilessly ordered all their heads to be chopped off and their bodies hacked into pieces with swords before being trampled under the hooves of horses until they were beyond recognition. The wives and children of the dead were taken prisoner and led through cities and valleys with their hands shackled. They were robbed of all their possessions, and their jewelry was violently ripped from their ears, hands, and necks.

"We Muslims call them martyrs, since they were killed for a holy cause. For Muslims, the highest, most sacred title is that of martyr, which is bestowed upon soldiers."

"What a horrifying event," Willie said. "I wonder why I've never heard a word of this. And what's your connection to those two followers?" Willie didn't know what to call them since he couldn't remember their names.

"The night before this tragedy, Burayr and Habib ibn Madhahir laughed and joked with their friends. When they were told, 'Your jokes are inappropriate—you should be serious during such a dangerous and worrisome time,' they answered that they felt joyful because they were about to be granted the exalted fate of a martyr. You know, Willie, Burayr and Habib ibn Madhahir weren't exactly comedians. History depicts them as very serious people. However, as death grew nearer, their joy knew no bounds. You know, it all comes down to a person's attitude toward death. I read about this event when I was only ten years old. It made such an impression on me that I couldn't stop thinking about it for a whole week.

"In our house, my grandfather hosted a big event on the anniversary of the martyrdom of Husayn and his followers. This anniversary is known as Ashura. During those days, everyone proclaims a time of mourning and grieves for the martyrs. Our friends, relatives, and the most influential people in our city used to visit us for this ceremony of mourning. My grandfather once invited a religious scholar, and he told the guests about the courage of Husayn and his followers, about their battles, their moral attributes, and the ruthlessness of their enemies. And I listened with great interest. Then a *rowzeh-khwan* with a beautiful voice arrived. Where we're from, that's what we call a man who sings sorrowful religious songs. When he sings, everyone cries. My father, noticing that I was gazing with astonishment at his streaming eyes, covered my eyes with his hand. Probably he didn't want me to see how he was crying. It was at these events that I learned about Burayr and Habib ibn Madhahir."

"It seems a little strange to me to be joking and celebrating right before dying," Willie said. "I don't get the point. Maybe it's a question of conviction and faith."

Wisam said, "For believers, if someone has done good in his life, upon death he emerges from a narrow confinement into a spacious and beautiful world. If you can expect to find transcendence and ease at the end of your path, it's very foolish to be afraid of it."

"You're not afraid of death?"

"Whether I'm afraid or not, it's still coming. So the best thing to do is to look into the eyes of death without fear. Why should you be afraid of something you can't avoid? And what's most important is what's waiting there for me: my family, my grandfather, my grandmother, and other loved ones. I have so little family left. They're nearly all gone . . . I'll be better off there. And as you can tell, my life is being spent at MD Anderson. It's like torture, being confined to this bed." Wisam said it with his usual smile. "Who could feel death's cold breath down the back of his neck better than I? But even so, your predicament looks more tragic than mine." This time Willie couldn't keep from laughing. They both cracked up.

"Yes, Wisam. If I'm in a bad mood, I always start to feel better when I'm around you. You're right. I'm living every day like someone under a death sentence with only one day left on this earth."

"What about you, Willie? Are you afraid of death?"

"It seems to me that this question is tied to the question 'Do you believe in God?'"

"Okay, then. Do you believe in God?"

"When I was a kid, I did. All children, as a rule, believe in a Creator. But now I don't know. I haven't really given a lot of thought to that question."

"If we're not going to believe in a Creator, many questions are going to go unanswered," Wisam said. "Willie, we consider God to be a being who created the entire universe and who wields absolute power. But it's not possible to truly understand what He really is. God sees and hears all. Nothing is brought to fruition in the universe without His knowledge."

"I don't want to get into a debate with you on this subject, Wisam. Human beings are just a little fragment of the natural world. Science has proven that they are a product of nature."

"In the eighth century, a movement known as the Dehri began to spread," said Wisam. "The Dehri were forerunners of the materialists, who believed that nature and time were the creators of all things. Once, a disciple of His Lordship Sadiq, a man named Mufazzal, asked him about the philosophy of the Dehri. His Lordship responded, 'The Dehri believe that human beings are a product of the natural world. But we should ask them whether the natural world that produced humans has knowledge and power — if it is alive. If they say no, then we will ask them how something lifeless, with no knowledge or power, could produce a living human that possesses both knowledge and power. But if they say that nature is a living being with knowledge and power, then we will tell them that there is no difference between their beliefs and ours. We both have faith in a creator of the universe and of mankind. We just call that creator by different names. They call Him nature and we call Him God.'"

"There's truth to what you're saying," Willie said. "To be honest, I've never had the time or the patience to think about God, the Creator, or about life after death. So I developed my opinions on this subject on the basis of commonly-held ideas."

"Willie, life itself hinges on questions like 'Does God exist?' and 'Is there life after death?' And you need to find the answers while you're still here on Earth. Because your answer will completely change your view of the world and change your life. 'When You were hidden from us, so as to require arguments to prove Your existence, when You were far from us, so we needed to grow closer to You . . .'"

The two friends fell silent. After some time had passed, Willie said, "I think I most regret that I was born into this world."

"I have liked being been born into this world if only to have seen a few things, met a few people, and to have beheld the splendor surrounding me. I would have come here if only to be the grandson of Judge Badr, eat my Grandma Hafiza's sweet *halva*, feel my father, Jafar, gently stroking my head, to hide behind my grandma's back from my mother's angry looks, and to gaze at the innocent face of my sister, Havra, who is thin-skinned and easily offended.

"And also to meet a great guy like you, Willie. That is worth being born into this world. I would be born to see the medical staff at MD Anderson Hospital, as well as my sick friends, and even to get to know Dr. Stevens, who irritates everyone with his inappropriate jokes. Life is wonderful from any perspective. It's wonderful, believe me! If a sick man who's living out his final days can recognize that, you know it must be true."

# IT ONLY TAKES TEN SECONDS TO GET HAPPY

*If, when you look around you, you see everyone as disappointed and the whole world as dirty, then think about the fact that there are people who can't see at all.*

"People are like pencils, sketching out their own lives. The more they sketch, the duller they become. And when they get dull, they can't sketch as accurately. So sometimes we need to be sharpened." Because of his positive outlook, all kinds of patients came to talk with Wisam from other rooms. Sometimes they invited him back to their rooms for tea. This young man with his big eyes and ready smile found his way into everyone's heart.

"In the Middle Ages, there were buildings called *khanqahs* where the Sufis gathered. Students who wanted to follow the spiritual path came to these khanqahs. But not all were accepted. Students went there for lessons on life and truth but had to pass exams given by the elderly master of the khanqah, who had taken the spiritual path and attained the highest spiritual rank. For forty days prior to the exams, they were not allowed to leave but were taught by a wise 'pir,'[7] who prepared them for the examination that the khanqah master was to administer. When the forty days were over, the wise teacher tested them. Students who passed this exam were given the opportunity to study with the master himself.

"When the day of the examination arrived, the master led them to a garbage dump next to the khanqah. Showing them a dead, rotting dog, he asked them what they thought about it. Some of them said

---

[7] This is the name given to the teacher who offers moral instruction to the students.

that it was a stinking corpse, others, that it was carrion covered with insects, and a few called it a source of contagious diseases. Then the teacher bowed his head in distress and told them that none of them had passed the exam. He turned to all his students and said, 'Not one of you noticed that this dog has teeth as white as pearls!' Only then did they see that the dog truly did have beautiful teeth as flawless as pearls. You can find clear evidence of beauty in every example of ugliness. The most important thing is to pay attention to that beauty and perceive the good in everything.

"We see forty days as a sacred period of time. If during that period a person learns worthy lessons from a worthy master, then the secret truths of his soul will become manifest, and he will see the true essence of all. But if he does not see this, it means that either he was not a worthy student, or his lessons were not from a worthy master. Forty days, Willie, is easily enough time to fundamentally change someone."

This episode greatly impressed the patients in the room, particularly the explanations based in *Irfan* that Wisam offered for it. He said that this type of trial undergone by students in the khanqah at the hands of a wise elder was done in imitation of Jesus Christ, who was known as *Ruhullah*. He was the first to teach the people in such a way.

"Willie, when you go home, you're worn out from work because you've been dealing with many problems all day long. At home no one greets you. You flick on the light in dark rooms. There's total silence all around. You sit down on the couch. You think, is this loneliness? No! It's freedom and peace." When Wisam spoke these words, many, like Willie, decided that this was aimed directly at them.

When Willie went home that day, he tried to look at what he considered to be loneliness, but this time using Wisam's eyes. As always, his children were late opening the door.

*This is nothing but a slight delay.*

As usual, Kevin was playing a game and paid no attention to Willie. *He's still a child with nothing but games in his head.* Sarah was again watching her TV show. *She deserves this. She works all day long, from morning to night. Why shouldn't she relax a little?*
*It seems to be working.* He smiled.

To Wisam, optimism and pessimism could not be affected by specific situations or the circumstances of life. The difference between an optimist and a pessimist came down to their differing views on the world around them. And this philosophy of life was what made

Wisam different from the other patients. For this reason, only positive thoughts ever occurred to him. Wisam was accustomed to this way of thinking and looking at events.

Once, Wisam said that they needed to decorate the patient rooms for every holiday. Although there was some initial pushback from the staff who were responsible for this, in the end, they gave their permission as long as there were no major changes to the rooms. One day Wisam suggested that they occasionally alter the layout of the room because the monotony was wearing on the patients.

"No way," Stevens said, pointing out that the "angels" were just temporary guests there. "That's just too much. And anyway, these patients never get a chance to get bored by the monotony."

Wisam was not at all upset, even when his requests were turned down. "What a wonderful nickname — 'angels.' Illness truly does make one as pure as an angel because it washes away all your sins. Looking at it like that, patients like us really are angels. Heaven is waiting for us. MD Anderson is like our *barzakh*. The barzakh is a spiritual world that exists between one's earthly life and heaven. You know, Willie, the barzakh is the world where our souls wait till Judgment Day."

But Stevens said that MD Anderson was more like Montfaucon. The Gibbet of Montfaucon was a thirteenth century execution site in Paris, with a multilevel scaffold, twelve to fourteen meters tall and made of stone. Each level contained compartments where prisoners were hanged. Up to fifty people could be executed at once. Those who had been executed were left hanging for a while within these compartments as a warning to the king's enemies.

"Dr. Stevens, then you probably see yourself as Enguerrand de Marigny, the man who built Montfaucon?" Most people tried to steer clear of Dr. Stevens, but not Wisam. He was very comfortable talking to him and not shy about expressing his opinions.

"Perhaps, perhaps . . ." said Stevens, not taking Wisam's question very seriously.

"Then you need to be extra careful, Dr. Stevens, because in the end, Marigny was also executed at Montfaucon."

Willie was always astonished at how much Wisam seemed to know. But later, when he learned that Wisam had graduated from several different schools and had an advanced degree, everything made more sense to him. He also learned that Wisam's family was considered part of the Lebanese aristocracy and that Wisam had studied in special schools ever since he was a child.

It was clear that Wisam's remarks were really keeping Stevens on his toes. Stevens wasn't as rude to this ill young man as he was to the others. Wisam's bravery also influenced Willie and encouraged him. Once when they were alone together, Wisam said, "Willie, our Prophet said, 'There are several groups of people who will act boldly toward you unless you transcend them and demonstrate your transcendence to them. And vile people are among them.' Of course, you have no right whatsoever to humiliate or fight them; that's out of the question. An insidious, vile man always should feel the severity of those above him, or else he will be too harsh toward the weak, and nothing will stop him." Willie knew what Wisam meant by that, but that was just like the young man—to always offer a full explanation to avoid any misunderstanding.

Wisam liked to say, "Willie, you only need ten seconds to feel happy." One day Willie asked how. Wisam answered with his usual grin, "By thinking about people like me!" When Wisam said that, Willie's eyes filled with tears. Wisam was right. Never in Willie's life had he truly valued what he had. He had always been dissatisfied. And as a result, he felt unhappy and unfortunate despite having everything he needed to feel happy. He had never sensed the sweetness of breath, the scent of flowers, the longings of his own children whimsically playing next to him nor had he appreciated his wife's hard work as she ran around from morning till night in the hopes of a fleeting smile from him.

On one occasion, Wisam said, "My grandfather always said, 'It's important to know that everything happens in the first ten seconds. We get angry in the first ten seconds; we speak rudely in the first ten seconds; we lose our self-control in the first ten seconds; and we allow negative thoughts in those ten seconds. But in those same first ten seconds, we can muster patience, think about things in a positive way, and act appropriately. It all starts with those ten seconds. Everything can begin in ten seconds. And the beginning is an important step to any undertaking. In ten seconds, a person can be bad or good. Ten seconds is sufficient to ensure that we have focused our thoughts in a positive or negative direction.'" Wisam did not often speak about his grandfather. But he occasionally borrowed some of his wise sayings.

"There are many who would not agree with your grandfather," Willie said. "Happiness is something that takes years to attain. Some travel a very long path to get there."

"No matter how long it takes them," Wisam said, "in the end, they realize that happiness was always right there next to them, and they didn't need to spend so much time searching for it. All they needed was ten seconds. Yup, in ten seconds we can make ourselves and others happy. Pleasant words such as 'I love you,' 'thank you,' and 'you're very kind' that we can use to gratify the people around us only require ten seconds. Words spoken to someone you love will always find their way into that person's heart. And if that word remains in someone's heart and delights him, then that word is happiness itself for him. Never deprive someone you love of that happiness, Willie. If you have a chance to make someone happy, don't be stingy, my friend; do it."

"It's all so simple for you. It's easy to talk."

"And to do! You just have to want to. You don't want to; that's why you don't. Don't forget that dreams only come true when desires are coupled with actions."

"You talk about making others happy in ten seconds. But sometimes I don't want to make anyone happy. And sometimes even if I wanted to . . . I don't know. The problem in our family is that we have nothing to talk about. We don't converse very much even when my wife and kids and I are all together."

"Sometimes we're quiet not because we don't have anything to say but maybe because we want to say so much more," Wisam said. "We just don't know where to start."

"Yeah, maybe. Sometimes I want to talk and unburden my heart, but I don't know how. And when I feel like that, I spend hours in indecision. And then I notice that a whole day has passed, and we're still silent." Willie shook his head.

Wisam said, "Sometimes you have to be silent to draw attention. Occasionally this happens when we feel incapable of expressing our feelings in words."

"When I was a kid, I felt sorry for my mom and dad," Willie said. "They didn't get along, so I wanted to draw them out a bit. But I had the same feeling that I had at school when I would be standing in front of the chalkboard trying to demonstrate something from our lesson, and my mind would go blank. And so I decided to do like I did in school, which was to write out some crib notes on the topic of our upcoming conversation."

"And what happened? Did that help?"

"No. It was all pointless. Using crib notes turned the conversation into a dry, contrived dialogue. In the end, I decided I'd rather not say anything. There were different reasons for my silence, but sometimes my parents reacted to my words in a sharp, rude way, making it clear that my thoughts were utterly meaningless to them. So I stopped talking. And the next time, I'd be afraid of being treated with that same irritability and rudeness. Wisam, you'll never understand me. You haven't lived my life."

"Or you mine."

"Yes, and for that reason, we should probably be quiet."

"We won't be able to reach a reasonable conclusion, because we want to solve our problems silently," Wisam said.

Willie didn't say a word. He was lost in thought.

"The expectation of celestial happiness and the dread of future tortures only served to prevent man from seeking after the means to render himself happy here below." Willie quoted d'Holbach as though those were his own words even though they were irrelevant to the discussion they had been having.

"So why are you unhappy?" Wisam said. "You don't seem worried about suffering in your afterlife. And you're not thinking about otherworldly happiness. So what's stopping you?"

Willie was silent for a moment. "I don't know the answer to that, Wisam. I know I'm unhappy, but I don't know why."

"I think you're searching for happiness everywhere but right around you and inside of you, Willie. At that rate, even if you circumnavigate the globe in search of happiness, looking for it night and day, you won't find it. Because you're not looking in the right place. You'll understand this once you completely lose hope of finding it. Happiness is very close to you. When you realize this, you'll find true, eternal joy. Don't forget that a man will never be unhappy if he doesn't want to be."

"I've spent my entire life struggling with hardships and disappointments," Willie said. "I've fully felt, firsthand, all the anxiety and suffering of people living through the most awful tragedies. I've always been afraid of someone losing their temper or walking out on me. I endlessly worry about events that never happen. And then there's my past. I can't seem to shake it. I blame only myself for what happened in the past. Not a day goes by that I don't think about my past. I've thought of hundreds of things I could have done back then but didn't. I've wondered about what would have happened if I had done this or that—maybe everything would have been so much better. All these 'ifs' get tangled up at the same point. If I'd never been born, then what? Yes, as soon as I entered this world, I ruined the lives of my parents. I, and only I, was the cause of that. It all started with me."

"Willie, you're making the same mistake that most people make. You're living in the past while simultaneously wanting to stay one jump ahead of time. And if you're always trying to get one jump ahead, that means you're living in the future. Agonizing over unpleasant events that have not yet occurred keep you from fully living. That kind of person imagines the death of loved ones who are still alive and begins to cry and mourn. Life is very simple, but we make it complicated. Life is glorious, but we paint it black. Don't bury those who aren't dead yet, Willie. If we're going to live with peace of mind, we can't worry about events that have not yet occurred. We must force ourselves to live in the present and not the future.

"You still haven't forgotten your past. But it's passed. Confused, you're left moving between the past and the future. 'Only a man who lives not in time but in the present is happy.' These are the words of Ludwig Wittgenstein.

"If you pay attention to your thoughts, you'll notice that you're mostly in the past or in the future. When you're working, eating, watching TV, with your family, talking to friends, or even relaxing, your thoughts are in your past. At that point, a person can't enjoy the food he's eating, find pleasure in observing the beauty of nature, feel like a significant figure during the time he spends with his children, or find delight in a child's laughter and joy.

"Willie, you must accept the fact that it is impossible to change the past. That's important. If you don't do that, then unfortunately remorse and grief will keep you from building a better future for yourself or taking advantage of any new opportunities that come your way.

"Don't forget that your happiness today depends on your attitude toward the past. Willie, unless you close the dark door of the past, you won't be able to move into a bright future.

"Enough already, stop agonizing so much over your past! What once was is no more. Do you know why it's called the past? It's called that because it buries everything that's happened inside of itself and flips through the pages of the painful and sweet events in the book of our lives bringing us to a new page called today. But today will never arrive for us until we stop regretting and thinking about the events of the past. Willie, so many people live in the past, even though they're actually in the present."

"Willie, the chief physician wants to see you," said the nurse on duty.

Willie was glad of an excuse to break off what was a difficult conversation for him. "Okay, I'm outta here. Plus you need to rest!" He stood up to leave the room.

"This conversation isn't over yet," Wisam said with a smile.

When Willie left the chief physician's office, he did not dare to continue the conversation with Wisam. But all the way home, Wisam's words were spinning in his head.

# IT IS NOT TIME, BUT PEOPLE, WHO CHANGE US

Wisam had grown on Willie so much that he started getting to the hospital earlier than ever and going in to visit him first thing. His words, actions, and thinking were having a deep impression on Willie. From the moment they'd met, Willie even began to appreciate certain parts of his body that he had always been oblivious to. Particularly his lungs. Every time he took a deep breath, he thought of Wisam. When Willie opened the window in his room, Wisam would grin and say, "Willie, breathe for me too! Look what a glorious day it is!" Willie didn't know whether to smile or weep.

The most surprising thing was that he never saw sadness in Wisam's face. He was a very cheerful, smiling, entertaining person. All the medical staff and patients raved about him. They all talked about him. Although he was sick, he gave everyone an appetite for life and inspired them to live. There were times when he had regular procedures done to drain the accumulated fluid from his lungs. Willie knew those treatments were very painful. Wisam also knew, because he had undergone them more than once. But whenever they were taking him from the room, he always smiled as he said good-bye to Willie. When Wisam came back, however, he looked exhausted and haggard. But nevertheless, his big, sunken eyes of that celestial color were still smiling. Although his body was a hostage in the hands of death, the will to live never left his eyes, even for a minute. Wisam's body, which was struggling to live, had begun to surrender. Willie sensed that Wisam was weakening every day. Although Willie tried to hide this from him, Wisam understood Willie's thoughts from the expression on his face.

"I guess I look pretty awful, don't I?" Wisam said, looking at Willie with a grin.

Willie pretended he didn't understand. "How do you feel today?"

"Yes, clearly this means that things are very bad."

"Why do you think so? I didn't say anything like that."

"No, Willie. You didn't say it, but I can easily read it in the eyes of every doctor and nurse. And even in yours . . ."

Wisam did not normally linger in sad or distressing moments. As soon as the atmosphere began to feel strained, he deftly changed the subject.

"Willie, I know you keep an eye on me while I sleep."

Willie didn't know what to answer. That was true. Whenever Willie went into Wisam's room and found him asleep, he would watch him with great compassion. At those moments, Willie thought what a pity it was that he hadn't meet Wisam under other circumstances, somewhere away from here—anywhere but a hospital.

Willie didn't know how to answer him. "Why do you think that? After all, you're sleeping."

"When I wake up, your gaze has left its traces on me," said Wisam, beginning to laugh.

Wisam often said sweet, engaging things like that. One time he told Willie a mother-in-law joke: "Once there was a son-in-law who joked that old women couldn't go to heaven. So of course, his mother-in-law really began to worry and almost started crying. And so then the son-in-law smiles and says, 'Old women can't go to heaven because God makes them young again before they get there.'"

"Oh, you're just trying to get in good with mothers-in-law," a patient in the room said. "What kind of joke is that? It works out for the mothers-in-law in the end."

Wisam smiled but didn't say a word.

"I've got one," chimed in Mason, the electrician who had come in to install a new light fixture.

"So, the son-in-law comes in from chopping wood, and he's carrying an axe. He goes in the house and sees his mother-in-law. The son-in-law throws her the axe and says, 'Mother-in-law, here you go! Hey, why are you so quiet? Why couldn't you catch it?'"

Everyone laughed at Mason's joke. Wisam looked at Willie and smiled. In his offhand way, Wisam managed to draw Willie into these discussions, and he began to feel like he was one of them.

Willie watched every move Wisam made.

Once, one of the nurses took Wisam for an exam. As he got out of bed, he accidentally stepped on the foot of Dr. Stevens, who was standing next to the nurse. Wisam apologized, adding that he hadn't meant to do it. But Dr. Stevens looked at him with great annoyance and left. Noticing the doctor's disgruntled silence, the nurse made it clear that it wasn't worth apologizing over. The other patients also told him that there had been no point in begging Stevens's pardon.

"That Stevens is clueless about anything like etiquette or civility, anyway."

But Wisam said, "When the queen of France, Marie Antoinette, was being led to the guillotine, she accidentally stepped on the executioner's foot. And do you know what she said? 'Pardon me! I did not mean to do that.' And those were her last words. Also, Gandhi, before his death, made a gesture with his hand that showed that he had forgiven his assassin."

This was a sign that he came from a fine, well-mannered family, but Willie knew not everything goes back to the family.

Wisam meant that compassion and tenderness should be the response even to rude behavior. In these moments, Willie felt that his own outlook was slowly changing. Now he remembered a conversation he'd had with an older gentleman in the park about a month earlier. Sitting next to Willie, the man began a sad monologue.

"In this life, everyone's just out for himself. I often sit here for hours. And not one person comes up to me or takes an interest in me. It's because I'm no use to anyone. I'm not of interest to anyone in this life. If I doze off here, they'll just walk on by, and no one will care if I'm alive."

Willie inadvertently turned to the side where the sound was coming from. Next to him sat a man about seventy years old with a cane in his hand and a fishing cap on his head. Willie wanted to tell him how much he agreed, but he didn't have the energy to speak up.

"This city is empty of people!" the man said. "It looks crowded, but there's no one to offer a shoulder to cry on. There's no one who understands you or will hold out a hand to help you up when you fall. There are millions of people in this city, but you're on your own, alone and invisible! All cities are exactly the same. And since every country in the world is made up of such cities, you'll find yourself all alone no matter where you go."

The old man uttered these words with such heartfelt sincerity that Willie decided the man must be reading his mind. And indeed, for fifteen years, Willie had been sure that this city was empty of people. It seemed to him that every city was completely uninhabited, and he lived alone in a vast wilderness. After listening to the old man's musings, Willie began to think that everyone who feels completely alone experiences the same emotions. Their grief was probably identical. Their suffering was identical, even if they'd had different reasons for their grief. He began to feel mixed emotions—admiration, astonishment, and pain.

"When you let people get near you," the old man said, "you're making yourself a bigger target for the rocks they start throwing at you the first chance they get. No one else has the slightest interest in your problems or how you're doing. Until they suddenly need you for something. Then they start to put on a real show. They come find you and suddenly have all kinds of questions about your life and how you're doing. As if they really care."

Willie was silent. It seemed to make no difference to the old man whether Willie spoke or not. The more the man talked, the more astonished Willie felt at the similarity of their ideas. He realized that, having been visited by these painful thoughts in his youth, they would likely be much worse by the time he reached the old man's age if he lived that long.

"Don't be deceived by people's sweet talk and open your heart to them!" The old man offered some guidance on this. "They will steal the most precious things in your heart: your hopes and joy. Once you're truly lonely and your heart has been gutted, you'll realize you've been betrayed.

"The hypocrisy of these people makes me crazy. We live in a time when everyone values material things—they chase after money and wealth. These days everything has a price: dignity, love, honor, and even human beings. People are now seen as objects to be bought and sold.

"I watch the people walking by, smiling their fake smiles at each other. Then they go about their own business. They talk about big, important things. But on the inside, they're painfully aware of their own limitations."

To keep the conversation from being completely one-sided, Willie felt it was only polite to ask the man a few questions but got no response. The old man only talked about his feelings. He just wanted to vent. At that point, Willie felt more pity for him than for himself. *Lonely hearts and sad glances – that's just how it is for people.* At that moment, Willie could have uttered hundreds of words that agreed with what the old man was telling him.

Willie didn't speak. He was thinking about other things at the time. Sometimes a single month could be enough to change a person. Wisam had told Willie a story about a wise man from the Middle Ages. To change yourself from the inside, you needed to become a wise man's pupil for forty days. Willie felt just like a pupil entering a khanqah, a pupil seated before a wise elder. But he had yet to take the exam covering this forty-day spiritual odyssey. Willie smiled at his thoughts. *I wonder what tests the 'wise elder' will subject me to, in the name of life, after forty days?* Right now Willie was taking lessons, but it was likely that his test lay ahead.

*Perhaps I really haven't changed so much over the years. My heart has simply become covered with dust, and my sense of dissatisfaction with my fate has suppressed every happy emotion inside of me. But now those are gradually beginning to stir.*

"Why is this city empty of people?" Willie asked. Wisam seemed to immediately understand this simple question and smiled.

"It's a philosophy of life, Willie. A philosophy that expresses one's emotions." That was Wisam—an "angel" who always had his own view of life. He said, "I would have phrased the question without the 'why': 'Is this city empty of people?' and at the same instant, I would have answered, 'Of course it isn't!'

"This city is full of wonderful people," Wisam said. "It's possible that someone doesn't notice you because he is somewhat preoccupied, not because he is thoughtless. Everyone has someone near them. You just have to notice them. I am also near someone. Perhaps the person next to us is just like us and is thinking that there is no one near him. We are right next to people like that—the people who look at life and say, 'I am alone.' If everyone says 'I am alone,' just like we do, then everyone will become lonely."

Hearing these words from this man who always had a smile on his face and seemed to view life from a higher vantage point, Willie felt as though he were emerging from the desert into a large, bustling city.

"'This city is empty of people' is a statement, but perhaps we should phrase it as a question instead. 'Is this city empty of people?'

This is indeed the question. You see, Willie, that's exactly what I meant when I spoke of the philosophy of life."

Willie remembered the words of that lonely old man again. ".

Time has made us this way. Time is what changes a person, for good or ill."

But now Willie believed that it was not time, but people, who changed us. Now he didn't agree with those thoughts, which seemed so dear to him a month ago.

# A CITY MENTIONED SEVENTY-SIX
# TIMES IN THE BIBLE

Wisam didn't talk much about himself. Although sometimes he would answer when Willie asked a personal question, he never offered many details. His past was a difficult place for him to revisit. However, Wisam's aunt was more talkative. She seemed to be searching for someone to whom she could pour out her heart.

Wisam was born in southern Lebanon in one of the country's largest cities, Saida. Knowing that the city of one's birth and youth had a very powerful impact on the formation of one's personality, Willie went to the library to read about the history of Wisam's native city. Saida was located south of the Lebanese capital of Beirut on the Mediterranean coast. The city, which was thought to have been built prior to the year 4000 BC, was the largest, most famous center of international trade during the ancient era. And because of its importance, the city has been frequently attacked and subdued by various conquerors, dating back to antiquity, and has been the site of many battles.

In ancient times, it was the capital of the massive, powerful state of Phoenicia. During that era the city was called Sidon. In the early sixteenth century, it was conquered by Sultan Salim I, who incorporated the city into the Ottoman Empire where it was given the name of Saida. Saida in Arabic means "fishery." It was the most important branch of the local industry.

Since ancient times, the city of Saida has been the birthplace of courageous individuals. Its population has fended off repeated attacks by its enemies, always offering robust resistance. When the king of Persia, Ahasuerus of the Achaemenid dynasty, wanted to conquer Sidon, its inhabitants locked the gates and set fire to the whole city rather than surrender. As a result, although the city's population of forty thousand burned in that fire, they did not capitulate to their enemy. Afterward, the gravely-weakened city of Saida was unable to withstand attacks by Alexander the Great and fell under his rule. Alexander the Great completely rebuilt the city and staged the Olympic Games there. The city of Saida has been destroyed and reconstructed many times throughout history. It is even mentioned a few times in the Bible, and Jesus Christ was said to have visited.

During the Crusades, this area was a hotbed of bloody battles between Christians and Muslims. In 1099, the Kingdom of Al-Quds was established after the Crusaders captured its capital during the first crusade. Sidon was attacked and conquered by the ruler of that kingdom, Baldwin I. Baldwin I then drove out the Muslims and consolidated his rule there. Later, Norway's King Sigurd I again attacked this city to destroy the Muslim forces that had been established there in the early twelfth century. A century later, England's King Richard I accompanied a crusade to Sidon to restore the Christians' diminishing influence there. Sidon was a city that had been repeatedly destroyed and rebuilt, and by the time it passed into the hands of the French king, Ludwig IX, in the mid-thirteenth century, it had been gutted. It is said that, at times, Ludwig personally had to drag stones and help his workers rebuild the city.

After the Khwarazm Shahs weakened the Kingdom of Al-Quds in the thirteenth century, Christian influence in the region began to decline. And after the collapse of the Kingdom of Al-Quds, Muslims regained their former influence in Sidon. Saida always was a very troubled city and remained so even into the modern era. For example, in the nineteenth century, the city returned to its history of warfare when it was bombed by an English-Australian air force.

Willie could not understand the reason for the bloody wars that had been fought throughout history between these two religions, both of which were thought to have been handed down from heaven.

If, as Wisam claimed, both these religions were a gift from the same God, then why were they so hostile to one another?

History — which has witnessed periodic attacks on the other by both Muslims and Christians — showed this painful truth. This was a violation of every religious law known to Willie. When he read about these sectarian wars, he felt very distant from Wisam. One day, Willie, unable to restrain himself, asked him about this.

"Willie, you have to make a distinction between a religious person and his religion. Religion is something sacred and divine, while a religious person is just an ordinary human being. Religion shows us the true path, while a religious person is just someone who is trying to follow it. Sometimes he follows it correctly, and sometimes he goes astray. A religion can't be judged by the acts of a person professing that faith. We were all created by the same God. We were all created in the same manner, as alike as the teeth of a comb. We are all people. There is no difference between us."

And yet it was very difficult for Willie to understand the actions of these "pseudo saints," both Christian and Muslim, who murdered under the guise of religion.

Willie jokingly said to Wisam, "Our ancestors fought each other for centuries. It's an odd fate that we've become friends."

"God wants people to be friends, Willie. It's the devil who hopes that they will become enemies."

Willie found Wisam's stories about Islam to be very interesting. It was all new to him. The more Wisam spoke, the more Willie noticed similarities between the two religions.

"Wisam, it is astonishing how fate brings together what history could not. A glance at history shows that the plots and story lines have remained the same up to the present; only the names of the heroes and tyrants have changed."

"You're right. You know, in my country more than half of the population is Muslim and the rest are Christian. Lebanon is home to more Christians than any other Arab country. Muslims there are, for the most part, either Shiite or Sunni. And most of the Christians are Maronites. When Lebanon became an independent nation in 1943, the leaders of the Muslim and Christian communities signed a treaty, in accordance with which the president would be elected from the Maronite population, the prime minister would be a Sunni, and the speaker of the parliament, a Shiite. Clearly they found an interesting solution to the problem of how to preserve the balance of religions. However, despite attempts to build unity between the different faiths, outside influences have sparked bloody wars between these three religious communities for many years. These wars scarred the futures of thousands of people, including my family." Wisam frowned, and Willie decided to change the subject.

"You know, Wisam, I know nothing of Lebanon but its name. I pictured it as one of those backward Arab countries."

"The Lebanese have a deep respect for education and science that dates back to the days of our distant ancestors, the Phoenicians. The world's first alphabet was created right there in ancient Lebanon. Lebanon is mentioned seventy-six times in the Bible. Some scholars claim that Jesus Christ performed his first miracle there. Scholars also believe that the world's first inhabited city was the city of Jubayl (also known as Byblos), which is in Lebanon.

"Lebanon is home to about fifty universities and has a literacy rate of as high as ninety percent. Only few segments of Lebanese are monolingual; most people speak two, three, even four languages. I myself speak French and English fluently.

"Lebanon is known as 'the Switzerland of the East.' You know why? There are about a hundred banks in Lebanon. In these banks, as in Switzerland, all information is kept completely confidential.

"Lebanon is the only Arab country that is not ruled by a dictatorship. It is a country where both secular and Sharia laws apply. Sharia law prevailed within the country until the mid-nineteenth century. In the latter nineteenth and early twentieth centuries, Ottoman legal standards began to influence those laws. French laws were later gradually introduced. In some cases, Sharia law is now slowly making a comeback. And several legal systems are used simultaneously at the highest levels of the judiciary."

"An interesting form of government, I never heard of it . . . Apparently, if it wasn't for the endless wars, Lebanon would have been able to develop much better."

"Lebanon has important geographical position and other assets. This is why it has continually found itself under attack. Achaemenid dynasty, Alexander the Great, the Sassanids, the Greeks, Roman and Byzantine emperors, Arab caliphs, Crusaders, and Ottoman Turks. Lebanon, which eventually became a French colony, was occupied exactly fifteen times by various countries at various times. And its capital of Beirut was destroyed and rebuilt seven times. There are four million Lebanese living in the country. Most of us, somewhere around twelve million, live abroad. If you can call it living . . . You know, Willie, I never thought history would repeat itself. I never thought my hometown would once again turn into boiling lava and swallow my family . . ." Wisam faltered.

"Well, I don't even know what to say, Wisam. It's not always up to us . . ." This time Willie quoted Wisam.

# THE BLACK SQUARE,
# OR THE EMPEROR HAS NO CLOTHES

Wisam had an idea to stage an exhibition of paintings in the hospital lobby. As always, he first shared his notion with Willie, who didn't take it seriously. But when Wisam began to discuss the issue with other hospital employees, Willie realized how determined he was to follow through on his intention. Wisam believed that in addition to medicine, sick people also needed a shot in the arm for their spirit. And if a patient had a goal in life to fight for, it was much easier for him to make headway against an illness.

"The biggest thing our hospitals are doing wrong is that they're only trying to cure the patients physically," Wisam said. "They forget that they're also depressed, which negatively impacts their recovery. Sick people need to do something useful and become involved in some kind of work so they feel they have a connection to life." This argument won over the hospital administrator.

Every patient in the unit was given ten days to draw an interesting picture. They were provided with all the tools they needed. Most liked this idea very much, although there were a lot of grumblers who said things like, "I don't feel like drawing," and "Is this really the time to be making art?"

A few patients from other rooms gathered with some doctors in Wisam's room to discuss the exhibit.

"If a picture is going to spark interest, it needs to be exceptional and beautiful," Dr. Stevens said. "Pardon my saying so, but what can we expect from pictures drawn by 'angels'? They'll either draw demons or devils."

No one paid attention anymore to Stevens's clumsy jokes or objections, yet Wisam tried to explain it to him. "Dr. Stevens, you don't need great artistic skill for what we're doing here. Exhibitions of amateur art have been going on for about fifty or sixty years now. Jean Dubuffet, a French painter and sculptor, came up with this idea back in the 1950s: an art movement that was not subject to traditional conventions or cultural or national formulas. This became known as 'outsider art' or *'art brut.'* 'Outsiders' are nonprofessional artists. I took part in several such exhibits in Beirut—"

"Yes, yes . . . I've heard of them," Stevens said, interrupting Wisam. "That's an artistic movement that promotes the work of the insane, the incarcerated, and the disabled—of people who have been rejected by society, in other words," said Stevens.

"That's not entirely true. Artwork created by outsiders is big news nowadays. They say that the idea first occurred to Jean Dubuffet when he read about the creativity of the mentally ill in psychiatric journals. He considered it a spiritual need of the psychologically weak. He believed that drawings created by children, the mentally ill, the self-taught, and simple dabblers more accurately expressed the truth than the work of professional artists. Over the course of his lifetime, Jean Dubuffet amassed about five thousand examples of outsider art. Many museums all over the world collect these kinds of pictures. According to some assessments, work by such artists is worth quite a lot of money. For example, the sketches of Adolf Wölfli, a diagnosed schizophrenic, are now estimated to be worth one hundred thousand dollars. And by the way, do you know where he took up drawing? At the Waldau psychiatric clinic."

"That's what I'm saying. Only people with psychiatric problems can do this. Normal people aren't capable of it. People with psychiatric problems draw these pictures."

"On the contrary, psychologists say that it soothes the soul to create art and draw pictures," Wisam said. "Your fellow American Judith Scott, who had Down's syndrome and only lived to be sixty-one, was involved in exactly this sort of creative endeavor. If she lived through so much with her condition, that means that this art has a direct impact on the human soul."

"Whatever you say, I absolutely reject this kind of movement and style," Stevens said. "What really matters is creating artwork that's worthwhile. And if you can't do it, then step aside."

"Not necessarily," Dr. Anna said. "For example, look at Kazimir Malevich's *Black Square*. It looks just like a square that's been colored black by a fourth grader as part of a geometry lesson. But it sold at auction for a million dollars. That goes to show that a painting becomes more valuable the sillier and more pointless it is.

"The story of this black square's creation goes back to 1915, when Kazimir Malevich was invited to take part in an exhibition of paintings in St. Petersburg. He intended to enter a wonderful work, but despite his efforts, it wasn't turning out as he had hoped. Because so little time was left before the show, he became angry and painted a big square over his drawing. And at that very moment someone walked by and said rapturously, 'This is brilliant!' Then Malevich decided to submit this blacked-out *Black Square* for the exhibit. And to give the work an unusual and interesting backstory, he pretended it had some extraordinary secret significance. So, who knows, perhaps future *Black Squares* will emerge from this exhibition."

A nurse named Ella spoke up. "It works that way with everything. Even with fiction. The more unconventional and meaningless the author's writing, the more everyone gasps in admiration. You have to wonder at such a strange approach. Why are meaningless and boring works so elevated and their authors so revered? Look at Dostoevsky, the Russian writer who is so renowned all over the world. He wrote a novel called *Poor Folk*. I read it. Trust me, it consists of nothing but meaningless correspondence between a man and a woman. He writes, she writes. You feel your soul atrophying from boredom while reading this novel. It's devoid of all sense and logic."

"That's true. It's not one of Dostoevsky's most successful works. If you want to get to know him, you should read *The Idiot* or *Crime and Punishment*," countered Dr. David.

"Okay then, what do you think about the contemporary writer Gabriel García Márquez? After all, he's famous for having written *One Hundred Years of Solitude*, *No One Writes to the Colonel*, and *Memories of My Melancholy Whores*. And those are awful."

The doctor pursed his lips, and having thought for a moment, he backed her up.

"To be honest, I still can't think of a good reason he got a Nobel Prize. His plots spin out like a spider's web. It's all very convoluted. And his books don't really reflect life. They're so hard to read, it's as if Márquez is actually trying to wear his readers out."

"That's what I'm saying," Ella said. "Nowadays people need fanfare. Once some person and his book become front-page news, that person is suddenly a genius, and his work a masterpiece. *One Hundred Years of Solitude* got so much praise that there was even a ubiquitous ad campaign that featured that windbag's words. When I read his book, I didn't understand any of it. But I didn't want to seem stupid and behind the times compared to everyone else, so I also began to sing its praises. But one day, on an online literary forum, I ran across some harsh criticism from various book critics, as well as readers, directed against this book. After that, I felt better and realized that I wasn't so dense and wasn't the only one who thought the way I did. I realized that I wasn't the problem."

"It was like everyone had been brainwashed, like in Hans Christian Andersen's *The Emperor's New Clothes*. At that moment, no one was brave enough to shout, 'But the emperor is naked,'" said Dr. Anna.

"But what does 'the emperor is naked' have to do with what we're talking about?" asked the janitor, Taylor, who had been quietly tidying up the room all the while. He suddenly leapt into the conversation, seeming to find this a curious expression.

"You don't understand such things," Dr. David said, paying no mind to Taylor's question. "The reason writers like Márquez became famous was because of the imagery present in their works, as well as their innovations and the unconventional genre they introduced. Márquez, for example, won fame for introducing the genre of magical realism, and for that he was awarded the Nobel Prize.

"There's deep meaning to his work; you just need to feel it. You have to read the works of geniuses like that with your heart and emotions, not with your mind, then you'll get it."

Dr. Anna said, "You can call it whatever you want — innovation, imagery, genre, and so on — but if there's no meaning, no scholarly significance, then it's still a bunch of hooey, hogwash, and hot air! If it's come to that, then just let everybody introduce his own innovation and get a Nobel Prize. Just because something is innovative, doesn't mean it's beautiful or true. You need to get that through your head once and for all!"

"But what does 'the emperor is naked' mean?" Taylor once again tried to get someone to clarify this expression that he found so interesting. Not once during the entire conversation had anyone paid any attention to his question. After everyone had left, he caught Dr. Anna in the hallway and asked her about it one more time.

"Two tailors promised to make the emperor an unusual suit of clothes. After a while, the con men claimed that they had sewn him some clothing that was invisible to the stupid and which only intelligent people could see. When the king put on his invisible suit, he and the members of his court realized that they couldn't see it. But they lied and pretended that they could, so that no one would call them fools. In the end, the emperor paraded before his people stark naked, and everyone pretended to marvel at his new suit. Except for one small boy who noticed this travesty and bravely shouted out, 'But the emperor is naked!' Only then did the people understand that they had been deceived and gained the courage to stand behind the boy. But nonetheless, the emperor and his court decided to completely dismiss the boy's words. And the con men, who had already gotten a great deal of gold from the king, made a run for it."

In the days leading up to the exhibit, Wisam sat propped up in bed, deeply immersed in his drawing. But he didn't want to tell anyone in advance what it was.

"Wisam, what are you submitting? Why won't you let us see?"

"It's a surprise, guys."

The day of the exhibition was drawing near. Willie and his fellow workers collected all the pictures and hung them in the lobby. Many patients took part, and even those who considered the show to be inappropriate or silly drew some small pictures. Two labels were placed under each picture. The first had to list the name of the artist and the second, the title of the sketch. The youngest patient in the hospital unit, Bill, drew his family. Nancy, an elderly patient, sketched her grandchildren. Even Dr. Stevens had a picture hanging there. He drew a big football stadium with a lot of players on the field. One of the players looked different from the others; he was wearing the sort of scrubs worn by the staff at MD Anderson. That player really stood out in the picture. It was obvious Stevens had drawn Willie. Everybody looked at Stevens's drawing, grinning. No one noticed Willie's embarrassment; he didn't know that Stevens and the other employees knew about his football past. Wisam did not submit his picture for the exhibit. When asked about it, he said that he had changed his mind. He didn't explain why. In the last few days, his condition had deteriorated noticeably. Willie decided that his friend could not complete the drawing and no longer insisted.

These days MD Anderson was so different that even Dr. Stevens sensed the positive atmosphere. The patients viewed their creations with great enthusiasm. Gazing at their pictures, they realized that despite all its hardships, life still went on, and not all was yet over for them. As long as they were still alive, they should create, refuse to give in, and not live as if under a death sentence. They also realized that they were all still relevant and could do something worthy of attention. This forced them to forget their illnesses, at least for a while.

Everyone who passed through the lobby — the patients' families, nurses, and doctors — all stopped to look at the sketches the "angels" had drawn that displayed such optimism and love for life. There was a subtle message for everyone who saw the pictures. Viewers realized that the "angels," like everyone else, had the right to a completely normal life. No one should be deprived of the right to live. And while you're still here, no matter how deadly your disease, you want to live a rich, full life. Even if your body has been sentenced to death, there's no way to kill the yearning of the human soul for beauty and perfection.

Willie felt even more drawn to Wisam as he viewed the exhibition. Halfway through, Willie left to go find his friend. He approached the door to Wisam's room but did not enter. He stood watching him from a distance. Wisam lay unmoving in his bed. The procedures he had undergone the day before had been quite punishing. Nevertheless, Wisam's face bore a look of contentment. Willie could sense that he was joyful.

*My God, where does anyone get so much energy? How can this sick man, with all his physical infirmity, keep fighting and never for one moment have the urge to give in? What kind of creature is he? A man? How can a man who is living out his days in agony spend his time thinking of other people and trying to instill in them a love for life? He gets enjoyment from giving hope and cheer to others . . . I 'm gonna miss you so much, Wisam. Hold on, friend, don't leave us too soon . . .*

# THE FEAR OF HAPPINESS

*Do the thing you fear most, and the death of fear is certain!*

~ Mark Twain

Wisam noticed that some sick people did not see themselves as worthy of happiness. They had lost all hope because of difficulties, miseries, and terrible illnesses.

Wisam heard them say things like, "I don't deserve to be happy. I've always had a suspicion, but now I'm quite certain. I'm not worthy of happiness," or, "The bad comes with the good in life. Alongside joy there is sadness; alongside health, illness; alongside blessings, harm; alongside safety, danger. So when you hear glad tidings, you also need to be prepared for the other side of the coin."

One patient told Wisam, "I obviously have rotten luck when it comes to good news and joy. How can anyone be happy when you don't know what will happen tomorrow and you live in a state of uncertainty? What about this life should make me happy or smile?"

Some of the patients became greatly distressed over the prospect of birthdays, holidays, celebrations, or any joyful occasion. They didn't want to celebrate, and when confronted with such events, their spirits suddenly flagged, and they were overcome with fear and anxiety. Out of fear, they avoided the festivities and holed up on their own. Such patients typically distanced themselves from others and retreated into their shells. After spending time with them, Wisam felt that they didn't understand what there was to be happy about in life. They couldn't let happiness in their lives, especially the ones who were doomed to die. Wisam said to Willie, "They are afraid to be happy."

Willie understood them very well because he had noticed all those same symptoms in himself. When Wisam described them, Willie thought he was talking about him. Since he wasn't sick, Willie wondered why he was in the same emotional state as these patients. *But apparently my body is healthy, but not my soul . . . So this means that the human fear of happiness is not only caused by physical disease. One's mindset and standard of ethics are the most important thing. And a wrongheaded philosophy of life is enough to mess you up.*

Wisam spent a lot of time with such patients. Several times he asked Dr. Stevens to invite the departmental psychologist to come meet with them.

"Dear boy, this is a cancer hospital, not a psychiatric ward."

Wisam and Willie talked about this quite a lot, usually in Wisam's room. Willie felt that Wisam wanted to have these sorts of discussions within the earshot of the other patients, wanting them to join in the conversation and get some use from it.

"People have everything they need to be rich, glorious, and wise, and only one thing—fear—prevents them from being happy when they achieve all this."

"Okay, Wisam, so how do they overcome this fear?" Willie said. "It's not within our power to not be afraid."

"It's very simple. If you're afraid to be happy, then try to be happy! Then fear itself will be afraid of you."

"How does that work?"

"Dismiss your fears, and do what gives you joy. But perhaps first you need to begin by making others happy. Buy someone flowers, for example. But under no circumstances spend any time thinking about how to rid yourself of this fear. Just live! Do what makes you happy, and before long, happiness will come to you.

"If someone says he won't be happy, then he certainly will not be happy. People have to live out the fates they have mapped out for themselves. It is written in our *hadiths* that 'God treats human beings in accordance with their views.' If someone considers himself to be unhappy and unlucky, his life will follow suit. The universe moves in accordance with the signals it receives from our souls."

Wisam stopped to catch his breath. When he spoke a bit more than usual, he got winded. But nonetheless he went on. "We keep making the same mistake; we keep waiting for the perfect existence. We believe that everything in life needs to be flawless—our family, friends, teachers, and even life itself—although we don't meet these standards ourselves. We won't search for any life except our own. But this is life! Life with all its hardships, illnesses, deaths, and disasters is still life. Life is not just health and happiness. Life is both night and day, the beginning and the end. This is very important! Until we figure this out, we can't taste real happiness.

"Disease and health, misfortune and joy. It's hard to take all this as a whole. There are so many unpleasant things in life, and so much is sheer chance. Some people are just lucky. And others . . . What kind of life is this, to be born into a family where you're not loved? It's nothing but agony.

"You're thinking that because you don't see the connection between the past and the present, the present and the future. It's like there is only this time and this place. Sometimes, the connection between events that happened at different times is too deep and invisible to realize. We look at life from the inside and see events as accidents that lack meaning, reason, and connection. But if you look at it all from the outside, you'll see the perfect harmony, order, and meaning reigning in the universe. At this point, a voice will whisper from the inside that you are not alone in the universe, that there is an invisible, strong hand behind the veil. You will feel with all your being that there is no room for chance, that there is sense in everything, and that you are a very important creature. This whole life, this universe, exists for you. You're not a bitter and meaningless plaything of nature. Happiness is yours."

# THE MOVIE IS JUST AN EXCUSE

*In a moment of indecision, act quickly and try to
make the first step, even if it seems unnecessary.*

~ Leo Tolstoy

Once Wisam got a bit better, he came up with the idea for a communal cinema in the hospital. He said it would be more interesting to watch movies as a group, and it would lift spirits to watch movies in an interactive way, rather than passively viewing them all alone. When Wisam talked about watching a movie interactively, he meant that the patients should express their feelings while watching it, voice their opinion about the film, and discuss it among themselves. "But the main thing isn't to watch the movie. The most important thing is to have a good time hanging out together, and the movie is a good excuse."

Although the rooms had televisions, the hospital administrators had no real objections to the idea. A place like that had been previously allocated for the hospital staff. No one had used it for a long time, however. Now it just needed to be made serviceable once again. After it was fixed up, they began showing interesting movies to the patients on certain days. A bunch of comfy armchairs were arranged around a big TV, and some hardback chairs were placed next to them to handle the overflow. Thus, a mini cinema was created, with seating for approximately thirty people.

"I've seen this movie more than once, but each time it seems new to me," said Betty, who suffered from stomach cancer.

"Yeah, I saw this for the first time in the theater," another patient with throat cancer said.

"But it's ridiculous how these samurai behave," said Dr. Stevens, who had just entered the room, "running out in front of guns with nothing but swords. They're sure to die. It's stupid to launch an attack that's destined to fail."

"The most important thing is not whether you're defeated, it's the fact that you're doing something and not running away from your responsibilities," Willie burst out. "Socrates respected the laws of his city and didn't run away but accepted death bravely. Jesus Christ could have saved himself from death as well. But he didn't run away from the city he was in. He fully surrendered himself to the will of God and accepted all his suffering. This is why the Bible exalts and praises him. And consequently he's become a model of self-sacrifice for everyone."

"Christ and Socrates from the ancient world are completely inappropriate examples here," Dr. Stevens said. "Bravery, to the Greeks, meant being killed in battle. So using that criteria, Socrates can't be called a hero. And the martyrdom of Jesus Christ as he was nailed to the cross exemplified a totally new version of heroism for Christians." Dr. Stevens wanted to say that neither of those examples was an example of heroism. "After Jesus Christ, a Christian associated heroism with compassion and humility."

"Self-sacrifice without a fight is not heroism but a clowning without spectators," said Adam, a patient suffering from brain cancer.

"Adam, it sounds like when they operated on your brain, they must have taken out your good sense as well," Tomas, his hospital roommate said.

"The fact is that all these differences of opinion stem from differing interpretations of heroism," Betty said. "So to really get to the heart of this question, we need to define the word 'heroism,' which is impossible to do. Heroism is a multifaceted concept."

"What is heroism?" Charlie said. "Heroes are soldiers from any country who die in combat, who were dismissed and undervalued while they were still alive." Charlie's father had been crippled in Vietnam and, after his return, had suffered for many years from the injuries he received fighting there. Charlie claimed that his father had been decorated many times for his distinguished service during that war. Nevertheless, upon returning to his native shores, he had been completely forgotten. When he died, no one came to his funeral except for a couple of old army buddies. "Heroes are only needed at times of danger, during battles. But then once the threat is gone, they're just a useless burden for their country . . ."

"But both Christ and Socrates were alike in their courage, in their mastery over their human, yet despised, animal instincts." Willie said. "They're both symbols of heroism and bravery: one divine and the other human. And they both courageously undertook a just pursuit." It seemed as though Willie had not been paying attention to what had been said about heroism. He was thinking about the words of Dr. Stevens, who had earlier thrust himself so curtly into the conversation. Willie hadn't been able to get those words out of his head.

"Again you're taking the subject into a spiritual realm," Stevens said. "Everyone says, 'What's inside a person is the main thing,' but for some reason, when it's time to get married, everyone wants a fashion model." This was met by a smile.

"Heroism is heroism, whether it's divine or human," Willie said.

A patient named Larry, who suffered from colon cancer said, "Yeah, these days you really have to be a hero to live on a small salary in today's economy. And if you throw in supporting your daughter and son-in-law, then you're a real superman."

"I agree with Willie," Wisam said. "Fighting for what you love and for the noblest causes, regardless of how it turns out, deserves praise. Very often, we don't understand what true victory means. For some, victory means achieving your ultimate goal. But maybe in some cases, the road to victory will pass through what looks like failure to the outside world. Husayn ibn Ali was a ruler in his day. After a battle against Muawiyah, the ruler of the city of Shaam, who had rebelled against him, Husayn signed a treaty with him and relinquished power. Some at that time saw that peace treaty as a defeat and sign of cowardice. However, from a political perspective, historians consider it to be one of Husayn ibn Ali's greatest victories.

"The same can be said about the uprising in Karbala that occurred in the seventh century. There, seventy-two men fought against an army of ten thousand from a dictatorial regime. The uprising ended in the martyrdom of those outnumbered, freedom-loving people. However, this uprising has been remembered for thirteen centuries as a symbol of the perseverance and resistance of those who love freedom against oppression and dictatorship. All Muslims remember this day every year and mourn for those who were martyred in this uprising."

Willie, who knew a fair amount about Husayn from talking with Wisam, said, "Many centuries have passed since the tragedy at Karbala. And it's true that Husayn and I come from different countries. But even if you have a heart of stone, you would have to be upset and impressed by the stories of the injustice, mercilessness, and atrocities suffered by Husayn and his followers. Or you have to at least try to find some sympathy for people who rebelled against tyrants for the sake of justice."

"Of course," Dr. Anna said. "It's always been that way. Throughout history, in every age there have been stouthearted people like that, from all different nations. When values are forgotten and courage melts away, one person always emerges to change the entire system."

Stevens became quite flustered because he felt his opinions had been rejected by the others.

"Yes, you're all so clever, and I'm the only one who apparently doesn't really get it," Stevens said. "But the heroism you're talking about only takes an hour. Living as an honorable citizen requires a whole lifetime. Your version of heroism is nothing but a way of dying. But the heroism I'm talking about is a way of living. That's the difference between you and me."

"It's always great to be the exception to the rule," Dr. Anna said. "Cowardly people have always dreamed of doing something heroic without getting hurt. Stevens, another word for the way of life you're talking about is 'cowardice.'"

"Hmm. You must think your impudence is some kind of heroism. You're wrong. It's sheer stupidity. You know why? Because I never forget what is done to me."

The room fell quiet. At that instant, a comedy program began playing on the TV.

"These comedy shows with their laugh tracks always make me sick. I feel like an idiot watching them because they tell me when I'm supposed to laugh." Ella changed the channel.

A football game was being televised just then. This time Willie objected in a low voice.

"Okay, we watched the movie, and now we're done!" Stevens ended the talk. "Everyone back to their rooms."

When the patients left the film room, Dr. Anna and Stevens began to talk loudly behind the closed doors.

# THE MIGRANT WHO COVERED
# A CENTURY-LONG PATH IN A SINGLE DAY

Of all the people Willie had met over the course of his difficult life, no one had ever had such a profound effect on him as Wisam. Willie found meaning and deep wisdom in everything Wisam did, even in his glance. Upon first acquaintance, Willie had the impression that Wisam's life had been interesting and enlightening. But that enlightening and interesting life was concealed behind Wisam's cheerful, smiling face. It was almost as if he were a miser who didn't want to share the profound treasure of life on which he sat.

Wisam's relatives, especially his aunt, who was his most frequent visitor, saw how well he got along with Willie. After a time, she also grew closer to him. Wisam himself was partially responsible for this. He occasionally talked to his aunt about what a trusting and good-hearted man Willie was. One day, Wisam's aunt invited Willie to their home. Willie was very surprised but accepted without hesitation.

When Willie got there, the door was opened by Bana, Aunt Bayan's daughter. Entering the house, he realized that the aunt had taken ill. In fact, the doctors claimed she had little time left, and this was why she had wanted to see Willie. He went into the room and saw Aunt Bayan lying in bed, half asleep. She was on oxygen. With her head, she signaled Willie to come closer. Willie moved the chair toward the bed and sat down. After some silence, Aunt Bayan went directly to the heart of the matter, without wasting words, as though they were old friends. It was as if the woman knew she was in a race with death and needed to hurry and tell him about something that was bothering her.

"Wisam is an ordinary person," she said. "He's like one of the thousands of people around us to whom no one pays any attention as we pass by indifferently. We ask ourselves what sort of meaning can there be in the lives of these wretched, unhappy people who have migrated from the other side of the world, from a backward, second-class, undeveloped country? What could anyone learn from their wretched existence? What's the point of them causing so much inconvenience here anyway?"

These words seemed strange to Willie. They were so contrary to how he felt about Wisam. It was true that Willie heard these kinds of comments from many other people, but he didn't think like them. Willie couldn't understand why this woman, who was so close to death, would say all this to him. *Perhaps she's heard Dr. Stevens say this? Maybe someone's said something to her . . .?"* Hundreds of conjectures flooded Willie's mind.

"Please don't think that I assume you also believe this. If that were the case, I wouldn't have mentioned it to you," Aunt Bayan continued in a hoarse whisper. "But if people can summon a little humility and patience and ask these strangers about their lives, they will see how those lives are deep, meaningful, and full of wisdom. Age is not the most important thing. Not at all. Where we're from, they say, 'Some people take a journey of one hundred years in a single day.'"

# THE WATCH THAT PROTECTS
# FROM THE EVIL EYE

"Wait a minute!" Jafar said, hearing a knock on the door. Upon opening the door, he saw Said, a criminal investigator who worked with his father, and greeted him with a smile. Said was almost a father figure to Jafar and a favorite guest in their home. He had a very close relationship with Jafar's father, Judge Badr.

"Hello, Uncle Said. How are you? Please come in."

"No, Jafar, I'll wait. Go get your coat. You need to come with me."

Jafar was surprised by the serious expression on Said's face. Uncle Said always came into their home with a smile and a joke for Jafar.

"Where are we going, Uncle Said? Has something happened?"

"To the police station. A charge has been lodged against you. I have an order from Judge Badr."

"An order from my father? Why? What for? What kind of charge?"

"Let's go. We'll sort it out at the station." Jafar was alarmed by Said's formal manner and realized that this was a serious matter.

Jafar went upstairs to get his coat. Grandmother Hafiza, seeing Jafar so pale, asked what was going on. Jafar said nothing but tossed something over his shoulder and went downstairs to where Said was waiting.

On his way down the stairs, he repeatedly asked his mother not to say anything to his wife, Asma.

At the police station, even though his father was a district judge, Jafar was interrogated just like anyone else facing an accusation.

It was almost evening before he was released. When he arrived home, everyone—his mother, Hafiza; his wife, Asma; his seventeen-year-old daughter, Havra; and his youngest child, fourteen-year-old Wisam—anxiously awaited him.

"What happened?" his mother said. "We practically worried ourselves to death."

Jafar said nothing and sat down on the couch in the living room. He opened his eyes wide and looked at the clock on the wall, on the inside of which were inscribed Arabic prayers for protection against the evil eye. He wondered if his happy family had fallen under the evil eye of some envious people. The family had never done anything against the law. *But now to face such an accusation.*

His father, Badr, was greatly respected and known even in the highest circles. He was a slim man, with deeply-creased skin on the back of his neck and forehead. Whenever his expression turned serious, or when he was pondering some issue, those creases became even deeper. He was dark-complected and the signs of aging were visible on every part of his body, with the exception of his large, expressive eyes. Youth, wisdom, and resolve could be seen in those eyes, which were of a celestial color, like the infinite heavens above, and hinted at his deeply spiritual nature. Although Badr was no longer young, his body was still strong, and he carried himself gracefully. Wisam bore a strong physical resemblance to his grandfather. Particularly in his eyes. They also had similar personalities. Like his grandfather, Wisam was reserved, quiet, and forbearing.

Badr had been a judge for many years. Although everyone knew him as a strict man, he was also very kind, caring, and wise. Jafar's family was well respected in the city. They were also comfortable financially. Badr was so respected because he was deeply knowledgeable and strictly upheld the standards of justice and the law from the bench—qualities that distinguished him from other judges.

Jafar and the members of his family often heard a story recounted by Judge Badr about the ruler Ali ibn Abi Talib, who is renowned among Muslims as a symbol of justice.

During the reign of Ali ibn Abi Talib, Abu Rafi' was the treasurer overseeing the entire Muslim budget. A very expensive pearl necklace was part of that treasury. One day, Zaynab, the daughter of Imam Ali, sent a messenger to Abu Rafi' to tell him that she wanted to be entrusted with this necklace for three days. Zaynab wanted to wear it during a major sacred Muslim holiday known as Kurban. Abu Rafi' told Zaynab that he could lend it to her on the condition that, if the necklace were damaged, she would be responsible for repaying the treasury for its cost. After Zaynab agreed to this condition, Abu Rafi' entrusted her with this necklace for three days. That very day, Imam Ali happened to notice the necklace around his daughter's neck. When he asked his daughter where it had come from, Zaynab answered that Abu Rafi' had given it to her. Imam Ali immediately summoned Abu Rafi' and asked him why he had done this. Abu Rafi' told Imam Ali what had happened. Then Imam Ali condemned the actions of Abu Rafi', saying to him, "This is a betrayal! The treasury belongs to all Muslims, and it was entrusted to you. To take something from there and give it to someone else, you must have the permission of all Muslims. If you ever do this again without my approval, I will punish you harshly. If Zaynab had taken this necklace without permission and without your conditions, I swear before God I would have cut off her hand for theft." Then Imam Ali ordered Abu Rafi' to immediately take the necklace from his daughter and return it to its place.

Zaynab was upset when she learned of this and went to her father. Ali ibn Abi Talib said to her, "My daughter, you must not wish for everything your heart wants. Many women like you will attend these festivities, but they will have no opportunity to wear such a necklace. You are not superior to them, and they are not inferior to you. It would have been unfair for you to wear this necklace."

Judge Badr had said, "It is difficult for a judge to see the closest member of his family stand accused. At that moment, a judge's true faith is revealed. That's when justice and faith like that of Imam Ali are needed in order to render an honest verdict. It costs nothing to pronounce a sentence on a stranger. Being forced to choose between my own child and justice is what I most fear in life."

"So what would you do if it happened, Badr?" asked Khanum Hafiza.

"I don't even want to think about it. But I would try to do as God wills."

Because of his fear, Badr did not permit Jafar, who was his only child, to accept a government job. "Jafar, my son, this is a very bad time. If you take a government job, you risk being slandered, and later you may not be able to prove your innocence. Whether such a thing would be to vilify me or reduce our family's influence, I don't know. There are so many potential problems. In my forty years on the bench, I've made a lot of enemies. It's all because I've issued just verdicts as commanded by law. I only have two years left before I retire. Then I'll take my pension and move to the village. I'll retreat into the mountains." Badr had done the best he could to protect his son, who had wanted to work in public service like his father.

His mother's trembling voice roused Jafar from his thoughts. "Do you hear me? Answer us. What happened? We've been worried sick ever since this morning." Jafar's wife, Asma, despite her anxiety, decided not to say anything around her mother-in-law. She simply waited nervously for her husband's response.

Without a word, Jafar jumped up, and as if remembering something important, he rushed down the stairs. He left the house, firmly latching the door behind him. Asma, barely able to control herself, ran after Jafar but could not catch up with him.

# A TERRIBLE ACCUSATION

Badr returned at midnight in a very agitated state. Jafar did not come home that evening. All night the family was under a great deal of strain. They learned about what had happened from Badr. Jafar had been accused of murdering a man named Marcus. There were witnesses to the incident.

"What are you saying? It's impossible. This can't be," Hafiza said, tears in her eyes.

"Hafiza, there are witnesses . . ." Badr had never experienced such a desperate situation.

"All right, what's the worst that could happen?" asked Asma. She was frightened and kept asking Hafiza a question the woman couldn't answer.

Badr didn't even want to think about it. Under court law, if the accused was shown to be guilty, the punishment was hanging.

Badr was deeply disturbed by Jafar's absence. In the morning, Jafar returned home, but he did not tell anyone where he had spent the night. After that day, Jafar was evasive and unapproachable.

He was frequently brought in for interrogation. Jafar insisted that he was being slandered, but witnesses claimed that he had taken part in the murder.

The man who had been killed, Marcus, was a Christian. Since Lebanon was embroiled in a civil war[8], the political situation made

---

[8] The civil war in Lebanon, which lasted fifteen years (1975–1990), took about two hundred thousand lives. About three hundred and fifty thousand were injured, and more than a million people left their country.

Jafar's case even more explosive. This civil war had been triggered by the Palestinian Liberation Organization's assassination attempt on the leader of the Maronite Christians. The attempt failed, but afterward, clashes broke out between Christians and Palestinians all over the country. Every faction in Lebanon eventually joined this war. Some foreign countries meddled within these factions, and the roster of their supporters often changed. The dead and wounded were counted in the tens of thousands.

Now, in the midst of this volatile situation, Jafar was accused of murdering a Christian. The investigation and trial of Jafar dragged on for six months. During this time, Badr's family was faced with great trials and tribulations that completely destroyed the stability of the family's routine. Everyone was on edge, particularly Asma. She was a very sensitive woman, and she suffered and grieved more than the others during those six months. During the investigation, even when facts emerged that showed Jafar's innocence, Asma was unable to regain her equanimity. It was as if she were expecting something terrible to happen. Noticing her condition, Grandma Hafiza began giving her a sedative the doctor had prescribed.

During this period of time, Jafar was repeatedly called in for questioning by the investigator, and he was confronted with some of his accusers. Sometimes Jafar's interrogations would last eight to ten hours. He was confronted with some of his accusers. The police also investigated the extent of the involvement of the witnesses in the case who were accusing Jafar. Out of respect for Judge Badr, the officers in charge of the investigation wanted to solve the crime as quickly as possible. The case had blown up so much that even those in the highest circles were following it closely.

Judge Badr appeared to be calmer than anyone else in his family. Outwardly he seemed coolheaded and composed; however, no one could imagine what was going on inside him. Everyone in the family, even Jafar, had someone with whom to share their feelings during trying moments. Only Judge Badr had no one. To those who didn't know him, he gave the impression of being indifferent and callous. No one dared ask the judge about his fears.

Finally, the investigation was over. Because of insufficient evidence and discrepancies in the witnesses' testimony during the exhaustive investigation into the case, Jafar was cleared of the charges. What the family had endured during this period had deeply shaken them and left them feeling powerless, but they now began to rally.

Life got back to normal. How the family yearned to return to their old life. The painful days were gradually forgotten, and the faces that had been shadowed with sadness now began to smile.

# THERE IS NO MORE MERCILESS
# JUDGE THAN THE CONSCIENCE

*You can bury the truth, but you can be sure that
it will emerge and face the daylight one day.*

Two months had passed since Jafar had been cleared. One day, Wisam came home early from school with some homework. As he entered the house, he overheard his parents arguing. That was very strange. That was a first in their family. Wisam cautiously climbed the stairs to the second floor. He heard his sobbing mother trying to explain something to his father. After a few more steps, the voices became clearly audible.

"How will this end?" Asma said. "I was so happy . . . I thought everything was looking up, that the black clouds over our family were slowly dissipating. But it seems we still have grim days ahead." Asma cried, pressing the collar of her sweater against her mouth. She didn't want anyone to hear her.

"Calm down, Asma, please," Jafar said. "It's all going to be okay. Pull yourself together, or my father will hear you."

"How can we live hiding the truth? What if everyone finds out and realizes what's happened?"

"There's no evidence, and besides, the case has already been closed. So no one will bring it up again. Trust me!" But Jafar's voice sounded uneasy.

"I didn't want this to happen," he said. "I didn't want you to find out. But you're always sniffing around in matters that aren't your business."

"I sensed something that night," Asma said. "When you came home, you had that package with you. I thought it was a present and wanted to open it, but you yelled at me. You were raving all night and slept very fitfully. You seemed so jumpy. I knew something had happened. And then when Inspector Said said that the murder had happened that very day . . . That's when I thought you had done it. But I wasn't really sure. Only God knows what I had to endure during the investigation. Fear that they might prove your guilt was tearing at my heart each day. But I still tried to convince myself otherwise. But today . . . Today, when I accidentally saw the gun in that package that you carried in that night, my worst fears were realized." Asma pressed her hands to her head.

"Hiding guns at home was a bad idea. I wanted to throw it away," Jafar said. "I waited until a little time had passed, but the right moment never presented itself. Asma, trust me, I will fix everything."

These words left Wisam horror-stricken. He couldn't move; he felt frozen where he stood. He made an effort to pull himself together, then he continued on to his room. Without getting undressed, he lay down on his bed. Wisam stayed there until evening. Despite his grandmother's insistence, he did not come down for dinner. Later that evening, Wisam began trembling. His temperature rose. During the night, an ambulance pulled up in front of the judge's house.

"Everything's all right," the doctor said as he left the house. "Just let him rest a bit, it's nothing serious. And tell him to take his medicine. In a day or two everything will be fine."

In a few days, Wisam seemed to come around although he wasn't talking, and he had no appetite. He remained in his room most of every day. Jafar's and Asma's attempts to talk to him were unsuccessful. Wisam didn't even want to speak to his grandfather, for whom he had the utmost respect. He always enjoyed his conversations with his grandfather, but now he felt awkward around him. Judge Badr took his grandson to see a wide variety of doctors, trying to figure out what was going on with him. They subjected the boy to a range of tests, but in the end, they determined that, physically, Wisam was perfectly healthy.

Meanwhile, the relationship between Jafar and Asma grew quite strained. Asma cried often and did not even want to talk to Jafar. All night she wanted to be near Wisam. But Wisam didn't want to see anyone, particularly not Asma or Jafar.

Wisam remained in his own world every day. The realization that his father was a murderer was horrifying. And it was even more horrifying that his father had escaped justice and had denied what had happened. Wisam understood the implications perfectly well. He was aware that if there was evidence of guilt, his father would be executed. Another question that deeply concerned him was what he should do under these circumstances. Should he tell his grandfather everything and ultimately cause his father to be executed? No, the idea of doing that was so painful that his mind felt dazed at the very thought of it.

Wisam was on the verge of losing his mind. It was better to keep quiet. But then he felt like a sinner whose actions conflicted with his own beliefs. It was unbearable for him.

And what about the harsh fate in the afterlife for those who concealed evidence? If he said nothing, would he bring down the wrath of God upon himself? Wisam knew what a major sin this was. How could he live the rest of his life with this burden, knowing that he had committed such a sin? He was in a desperate situation. Wisam had not forgotten about the hadith of the Prophet, which he had many times read and heard from his teacher at school:

'Anyone who conceals evidence or bears false witness that leads to the shedding of innocent blood will stand blackened and wounded before the people on Judgment Day. All creatures will know his name and his lineage. But if he gives evidence to preserve someone's rights, on the Day of Judgment, he will come to God with a radiant face. And all creatures will know his name and his lineage. God instructs us about this in the Quran: 'Give testimony for the sake of God!'

Wisam pressed his head into his pillow to muffle the voice of his conscience. It was very hard for him to resist its call.

*Maybe my testimony will not be admissible, perhaps under Sharia I am not old enough.* Wisam wanted to find a way out of his predicament, a way to justify his actions and deceive his conscience.

*Aaugh, what am I saying? I'm fifteen already.*[9] *That's quite old enough to give evidence,* he argued with himself.

*My grandfather said that two people were needed to testify. Perhaps my testimony alone will not be sufficient. What should I do? How can I find my way? Maybe I should see what Grandfather thinks?* thought Wisam bewilderedly.

*To go offer evidence against my own father! How? Against the one who brought me into this world and raised me? And what if my evidence is admissible and he is executed? But if I don't testify, I will be committing an even greater sin. I will be opposing God, my creator, the one who has more say over me than anyone else.*

---

[9] In accordance with Islamic Sharia, one requirement for a boy to testify in court is that he be at least fifteen years of age, according to the lunar calendar.

Wisam so tormented himself with these doubts that he was soon hardly recognizable. He became thin and sallow. Eventually he broke down. One night when the family gathered at the dinner table, Wisam, tormented by his thoughts, lost control of himself and began sobbing.

"I don't know what to do. I don't know . . . Help me, please. I can't bear it any longer . . ."

Asma also began to cry upon seeing her son in such a state. Grandmother Hafiza went over to her grandson and hugged him. Her eyes filled with tears, but she kept her composure. Jafar left the room. He could not remain unmoved by the sight of his son suffering so on his account. When Asma had mentioned the gun to Jafar, he had sensed Wisam's presence behind the door before the discussion had ended. But he had hoped that the boy hadn't heard them. Seeing the changes in his son after that day, Jafar became certain that Wisam knew about what had happened. Asma had also guessed the reason for her son's behavior. But she didn't want to think about it either.

Grandmother Hafiza questioned Wisam for a long time to try to uncover the reason for his distress, but the boy simply said nothing. He broke out in a cold sweat. Grandmother Hafiza telephoned Badr and asked him to come home early. Before Judge Badr arrived, Wisam had already been taken to the doctor. His therapist said that he was suffering from nervous tension, but he could not explain the root cause. Wisam was not having any kind of problems at school or with his friends or teachers or with his family at home. The school tried to figure out what was going on as well. But they couldn't find any rational explanation. The doctor prescribed a sedative. But no matter how Asma tried, she couldn't get him to swallow the medicine. Wisam grew worse that evening. During the night, he began to cry, calling out to God for help. His family was forced to summon an ambulance. With some effort, a nurse managed to inject him with a sedative. Soon he fell asleep.

Jafar didn't know what to do. Should he go make a confession to the police? Jafar knew very well what that would mean. *Now that my situation is looking up, should I go and ruin everything?* But if he didn't, he would have to watch his son waste away before his very eyes. Asma couldn't say anything to Jafar. It was very hard for her to have to choose between her husband and her son. She didn't want to lose either of them. Jafar knew that his son had a strong faith. He understood that Wisam was in a terrible predicament. He understood that if he didn't help Wisam make his choice, the boy would destroy himself.

In the morning, Jafar went into Wisam's room. He sat silently for a while beside his son. Wisam looked so much like his grandfather when he was asleep. He had very thick, curly hair. Jafar touched his son's head, stroking and gently smoothing his hair. He wanted to feel that curly hair between his fingers. Jafar remembered the most glorious days he had spent with his child: when he was born, took his first steps, began to speak, and started school. He remembered his birthdays . . .

"Wisam, after giving you life, I will not take it away from you. I will help you make this difficult choice," said Jafar. He drew closer to his son, kissed him on his sweaty brow, and left.

# SELFLESSNESS IS THE REALIZATION THAT SOME THINGS ARE MORE IMPORTANT THAN YOU

*The only certain happiness in life is to live for others.*

~ Leo Tolstoy

Wisam woke about three in the afternoon. His head ached terribly. He had a dim recollection of yesterday's events. The house was very still, which was unusual for that time of day. He called for his mother, then his grandmother, and even his sister, Havra, but no one answered.

Wisam lay awake for a bit, then decided to get up. The silence in the house alarmed him. He went into the living room. Not finding anyone there, he became quite distraught. Then the sound of someone wailing gave him a start. His mother came into the house weeping, with his grandmother, Hafiza, trailing after her.

"Jafar! Jafar!" Asma, who was always quiet and had never raised her voice in her mother-in-law's presence, was now shouting furiously.

Grandmother Hafiza did her best to calm her. Wisam's Aunt Bayan came over with them. She was also crying and trying to comfort her sister. But it was no use.

Wisam realized that his father had confessed to the murder. Jafar had gone straight to the chief prosecutor to make his confession. He hadn't wanted to force a difficult choice upon Judge Badr as well by telling him everything. Upon obtaining his confession, the prosecutor first wanted to discuss the matter with the judge. After Badr listened to the prosecutor, he was dumbstruck and sat silent, not knowing what to say. Then, having regained his composure, he told the prosecutor that the usual procedures should be followed. The prosecutor asked him if that was what he really wanted done, and the judge repeated what he had said. Then the prosecutor took Jafar into custody, pending his trial.

This news quickly spread throughout Saida. Everyone was astounded at the unexpected turn of events and utterly stunned by Jafar's sudden confession.

# THERE MUST BE A RECKONING FOR BLOOD THAT IS SPILLED UNJUSTLY

After hearing the news, everyone asked Judge Badr to help Jafar, to commute the sentence or offer some punishment other than execution. Even Asma's family tried to influence the judge. But he would not see anyone. Asma also repeatedly tried to talk to him.

"I have always been a good daughter-in-law to you. I have never asked you for anything before. Now, I beg you, have pity on Jafar. He's not some stranger — this is your own son. Don't make me a widow. Have mercy on my children," Asma said, sobbing as she tried relentlessly to change the judge's mind. But Badr silently pondered the fact that he could not act against God's will. Then the exhausted Asma began to cry quietly, pressing her head against her knees. Badr stood for a moment, then walked out of the room without saying a word. He left Asma weeping alone.

Respected elders from Asma's family came to see Badr and wanted to discuss the matter with him.

"Everything that happens to us is by the hand of our fellow Muslims," said Asma's cousin Saleh, breaking a long silence. "Those Palestinians are the root of the whole problem. At first, they were in Jordan. But they can never settle down. It all started with Yasser Arafat's desire to stage a coup. What had Hussein[10] ever done to them? When the Palestinians fled from the Israelis, they had nowhere to go, and the

---

[10] Hussein bin Talal was the king of Jordan.

government of Jordan offered them a refuge. And how did they thank them? By trying to overthrow the government. And in the end what happened? The military coup failed. Hussein crushed the Palestinian forces and expelled their armed brigades from his country. Then we Lebanese took them in. And now they're wreaking havoc in our country." Saleh, a journalist and political columnist, dealt with political issues all day long, so he usually turned conversations in that direction.

"Yes, you're right. You really have to watch out with them. But Hussein bin Talal didn't expel all the Palestinians! Only their armed brigades. About half a million Palestinian refugees currently live in Jordan and enjoy the same rights as full citizens of that country," claimed Walid, correcting his brother a bit.

"Yasser Arafat deals from both sides of the deck," Saleh said. "He always has. When the Islamists overthrew the shah in Iran, Yasser showed up there less than two weeks later. As a result, he became the first foreign visitor to arrive in Iran. Although Tehran's Mehrabad airport was closed because of the country's political issues, Arafat still landed his plane there. When they asked him, 'Why did you rush here so quickly without telling anyone you were coming?' he answered, 'Does a person really have to provide notice when he's coming home?' His visit to the newly-established Islamic Republic of Iran and his grandiose words demonstrated his brotherly affection for the Iranians and the fact that he considered Iran his home.

"However, when war broke out between Iran and Iraq, that same Arafat rushed to Baghdad to offer a 'brotherly' greeting to Saddam, to whom he officially pledged his support, promising that the PLO would be at his side in that war."

"Yes, I remember," Haidar, Asma's uncle, said without raising his head. "And right after the Iranian revolution, Arafat told Moshe Dayan, 'You can have America, Iran is enough for us!' And what happened then? Once they found a juicier morsel, they turned on Iran. But don't confuse those people with the rest of the peaceful Palestinian nation. Those poor sods have always gotten the short end of the stick. That's politics. It's a nasty game. There's no conception of justice, compassion, or courage. All that matters in that big, cruel game is what's in the interests of the country."

"The Palestinians have created a state within a state in our country," Saleh said. "The authorities can't do anything about it. They don't have enough power. The Christians and the Shiites who are concentrated in southern Lebanon suffer the most from it."

No one dared begin a conversation about Jafar with Badr. There-fore, Asma's father decided to wait for the appropriate moment to turn to the real subject they wanted to discuss.

"If the Palestinians are to blame," said Said, "then those who got them involved in these matters are also guilty. Palestinian refugees are currently a very big problem. The primary cause of that problem is the Arab-Israeli conflict. The Palestinians were also used as an instrument during the coup attempt in Jordan. The forces that took advantage of them didn't need to look far. They were found within the Jordanian government itself." It was inappropriate to talk about justice and fair-ness, given the circumstances. They were trying to imply that com-peting political interests were playing dirty pool with their country. And everyone wants to reap all the possible benefits for themselves. There's no place now for laws you can believe in and use to guide your actions.

A brief silence was followed a period of chatting, which then prompted a new round of political discussions on the previous topics. It was difficult for everyone to move on to the main issue. Then Badr spoke. "Maybe we could change the subject? And it would be even better if we could close this question without moving on to other top-ics. This is so hard and unbearable for all of us. All our strength has been depleted."

After these words from the judge, Asma's uncle, Haidar, who had kept silent until then, could no longer restrain himself and asked ner-vously, "Badr, do you truly not understand what is happening? Are you really unable to properly assess the situation? Everyone . . ."

But just then, Grandmother Hafiza entered the room with a pot of tea, so Haidar sank into silence, and everyone waited for her to leave. After Grandmother Hafiza withdrew from the room, Haidar said, "Badr—"

This time Asma's father interrupted Haidar. "There's already a war going on in this country between Muslims and Christians. Have you forgotten that they killed six hundred Muslims in Beirut?" He gestured nervously. "Now you're taking their side?"

"The same number of Christians were killed by the Muslim commu-nity with the help of the Palestinians in Damour," answered Judge Badr.

"All right then, how about the murders and attacks that occurred in Sabra and Shatila on peaceful Palestinian settlements?"

"Both sides are killing each other in this brutal war. But that doesn't give us the right to kill peaceful people that are not guilty of anything," said the judge, gripped by bitter emotions. His throat had dried up. He faltered and then continued: "If someone commits the sin of violence, should we do the same? Jafar killed a peaceful man. The murder of an innocent person, regardless of his religious affiliation, must not go unpunished. You can be assured that this is much more distressing for me. But I cannot act against Islamic Sharia. To send your only son to the gallows with your own hands and to thus cast a blight upon your lineage—this is a father's greatest nightmare." His eyes filled with tears as he said this.

Everyone in the room understood that there was nothing more to say, and so, filled with resentment, they departed without a word. They filed out, and the judge was left alone with his grief. It was their last visit.

# ABRAHAM'S SACRIFICE



*Paternal love is no different from self-love.*

~ Vauvenargues


The verdict was to be read out in the morning. As the day wore on, Judge Badr was so anxious he was unable to settle down. Never in his life had he felt this way. Recently he had spent most of his time reading the Quran to quiet his heart and find strength in the divine words, so that he could make the right decision. Late in the afternoon, the judge went to the detention center. He asked the guard to bring in Jafar, who greeted him as he entered the room. The guard left them alone. In measured tones, the judge offered a return greeting. Badr stood up from his seat and sat down next to Jafar. For a while, he did not know what to say. Then he put his hand on his son's shoulder. He gazed at him. But Jafar sat with a bowed head and said nothing.

"Jafar, you're all gray. I hadn't noticed until now."

Judge Badr stroked Jafar's hair. He examined the features of his face, as if seeing him for the first time. Jafar, without raising his head, remained hunched over with his elbows digging into his knees.

"In very ancient times there lived a prophet," the judge started telling a story that was known to Jafar since he was a kid. "His name was Abraham. For many years he had no children. The prophet Abraham greatly desired a son — a successor who would support him," His voice trembled. "When he was quite advanced in years, God finally heard his prayer and granted him a son. Abraham's joy knew no bounds. He named his son Ishmael. He watched the child grow and made plans for his future. Abraham often took him in his arms and stroked his head, saying, 'Son, when you grow up, you will be my successor and bring even more honor to the lineage of Abraham.'"

Jafar swallowed. Only now did he feel with all his being what suffering his father had to endure because of him. He wanted to say something, to save him from all this, but not a word came to his mind.

"But one day, God asked Abraham to sacrifice his son, who meant everything to him. It was the most harrowing trial of the Prophet's life. Abraham did not know what to do. He was hoping to find a different solution. But as he slept, God made it known to him exactly three times that there was no other way but to offer his son as a sacrifice to Him. Abraham saw that only one road lay before him.

"The day before the promised date, Abraham summoned his son Ishmael and informed him of God's command." The judge felt a lump in his throat. Quietly shedding tears, he went on. "It was very difficult for Abraham to have this conversation with his son. He didn't want to sacrifice his own child. What father would want to kill his only son? What father would want to execute his child — the rock of his support in all matters? What father would find that an easy thing to do?"

At that moment Jafar raised his head. For the first time since he had been imprisoned, he looked at his father very intently. Judge Badr had aged dramatically during this short period of time. His back was bent, his face looked haggard, his eyes were sunken, his hair had turned white, and he had lost a lot of weight. The well-fitting jacket now looked too big for him. The white dress shirt under the jacket was also rumpled. Some stains could be seen on the collar. The judge seemed diminished. Jafar's eyes filled with tears, but he steadied himself.

"Father, it doesn't look like Khanum Hafiza has been looking after you very well lately," Jafar joked.

Judge Badr looked down at himself. "No, that poor woman has been brooding for the last few days and is tired . . . awfully tired," he said.

"Yes, Father, I understand. I've turned everything upside down. I know it's all because of me."

After a brief silence, Jafar said, "'Oh, my father, do as you are commanded. You will find me, if God wills, of the steadfast.'"

The judge's eyes again filled with tears. He could no longer suppress the grief that had been building for months, and embracing his son, he wept as Jafar repeated the answer that Ismael had given to Abraham in the Quran.

"I'm sorry. I should have spent more time with you, Jafar."

"Don't be sorry about anything. You were a truly wonderful father. You were an example for me to emulate. You were always a fair judge and a true believer. It's too bad every judge in the world isn't like you."

"You know, Jafar, you've actually helped me. If you hadn't responded with patience and resolve, this would have been very difficult for me. Your submission to justice has truly helped me not to break morally. Had you acted otherwise, I don't know what I would have done. You're the one who's setting the example. You've confessed to your sin. And that requires a lot of courage and a strong faith."

"Father, I repent of my deeds. I was under some bad influences. The civil war in our country and the mass killings of Christians and Muslims had a negative impact on me. Because of this, I took a rash step. When an argument arose between Marcus and me, I was very angry. He said a lot of things he shouldn't have. I acted in the wake of all these events that have occurred in our country. I was unable to restrain myself. But I didn't want this to happen. When we argued, I only wanted to scare him and teach him a bit of a lesson. I repent of my actions. I didn't want this to happen, believe me . . ."

"Jafar, all expressions of remorse are acceptable to God. In accordance with Sharia, when a person is punished for his sin, he leaves this world free from that sin. And God does not punish him any further. Perform a full ritual of purification before your execution. And like a true Muslim, accept the penalty for your actions. In accordance with our faith, the body of a sinful man who has accepted his punishment bravely is like that that of a martyr — both are clean and not considered to be polluted, thus such people can be buried without a full purification ritual."

"Comparable to a martyr? My sin will be wiped away? Is this true, Father?" Jafar turned to his father like a child hoping to be comforted one final time.

Judge Badr smiled and embraced Jafar. Tears trickled from his eyes.

"Yes, God will forgive all your sins, my son. I'm sorry if I ever did something to upset you. Forgive me!"

"You are the one who must forgive. I have nothing to excuse. I almost lost my afterlife, but you have given if back to me again."

# THE LAST TRIAL

Although Judge Badr did not want to preside over Jafar's trial himself, he had no choice because the other two judges refused to do it. The court's verdict and sentence were known in advance. According to Islamic law, two impartial witnesses are needed to testify at a murder trial. But if there are no witnesses, guilt is considered proven if the killer confesses. So in this instance, the two witnesses were not needed. In accordance with Sharia, although self-exculpatory testimony from someone of sound mind might not be admissible, self-incriminating testimony is quite satisfactory as evidence of a crime.

Badr was still secretly nourishing a flicker of hope, which he couldn't admit to himself. He thought that perhaps Jafar might recant his confession and deny his guilt. Even without Jafar's confession, the crime weapon and other evidence was sufficient to convict him. Because this was a very sensitive case, the highest officials in the city of Saida were watching the affair closely. Many of those were Maronite Christians serving in the police force. Nor did Jafar want to back down, because his son, Wisam, was always foremost in his thoughts. It was easier for him to lose his own life than to lose his son.

During the trial, Judge Badr's body was bathed in a cold sweat. He was in anguish but could do nothing. Jafar, who was seated in the dock, did not look at the judge, both to avoid causing him pain and out of personal shame. He looked around the courtroom and was relieved not to see his family's faces. His father wouldn't let anybody in the family attend the trial. Jafar let his head down again, closed his eyes, and waited.

And now it was time for the judge to make his final statement and pronounce a verdict. He paused for an instant to think. At such moments, the human brain moves at the speed of light; many different emotions can flood through a person within a single instant. Judge Badr thought about how quickly time had passed. It seemed as if only yesterday Jafar had been a newborn baby handed to his father, as though yesterday Jafar had taken his first steps, begun to speak, and uttered the word "Grandma" for the first time. Jafar had been raised by Badr's mother, and the judge thought of her now as though she were still alive and watching Jafar go off to his first day of school. It seemed as if Jafar had just started a family and become a father to Havra and Wisam . . .

Badr had great hopes for his son and grandchildren. He dreamed of sharing their happiest days and their joys and even seeing the children of his grandchildren. But those dreams were tied to the future. Badr didn't want his hopes to turn into ashes in his own hands.

"Your honor, your honor," whispered the judge's aide seated to his right, rousing Judge Badr from his reverie.

"Yes, I'm here," he said, flustered.

"Everyone is awaiting your verdict."

The judge did not want to face reality. His dreams and his yesterdays seemed sweeter to him. The deputy's voice returned him to the courtroom, yanked him away from the happy days of the past. Badr's hand began to tremble. No matter how he tried, he could not read out the verdict. Judge Badr had admired Imam Ali all his life. He had always tried to mimic him and follow his path. The judge wondered for a split second what Imam Ali would have done at this moment. He began to repeat the words from the Quran, "So do not fear the people, but fear Me, and do not exchange My verses for a small price. And whoever does not judge by what God has revealed — then it is those who are the disbelievers." With some effort, he composed himself, and only then did he raise his head and look at his son. Sensing this, Jafar also lifted his head. Their eyes met, not as the accused and the judge, but as a father and a son. No matter how guilty and deserving of execution Jafar might be, the judge could not look at him as a criminal. For Badr, Jafar would always be a beloved child, a part of his soul.

Jafar's eyes proclaimed his support for his father. It was as if he said, "Father, do as you see fit!" Jafar, smiling, nodded his head. Judge Badr also smiled at him in response, but his smile was very different from Jafar's. For Badr, smiling was a challenge.

◆　◆　◆

"We sentence Jafar, son of Badr, to be hanged by the neck until dead."

After the verdict was read, the courtroom erupted in screams, weeping, and shouts of anger directed at the judge.

"Death to the judge! The murderer of his son!"

"Ruthless!"

"Damn you!"

The police were forced to intervene. They hurried everyone outside, and the judge was left alone with his last sentence. All his hopes and dreams had been shattered. Pronouncing the verdict had not brought him any relief. Although the story of the prophet Abraham and Ismael was one that Judge Badr had often read from books and told to many, it was agonizing to experience it firsthand.

*What a harrowing experience, Lord! Help me! Lighten my burden! How will I live with this pain, God?* In his mind he understood that what he did was right, and he had a clean conscience, but this . . . His heart was broken. He could not quiet it or bring it around. How was he going to look into the eyes of Wisam and Havra now? *If they ask me, 'Grandpa, why did you kill our father?' what will I answer? And his mother . . . What will I say to her? 'Badr, give my son back to me, return him,' she will beg, sobbing.* How difficult it was to follow the path of Imam Ali and Imam Abraham.

The judge lost track of time in the constant stream of consciousness. The door opened quietly, letting in light and the silhouette of a guard: "Uh . . . Your Honor, it's very late; I have to lock the doors . . ." Badr throw at him a petrified look, stood up, and walked heavily to the door of the courtroom.

# YOU WON'T BID ME FINAL FAREWELL

*A man kneeling before God can see much farther than the whole world can see even standing on its tiptoes.*

~ John Wesley

The day before his execution, Jafar was given permission to see his family. Escorted by the guard, he passed through the prison yard fenced with iron bars above and entered a small room. Grandmother Hafiza, Asma, Havra, and Wisam were waiting for him. Judge Badr did not come with them. The visit lasted several hours, and the members of the family cried and embraced Jafar. No one really spoke. Occasionally Hafiza would address an affectionate word toward her child.

But when the guard came in and announced, "Time's up!" no one was ready to leave.

"Listen, don't vilify my father," Jafar said. "He did the right thing. I'm proud of him. He did something that I wouldn't have dared. No one could have acted as he did." He could barely keep from bursting into tears in front of his family.

"I love you all very much," Jafar said in a weakened voice, "and I'll never forget any of you." He felt overwhelmed by what was happening and now wanted the visit to end quickly. Everybody got back on their feet as soon as he stood up.

Asma broke down and fell to his feet. She began to sob so loudly that a second guard opened the peephole in the iron door and looked in to see what was happening. Grandmother Hafiza steadied herself against a wall to keep from falling. And Havra was crying and clinging to her father.

"Papa, why is this happening?" she said. "I don't want you to go. Don't leave. Please don't leave. Come home. I miss you."

Wisam stayed silent. He didn't know what to say. He felt as if he'd done something wrong. He wanted to believe that all this was a terrible nightmare, that after a while, his father would leave this dark room and return home. A whirlpool of confusing feelings and thoughts overwhelmed him. Asma's screams jerked him out of his numbness. Choking with tears, he hugged and kissed his father. Jafar hugged his son back and whispered into his ear: "Wisam, son, your grandfather is old . . . Take care of your sister and mother."

Because it was such a difficult situation, the guard had done the best he could to extend the visit. But no matter how much extra time he gave them, it was very little compared to the long separation that awaited their family. Now he was forced to intervene.

The judge arrived late for his visit with Jafar that day. Father and son sat together in silence for a long time. Neither knew what to say. Their tongues were silent, but their hearts conversed as they talked with each other in their minds. They sat face to face, just looking at one another. Jafar was the first to break the silence.

"Father, Havra doesn't have any warm clothes. Let's buy her a nice coat. And Asma asked me to get her a new head scarf. But I keep forgetting to buy one."

"We'll buy all that Jafar, absolutely."

"I also want to get a present for Mother. I always forget about her when I buy something for Asma. And she needs attention and gifts too." Then he smiled a little. "Of course, it's actually her own fault. Whenever I buy her anything, she just says, 'Why waste your extra money on me? Buy something for Asma!'"

"We will, Jafar. And we'll get something for your mother too," said Judge Badr, without tearing his weary gaze away from his son. He knew perfectly well what his son wanted to say—he was making his will.

"Jafar, we'll buy whatever you want. Everyone in the family loves you very much."

"Father, do you think I've been too hard on Wisam? Sometimes I feel like I never manage to find much time for him. I feel like I need to really change the way I treat him and be more attentive."

"No, Jafar, you're doing fine. You're a very affectionate father. All fathers feel this way. Myself included."

"And the balcony hasn't been repaired," Jafar said. "Some work really needs to be done on it. Havra has been complaining that when her friends come over, no one wants to sit out there.

"I want us to hold Wisam's wedding in our village. As you get older, you start to feel the pull of your roots. You want to go back to your village. City life is tiring. I think we'll be better off in the village. Nature is very soothing. When you used to talk about wanting to go back to your village, I couldn't understand why you would want to leave behind everything you had in the city and go live in the sticks. Now I understand you very well.

"Wisam looks so much like you, Father," said Jafar, hopscotching from one subject to the next. His heart was full, and he didn't know what they should talk about. But at the same time, Jafar wanted to spend time with his father, sharing emotions and feeling his father's love.

The judge sat silently, gazing at his son. They were both agonizingly aware that it would soon be time to say good-bye. The judge felt like he should say something to his son — something very important — or ask him something. Jafar felt the same way, but no matter how they tried, neither of them could remember what that might be.

The time that Badr had asked the guard to grant them was already up, and he had to leave. But he didn't know how he would do that. How could he end a conversation he would never have again or part with a son he would never see again?

"Jafar, my son, I have to go. Truly I have no choice; our time was up long ago. You should lie down and rest." Judge Badr didn't know how he was able to say those words. For an instant he was dumbstruck. He felt those were the most ridiculous words he could have said to someone who was to be executed in the morning. But he had let them slip out without thinking.

Smiling a little, Jafar responded, "All right, Father! You go, and I'll rest. I have a long journey ahead of me tomorrow."

The judge could not bear to hear those words. He embraced Jafar and began to sob. Jafar also hugged his father tightly and cried. But more quietly, with tears springing from deep within. Badr kissed his son's neck and breathed in his scent. He would never forget that moment or that scent. The father and child stood clinging to one another for some time.

"Father . . ." Jafar held him in his arms and whispered quietly into his ear. "I've always known that someday you would grow old and die. When I thought about it, my heart would start pounding like it was going to burst. Everyone celebrated when you had a birthday. But I was always thinking about the fact that you were another year older and closer to death. Sometimes I would look at your wrinkled face and at your neck and hands. I would always jokingly tell you that you were holding up well and that the younger guys had nothing on you, but I was trying to convince myself that you still had a long life ahead. I couldn't imagine that you'd leave me first. I just couldn't . . . To commit you to the cold earth, leaving you alone and returning home to a house filled with your scent . . . You've always been my rock, my advisor. It was unbearable for me to think that I would lose you. You know, Father, this will in fact save me from living out my worst nightmare."

"No," Badr cried out. "It wasn't supposed to happen this way. A father should go first, and his children should be there to send him off. Now you're leaving and won't accompany me to my final place of rest. But I . . . How can I bury you? You haven't thought about how hard it is for a father to say good-bye to his child!"

There are moments when time seems to speed up. Another hour passed, during which the judge and Jafar several times mentioned that it was time to leave, but neither of them dared be the first to say good-bye. Badr would have spent the night with his son, but the warden had come personally to fetch the judge. He apologized but said that the judge needed to leave. Jafar asked the warden to take his father away first. He didn't want his father to have to watch him go and be left alone in the room where they had spent their final time together.

"Father . . ." Badr was slumped over and dragging his feet across the floor, hardly able to force himself from the room, but he halted at the doorway, not turning to face his son.

"Father, I was always happy to be an only child. I knew I wouldn't have to share my parents' love with anyone else. But now I'm very sorry not to have a brother. When I'm gone you'll have no one to lean on. Father, you must be very strong, do you hear? Be strong, Father! Don't pay attention to anything anyone says. Take care of yourself, and have Asma iron your clothes so they're smooth and clean, like always. Be sure to eat well. You've gotten so thin . . ." Jafar swallowed the lump in his throat with difficulty.

"Father, I will wait for you at the gates to heaven. I won't go in without you!" Jafar was making a reference to the hadith of the Prophet of Islam that his father had recited to him. The hadith says that children who have left this world before their parents will be waiting for them at the gates to heaven and will refuse to enter until their parents arrive.

The next day was Thursday. Jafar was to be executed early in the morning. He performed a full ablution. He lay awake all night. He spent those hours communing with God, worshiping, performing his traditional prayer, and asking forgiveness for his sins. He asked God to protect his family, especially his father. Jafar was a father too, so it was easy for him to put himself in his father's place. He knew that his father would suffer more than anyone else, because everyone would be against him and forsake him.

The judge returned home very late after meeting with Jafar. He didn't say anything to anyone. He went into the prayer room and locked himself in. He stayed there until morning. Wisam wanted to talk to his grandfather and confide in him. It was as if he sensed that it was only a matter of hours until his father's execution. He went to the door of that room several times that night but didn't dare enter. Wisam heard his grandfather crying miserably. Judge Badr typically did that on the anniversary of the martyrdom of Husayn ibn Ali. During those days of ritual mourning, the judge often disappeared into that room and grieved for Imam Husayn and did not sleep all night long.

No one in the family slept that night, and everyone was very tense. They only learned about Jafar's death the day after his execution.

# FORTY DAYS LATER

Forty days had passed since Jafar's execution. Everything had changed during that period. Judge Badr had submitted his resignation, with less than a year left to serve before he reached retirement age. Because of his situation, the presiding judge on the Supreme Court gave his consent. Asma took the children back to her native village and moved in with her sister Bayan. She, as well as everyone else in her family, held Judge Badr solely responsible for what had happened.

"Badr murdered his only son. He didn't set aside his cold righteousness for just one time in his life, even to save his son. He could have used his personal connections to free him. He could have fabricated evidence in Jafar's favor. But he did nothing. He sent his own son to the gallows with his own hands."

"Badr's ambitions were Jafar's undoing. Who today obeys the law? There are judges who take bribes. But he was guilty of a much greater evil; his hands have been steeped in his son's blood."

"Badr thought that by enforcing a meaningless form of justice, he would establish peace between Christians and Muslims. He thought that everyone would understand how important it is to be ready to sacrifice everything for the sake of justice. Badr was sure that everyone would then stop fighting and submit themselves to the idea of justice. But no such luck! The war flared up with renewed intensity, as did the momentum of killing."

Those forty days were like forty years for the family. Judge Badr had grown old from brooding and hunchbacked from grief. Until recently the judge had remained undaunted by old age, but now he was utterly drained. Hafiza's legs were giving out on her. She found walking difficult and needed a cane or someone's help to get around.

Nor did any trace of Asma's youth remain. Her hair turned gray, and her face was as ashen as an old woman's. Her eyes were sunken, and when she spoke, her voice was hoarse and barely audible. Havra cried every night. She could keep herself distracted during the day, but at night she kept her eyes on the door as if expecting someone to suddenly walk in. The girl still could not believe that her father was dead. She had decorated every wall in the house with photographs of him. The family was in mourning every day for Jafar. No one could forget him.

The last time Wisam saw his grandmother and grandfather was on the forty-day anniversary of Jafar's death. When Judge Badr wanted to say hello to Wisam, Asma cried out and stopped him.

"You killed Jafar, but now you feel free to hug his son? What are you planning to say to him? Are you going to tell him you killed his father? How dare you touch him! You've robbed him of a father's affection, and now you want to replace that affection with your lying, fake tenderness? You can save your breath because that's never going to happen! You're never coming near Jafar's children as long as I live!"

Judge Badr hung his head like a man condemned. Asma clutched Wisam's arm tightly and pulled him toward her. Embracing her son, she sobbed loudly. Havra watched them from a distance. She deeply resented her grandfather. No one in the family could understand the judge. They could not comprehend how it was possible for a man to execute his son in the name of the law and justice. It was difficult for anyone to understand that.

For Wisam it was also terribly hard to digest what had happened. But he didn't blame anyone. He still felt exactly the same toward Judge Badr. He wanted to defend his grandfather from all of them, but he was afraid that by doing so, he might further escalate a tense situation. Seeing the aggression against his grandfather, he wondered, *People who claim to believe that "all are equal before the law" start to see things quite differently when things get personal. Justice is all fine and well, as long as it's not in conflict with our own interests. It's amazing how easy it is to see ourselves as the exception to the rules that we uphold and apply to everyone else . . ."*

Although Judge Badr had not discussed the subject with Wisam, when he looked into his eyes, he sensed his grandson's staunch support. He really needed to talk to Wisam. In this regard, people are like trees that need water. The hotter it gets outside, the more a tree needs water. The fact that a tree is old and has a large trunk doesn't change anything. Big people, just like little people, need encouraging words and support when they find themselves up against a desperate situation. Everyone has his own trials and tribulations. And this was the biggest and most complicated trial of Judge Badr's life.

Sometimes Badr wondered how he managed to wander that thorny path. But he was absolutely sure that, if he went back in time, he would do the same again. The judge's actions were rooted in his beliefs, and for a person of faith, those convictions were a powerful driving force when they have been held for years. The judge's confidence and his anxiety were not irreconcilable feelings. He had been exhausted by Jafar's death because of his fatherly emotions; his anxiety over painful events stemmed from his human qualities. The death sentence came from his convictions, honor, and sense of justice. His eyes shed tears and his heart pounded, but he never said a word that went against his beliefs or could be considered a protest against God's will.

The forty-day anniversary of Jafar's death was the last time Wisam would ever see Judge Badr or his Grandmother Hafiza. Asma had nothing to be nervous about; Badr didn't try to look for them, despite his immense desire to see the children. He occasionally sent them money and letters. But Asma refused all of it. Even that small tie was completely broken when Asma moved to northern Lebanon. Three years after Jafar's death, Grandmother Hafiza bid this world farewell. Wisam heard this news when his Aunt Bayan told his mother. When Asma learned of her mother-in-law's death, she stopped dead in her tracks. Her whole life passed before her eyes in an instant—Grandmother Hafiza's kind deeds, good heart, smiling face, and wise advice, plus Jafar's gentle jokes, the happy days that were spent in that house, and all the pain that followed. Embracing her sister, she wept loudly.

# SUICIDE IS THE RESULT OF A LIFELONG CRY FOR HELP THAT WENT UNHEARD



After Hafiza's death, Asma's nerves deteriorated sharply. At night she was unable to sleep and was often troubled by terrible dreams. With her husband's help, Bayan was able to get Asma admitted to the country's biggest psychiatric hospital. She had not been taking the drugs the doctor had prescribed, and for this reason, she was under close supervision while at the hospital. But even then, she lied to the doctors every chance she got and threw away her medicine. The treatment was of no discernible benefit to her. After returning from the hospital, Asma's condition deteriorated further.

Then the night came when Asma killed herself. She overdosed on the medication prescribed to her. There was an empty medicine box on the table and a letter for Wisam. At first, they hid the note from him, but then Aunt Bayan, seeing Wisam's suffering, decided to give him the letter. His mother's soul was screaming from the paper:

Forgive me sweetheart. I dream about your father every night. He's calling me. I can't go on without him. I decided to do this on the day your father left us. But I always held back, thinking of you. I can't carry this burden any longer. Forgive me, I beg you, forgive me. I'm leaving you and your sister on your own, but I think you're already a grown man. I always saw you as an adult. You have a great force of will. You're much like your grandfather. Lately I often find myself dreaming about him too. At first I was angry when he appeared in my dreams. But now I'm ashamed. My head's a muddle. I can't get a handle on myself. I'm falling into a deep chasm and can't see the bottom. Look after your sister.

An internal flame burned brightly within Asma and could be seen in each word she wrote. The traces of her tears on the paper touched the soul more than her words. They conveyed all of Asma's suffering and all of the words she wanted to say but could not.

Asma was buried in the village cemetery. Wisam stood quietly, embracing his sister Havra. The mullah read the Surah Yaseen and offered prayers. As the dead body was being lowered into the grave, Wisam maintained his composure. He was now only worried about one person—Havra. He needed to be a tower of strength for his grief-stricken sister. She pulled away from Wisam's embrace and threw herself upon her mother's grave. "Mama, Mama, don't leave me, Mama . . ." With difficulty Wisam pulled his sister up from the ground. He hugged her and led her to one side.

After the burial, Wisam took his sister home. Havra cried so much that she was utterly spent. He put his sister to bed and stroked her hair.

"Now we're orphans, Wisam, lonely orphans," Havra said, sobbing.

"No Havra, no. I'm with you. You're not an orphan. Our parents are alive. Now they're watching us from a distance, and we mustn't distress them with our actions. *Inna lillahi wa inna ilayhi raji'un.* Surely we belong to God, and to Him we shall return. No matter what, we will return to God one day. Now we must be patient. 'He who created death and life, that He may try you—which of you is best in deeds; and He is the Mighty, the Forgiving.' We must not forget these *ayats.* It will all work out. I will keep you safe." Wisam wiped away his sister's tears as he spoke.

"Wisam, do you remember when we were little, and whenever I fell down Papa would come and hug me and then blow on whatever I wounded until it stopped hurting? As I felt the puffs of his breath, my pain decreased. I really wish he were with me now and could blow on my injured heart. Wisam, my heart is in so much pain, it truly is. It would hurt less if I could see him."

Wisam hugged his sister. As Havra spoke, Wisam's heart tightened even further. But he held himself together and refused to cry, because he wanted his sister to be able to lean on him.

Wisam stroked his sister's hair to calm her. He comforted her by telling her what he would do in the future for her and spoke about the happy days to come and how they would always be together. Before long, Havra fell asleep.

No matter how strong Wisam tried to appear, just like Havra, he needed support, someone who would comfort him with kind words. But he didn't have anyone like that. Wisam, looking up to heaven, wanted to ask God why He had taken his mother so soon after taking his father. Wisam had many unanswered questions. But the voice from within whispered that he should simply submit to God and rely on Him, that only this way would he find peace. Soon, he closed his tired eyes.

Wisam wanted to get in touch with his grandfather. He had not dared do this while his mother was still alive. Asma had strictly forbidden it. And the doctors had insisted that everyone in the family refrain from doing anything that might make Asma feel depressed. Wisam had focused solely on his mother's health during that time. But after her suicide, he felt an urgent need for his grandfather's support, care, and wisdom. No one answered at their old phone number. He wanted to call Uncle Said but couldn't remember his number. Then Wisam phoned the court in Saida and asked them about Judge Badr. He discovered that Judge Badr had left Saida long ago to return to his ancestral village, as Jafar had longed to do.

Wisam traveled to the village to find his grandfather, but he was too late. The judge had died several months earlier. Wisam tried to find out from relatives how his grandfather had spent his last days and what he had said, or if he had left anything for his grandson. Shortly before his death, he had fallen and broken his leg. He had spent some time confined to his bed because he hadn't been strong enough to stand, and those were the circumstances under which he had left this world. Wisam's relatives didn't know what to tell him, how to comfort him. "When he was ill, we often visited him, tried not to leave him alone. True, your grandfather used to be silent most of the time. He didn't talk to us much after he moved here. Anything he wanted to say, he said only to Grandmother Hafiza. Presumably he shared his grief with her." But Wisam, who knew quite well what Judge Badr was like, thought that, no matter what his grandfather had said to Grandmother Hafiza, he would never have shared any thoughts with her that would have caused her pain. Judge Badr didn't want to be a burden on anyone and had always offered support to everyone with his wise and comforting words. The invincible Badr, who could not be broken by the merciless blows of life.

Relatives said that, after Hafiza's death, the judge had descended into an even deeper silence. He was mulling something over, deliberating, and often holed up on his own. No one knew what he did then. From time to time, some saw him reading the Quran and taking notes. But afterward, despite exhaustive searches of the house, his relatives could never find those notes.

The day before he died, Judge Badr received a visit from a childhood friend and neighbor, Uncle Hikmat. When Wisam spoke with him, Uncle Hikmat said, "Badr was very calm. I sensed that hope and joy had rekindled within him—the same spark that I had seen in his eyes back when we attended the village school together as children. Although physically he was utterly debilitated, you could see the youth in his eyes. And he was more talkative than he had been in days past. We had a lot to say to one another. Before I left, the judge told me about a dream he had had the night before. Judge Badr had dreamed about Imam Ali. In his dream, he saw a small green valley in the middle of a large arid desert. Many people were standing in the desert, and no one was allowed into the valley. Imam Ali and his aide stood in that valley. His aide was seated behind an old table and was writing something on a piece of paper. When he finished, he asked Imam Ali a question.

"'O Emir! The list is complete. May I place a seal over it?'

"At that instant, Ali raised his head, looked at Judge Badr with his stern, meaningful gaze, and said, 'No, there is one final man left. The son of Abbas—Badr . . . Wait! It would be best if you write his name as Judge Badr.'"

Uncle Hikmat said, "Badr seemed very pleased. Probably it was on account of that dream that he was so happy that day. My eyes filled with tears when he told me about his dream. I remembered Jafar. He was almost like a son to me. After we were silent for a little while, I said good-bye and left. I didn't know that would be our last meeting . . ."

Uncle Hikmat, like many others, had a nuanced interpretation of what his friend had done. But he never said a word about that to anyone, even to Judge Badr himself.

Wisam maintained his poise in the face of all this. Everyone told him how brave he was. But Wisam mused, *No one knows what I'm enduring to seem so strong. How much strength does it take to know that you are alone, an orphan, yet at the same time to be resilient and show that you have pride and support — how difficult that is . . . How much strength does it take to keep people from guessing that you cry at night all alone . . . That's what no one knows.*

# THE SAME LIFE UNDER DIFFERENT LIGHTS

Wisam's aunt began her narrative about him with the day when Said came to their house and took Jafar to the police station. For Wisam, the most dear and memorable part of his life lay before these events. Sometimes, he'd mention the days when the whole family was living happily together. Everything that happened later wasn't quite real to him. Different people can hold two different views of the same life. In other words, it is feasible to view the same thing from different angles. And therein lay the central question that Willie had been pondering: *How is it possible that some see a glass of water that is half full, while others see it as half empty?*

The conversation with Aunt Bayan touched Willie to the depths of his heart. He understood why he had been invited. Aunt Bayan didn't ask him about anything. She only wanted to tell Willie about Wisam, thereby communicating to him her concern over the fate of the person who had been entrusted to her. Aunt Bayan thought it was necessary to consign Wisam to the care of some employee from the hospital. And she didn't know anyone more suitable for that than Willie.

It was very late when Willie left her house. He went straight to MD Anderson Hospital. He was filled with the desire to see Wisam and felt under the spell of Aunt Bayan's story the whole way there. The difficulties Wisam had endured had made Willie forget about his own problems. His mind was jumbled with thoughts about the similarities and differences between his life and Wisam's. *He's a truly amazing person with a truly amazing life. Who are we, really?*

It was quite dark when Willie reached the hospital. It seemed to Willie that the city turned into separate islands of light as the night began. When he got up to Wisam's room, his friend was already in bed. Willie decided not to bother him and quietly shut the door.

◆　◆　◆

The wind was flinging drops of rain onto the windows. Wisam was lying on his side, watching the drops roll down. Maybe he was watching the city's lights, like Willie had. Or perhaps his memories had taken him far away. Wisam was thinking about the thousands of kilometers that separated him from Saida, on the other side of the Atlantic Ocean. He had not come to the US, the country that bills itself as the birthplace of democracy, in search of happiness and a quiet life, like some immigrants. Now he was feeling like a helpless branch, torn off and flung into alien wilderness. Although he had arrived here, his path was not at an end. Another journey lay ahead. Wisam was preparing himself for that. That road would be the longest and the most difficult.

# IN SEARCH OF HAPPINESS

After his conversation with Aunt Bayan, Willie was unable to fall asleep that night. Until morning, his head spun with hundreds of different thoughts: his own past and Wisam's experiences, the confusion of life and its ruthlessness, the unforeseen, the uncertainty of the future. Willie could not escape the maelstrom of his thoughts.

The more he mulled things over, the more mixed up his thinking became. After what Willie had learned that day, he had developed a different perspective on his conversations with Wisam, on his observations and behavior. Willie wanted to refresh his memory about each and every word that he had heard from Wisam since making his acquaintance.

Everything Wisam had ever said now took on a different significance for Willie. He only now understood the extent to which those words had come from the depths of Wisam's soul. Wisam had undergone serious trials in his life. Willie was now affected more deeply to hear words full of hope from a person who had experienced such suffering. Wisam's words about the meaning of life and about the role of man in this world resounded in Willie's ears. Everything he and Wisam had each experienced in the last fifteen years—this onerous, taxing, nettlesome life filled with wars, hunger, deaths, diseases, and limitations—seemed meaningless, empty, and dispiriting to Willie. This period exemplified everything that was spent, tedious, and unintelligible. His desire to live had been snuffed out.

But Wisam looked at everything completely differently. What Willie saw as black and white, for Wisam, was painted in multicolored hues. Viewed through his eyes, life returned and spring bloomed all over the world. Illuminating everything around him, the dawn seemed to present a complete picture, pointing to the interrelation of all events and episodes. Only from Wisam's perspective could Judge Badr be fully understood. Otherwise, it was very difficult. *Very.*

Willie remembered one conversation with Wisam, who had said, "Willie, everything in life begins with faith in God. A person without faith is like a dried up tree, cut off from its roots."

"At times it's very difficult for me to believe in Him, Wisam."

*"Afillaahi shakkun faatiris samaawaati wal ardi."*

Willie chuckled. "What does that mean?"

"'Can there be doubt about God, Creator of the heavens and earth?' And besides, we're surrounded by so many arguments for His existence, how can you doubt it? The heavens, the earth, you, me, all of creation . . . Don't those signify anything to you? Aren't those indicative of the presence of a Creator?

"Willie, what's stopping you from believing? What bothers you about it? What's the reason?"

Willie hadn't been expecting to be suddenly bombarded with questions. Disconcerted, he sat thinking about concepts like uncertainty, darkness, emptiness, and bewilderment. After a brief silence, he forced himself to admit quietly, "I don't know."

"It seems to me like you're afraid. Yeah, you're afraid. You're horrified, petrified! With belief, you would embark on a new life. Belief would usher in new emotions that you're not used to, and the novelty of that frightens you. But it seems to me that what you actually need to be afraid of is unbelief, Willie. Belief will help you begin to live, and you'll be free from the unending fears that surround you in life."

"I forgot long ago what it means to be afraid," Willie said. "You're only afraid if you have something to lose. But I have nothing to lose in life."

"Everyone has something to lose, Willie. Even you. That's exactly what scares you."

Willie did not want to continue the conversation in this vein. So he approached the subject through a different question.

"Wisam, if this is really true, what you're saying, then why doesn't the Creator make some attempt to convince us of His existence? Why does He leave us so confused? Why doesn't He show us His way?

Why all the mystery? Shouldn't the Creator introduce Himself to the beings he's created? It's all so impenetrable and secretive."

"On the contrary, Willie; it's the other way around. He has introduced Himself to us. Our hearts know Him very well. Our souls are powerfully drawn to Him. In a miraculous way, He pulls everyone toward Him. That's why we search for Him all our lives."

"People search for happiness anyway," Willie said.

"Searching for happiness is the same thing as looking for Him. The happiness that we seek begins by finding Him, making our peace with Him, and accepting Him. Thus far you've been looking for a happiness that doesn't include God. Have you ever found it, Willie? Thousands and millions of people like you have returned empty-handed from that sort of search for happiness. God breathed His spirit into us. As soon as we are reunited with Him, our hearts will find peace because they are returning home. Even if a person achieves everything he wants in life, if God is not part of that life, there will be no meaning in anything. He will be in constant confusion and tension, and will be constantly searching for significance."

Wisam paused for a moment, then said softly, "Everyone can feel a force that is hidden, yet easy to sense, that is always watching over them, looking after them, and never leaving them on their own. Willie, even in solitude on dark nights, your soul can sense that it is not alone. It feels the warm and tender breath of a being that is always with it. Even when everyone is asleep, He does not sleep. Always. Do you hear, Willie? There is always someone there with us. He is indivisible from us. He even encompasses our souls. We are inseparable from Him, Willie. Just as a wave is inseparable from the sea, the sun's rays dissolve into the sun itself, and the whiteness of snow is indivisible from the snow itself. This is not hard to feel."

"In that case, how can you explain the doubts some people have about the existence of God?" Willie said. "If this issue is so obvious that there can be no question about it, as you say, then it should be clear to everyone, and there shouldn't be any disagreement about it. Everyone should be able to feel Him. But you can see that some people can't accept Him."

"Willie, sometimes an issue can be quite obvious, but people don't take any notice of it. A person hears so many conflicting ideas that this obvious issue gets sidelined.

"Life's various pursuits distract us. We deceive ourselves so with fleeting pleasures that we don't even notice how the day has passed.

In the end, life makes us forget ourselves. When a person becomes very attached to and places his trust in the things of the flesh that surround us, this dulls the longing for the divine found in the depths of his heart. The loud noises around us do even more to drown out what is already a faint inner voice."

"It's impossible to imagine life without problems and pursuits," Willie said, "so it's actually impossible to know God or to hear the call of the heart since it's not possible to shush the loud noises around us."

"No, Willie, that's not how it is. In life, we sometimes find ourselves in a situation in which we're in a position to hear the call of our hearts more clearly, and at the same time, we begin to feel the breath of the divine closer to us. In the most desperate and dangerous situations, when there is no hope at all and everything that we possess completely loses its meaning, then the influence from within becomes more pronounced. At that moment, the faint voice from within can be heard clearly and distinctly.

"When someone far from God falls into a storm of life and loses all hope, and when everyone abandons him, leaving him helpless, only then does one involuntarily begin to strive toward God. As a child who is far from home in search of happiness in a foreign country finds himself in a difficult situation, he begins to long for his native land and miss his home.

"In the thirteenth century, there lived a very great scholar. He founded a university that became famous throughout the Islamic world, where geniuses flourished and different sciences were taught. That scholar's name was Jafar ibn Muhammad. My father was named for him.

"One day, a man came to this scholar and said, 'Some people who do not recognize God have caused me to doubt. Present me with an argument that will dispel my doubts and increase my faith in God.' Then Jafar ibn Muhammad asked him if he had ever boarded a ship. The man answered that he had. 'In that case,' the scholar said to him, 'did the ship on which you were sailing ever encounter a storm and find itself in the midst of great waves? And then did your ship began to sink, and there was no other ship near you nor any strong swimmer who could save you, and as a result, you had no hope at all?' The man admitted that he had been in such a situation. Then Jafar ibn Mohammed said, 'At that moment, did your heart not direct you to one who holds the secret power to save you? In this situation, did you not sense the hand of the omnipotent upon you, who would pull you from this nightmare with ease?' This man admitted that such a feeling had then appeared in his heart, and that deep in his bones, he had sensed the presence of such a being. Jafar ibn Muhammad said, 'So you see, the power that your heart recognizes and pursues — that's God, the one who created you. He is the One, a being who can save you when all hope is lost and no one can come to your assistance. When all doors are closed, you feel with your whole being that one door is always open to you. And that's the door that belongs to Him!'

"Yes, Willie . . . I always have this feeling. Every instant I sense His warm breath, His tenderness and care for me. Who could recognize this better than I, who have lost all hope and whose ship of life is sinking into a vortex of misfortune, suffering, and loneliness? And I had already been in that state years before I got here."

*He's referring to his illness, isn't he? So didn't he get sick here?* Only now, remembering this conversation, did Willie understand what Wisam had wanted to say to him. "Isn't our thirst excellent proof of the existence of water?" Wisam said. "Don't our fears suggest the existence of the thing that causes our fear? If a person confesses his love, this indicates the existence of his beloved. If someone is tempted, it means that there is something to be tempted by. Thus, if our heart feels the breath of the divine, that means that the possessor of that breath also exists. If there is a sense of yearning for God, that means there is a God. This yearning manifests itself to a greater or lesser degree throughout a person's life. In their hearts, people feel the sway of a power that, in this world, draws them to truth, faith, and the awareness of the meaning of life. The power that prods them to seek out their own happiness is He! Isn't that right, Willie?"

Willie offered no answer.

"At times," Wisam said, "a person finds himself on a merry-go-round of emotions, and he loses the way that leads to God. He doesn't want to hear the cry coming from the depths of his heart. That person sees himself as helpless and alone and believes that God did not come to him during those moments when he needed Him most and so feels abandoned. At that point, God is resented.

"But in fact, a human being cannot fathom God's affairs and doesn't understand what God wants to do with him. A person is never cognizant of God's plans, which gives rise to misunderstandings, and then a bad opinion of God is formed.

"The hardest thing for anyone to do is to be patient with something when you don't understand the wisdom of what is happening. 'How can you remain patient about something you have no secret-and-true knowledge of?'

"Yes Willie, as the Prophet said, 'Any who can recognize the truth within adversity will exhibit patience. He who does not recognize it will see that adversity as abhorrent.'

"We are taught the sciences of the outside world, but we have very little knowledge of the sciences of life and truth. It's very difficult to grasp the connections and meaning of the life beyond the veil, and sometimes it's completely impossible."

"Yes . . ." Willie took a breath. "It's really impossible to understand His business."

"'Only one who knows the excellence and merits of the truth can show patience toward it,'" said Wisam, quoting Imam Ali.

"Do you know anyone who can be patient with what God is doing to him? Yeah, maybe such people existed long ago, but nowadays? There aren't any people like that, Wisam."

Wisam's eyes filled with tears. He swallowed a lump in his throat and suppressed the sadness and pain that welled up within him. "I knew one. I did," he said.

"I asked a wise, old man, whom I knew very well and who had seen much adversity while remaining stalwart and retaining a great force of will, about how he had endured all the difficulties he had experienced in his life. He gave an enigmatic smile." Wisam also smiled as he visualized how that wise, old man had smiled. "'Teach me how as well!' I begged. But he answered me, 'A mother does not have to be taught to cry when her child dies. When the times comes, life itself is the teacher.'

"Willie, back then I didn't fully understand what that wise man had said. But now I do. I looked at the painful things that other people went through and thought that I could never endure them if they happened to me. Yes, that's what I thought, until I found myself also faced with such events. I began to cry, having not learned that, Willie . . .

"Once, I asked him about the secret of life and its deeper meaning. He told me the story of Khidr and the Prophet Musa.

"The Prophet Musa was one of God's greatest messengers. He is one of the five prophets who became known as arch-prophets. According to the hadiths, after the Prophet Musa attained this rank, he believed that he had mastered all of the sciences and that no one's knowledge could be superior to his. Then God decided that he should meet a man whose abilities far surpassed his. This was how the Prophet Musa met His Lordship Khidr. Khidr was a master of the hidden sciences. And that holy man was, at the same time, a symbol of goodness and abundance. Dry earth turned green when he stepped on it, and the dead were resurrected at the touch of his breath. According to our Muslim beliefs, he still lives. He is among us and, with the permission of God, helps people with their tasks.

"God showed Musa where to find Khidr, which he did, traveling a long way and following the signs. Then Musa told Khidr that he wanted to study the science that uncovers the truth and peers behind events to see the real picture. Khidr agreed on one condition, which was that the Prophet Musa was to accompany him on a journey and make no objections of any kind to anything Khidr did during the trip. The Prophet Musa said that he was prepared to obey him, but Khidr warned him from the beginning: 'Indeed, with me you will never be able to have patience. And if you object, we will have to part.'

"When the Prophet Musa asked Khidr why he would not be able to be patient with Khidr's deeds, Khidr explained it this way: 'You, O Musa, are a scholar and a prophet of manifest knowledge. But I am the master of knowledge that reveals secret causes, meaning, and truth that lie behind the appearance of what seems to be happening. What seems true to you by its outward signs may turn out not to be, in accordance with the hidden science. You will not be able to understand the true reason behind my actions since I do these things based solely on hidden knowledge. As a result, it will be difficult for you to stomach what I do.'

"Another of Khidr's qualities was that he was invisible. Only His Lordship Musa could see him. Therefore, his actions were known only to the Prophet Musa. Since Khidr was a master of divine power, all his actions appeared to others to be natural events.

"Over the course of their odyssey, Khidr did a lot of strange things. First, he damaged a ship that belonged to a group of impoverished people. When the Prophet Musa saw this, he became greatly agitated. 'O Khidr, why do you harm people who are in such a difficult situation and are struggling to feed themselves? Is such an act worthy of a holy man like you? What you have done has made their predicament even worse.' Then Khidr reminded Musa of his promise not to protest against his actions. The Prophet Musa assured him that this would not happen again. But before long, Khidr again transgressed. He killed a young, innocent child whose parents were very good people. Musa said, 'Have you slain an innocent person without his having slain anyone? Indeed, you have done a terrible thing!' Again, Khidr reminded the Prophet Musa that he had given his word not to object to his actions.

"At last, they reached a city. The inhabitants of this city were very rude and greedy people. They mistreated Musa and Khidr and did not receive them as guests or give them food or drink. Such behavior by the inhabitants of the city angered the Prophet Musa."

"Hey, wasn't Khidr invisible?" asked Willie, who had so far been listening to Wisam with interest, not breathing a word.

"What?"

"You told me that Khidr was invisible and that only Musa could see him. But now you're saying that the inhabitants of the city were treating Musa and Khidr badly. That means they could see him."

"Khidr was invisible under some circumstances. When Khidr entered the city, he was wearing a different face. People saw him. But they didn't know it was him," said Wisam, smiling.

"Khidr worked to improve the city. For a short period of time, God lent him the strength to restore a wall that had been on the verge of collapse. And he did not ask the city's inhabitants for any payment for this. Upon seeing this, Musa once again objected. 'You saw how the inhabitants of this city acted toward us. We asked them for some food and water, but they gave us nothing. And you worked for them free of charge, helping them. We could have demanded some kind of reward for this work.'

"Musa's objections were natural. He had assessed and analyzed the situation and thought it unseemly for someone like Khidr to have behaved this way. He thought that it had been a mistake to do what he did. In the same way, we continually protest against the actions of God because we have a superficial view of events and do not know about the hidden reasons behind them. From our standpoint, an innocent person has died, someone who deserves better has suffered a loss or fallen ill, bad people have gotten ahead, the indigent have found themselves in even more dire straits."

"And Khidr didn't show Musa the hidden side of these events?" Willie said. "He didn't explain to him what lay behind it all?"

"Khidr did explain the wisdom of his deeds. In regard to the damaged ship, he said, 'If I hadn't harmed that ship, they would have taken it out to sea that day. For several days, pirates had been capturing ships at sea and sometimes killing the owners. I damaged the ship belonging to those poor wretches so they couldn't go to sea for a while. By the time the ship was repaired, the pirates were gone. So by inflicting a little harm on them, I shielded them from a great loss. I saved them, as well as their lives and property. As for the child, had that boy grown up, he would have become a very bad person. As a result, he would have caused his parents and himself great unhappiness.

Both he and his parents would have suffered. By killing him, I rid him, as well as his good-hearted parents, of this torment. And God will later present those parents with a worthy child.'

"So you see Willie, mercy and blessings can be found even in death and loss."

That day, the nurse took Wisam away for an examination, and their conversation remained incomplete. Willie was trying to figure out why Khidr had helped the people of the city. *I'll have to ask Wisam . . . Now I understand why he felt so bad when he said he knew a man who has withstood all of God's trials . . . Oh, my friend, why didn't you tell me about your grandfather, about yourself? How much you've been through in your short life!* Now Willie tried to view all events through Khidr's eyes. In this manner, he tried to understand the things that happened and see the meaning hidden behind them.

# AS LONG AS YOU'RE STILL ALIVE, YOU HAVE A CHANCE TO RAISE A WALL THAT HAS COLLAPSED

*Every life is like a painting. Parents provide the canvas; fate, the frame; and society, the colors. It is left to us to draw.*

Willie felt that everyone held many valuable blessings in their hands. He wondered how many of them were noticed. It was a great pity that sometimes people live their lives unaware of them.

To recognize how rich and happy they were, all people had to do was look at how many other people didn't have what they had. If they were distressed over their lack of shoes, they probably hadn't met anyone who had no feet.

It was true that people are often indifferent to what they had, yearning for what they don't. They become indifferent to a desired treasure shortly after acquiring it and develop an interest and attraction toward some other treasure they do not possess. This proclivity will accompany a person throughout life, unless desires are gotten under control.

If he wanted to manage his desires, Willie felt he should never look at people who possess what he didn't have. The best way to cultivate a sense of happiness and thanksgiving was to look at people who had less than him in terms of health or money or social status. Using this approach, he thought he could learn to value what he had. But people usually did the opposite. They spent more time thinking about what they lacked than what they had. And this naturally fueled feelings of frustration and ingratitude within their hearts. Behind most crimes lay the desire to forcibly acquire what one did not have. To be satisfied with little and to always be thankful were qualities that had great power to rein in human desires. Willie came to understand that if he examined what he already held in his hands, he would see that he possessed enormous advantages that cannot be measured by wealth of any sort.

"If someone asks you, 'How much for your hands?' what would you say?" Wisam asked one day. "And could you sell your feet, eyes, heart, tongue, kidneys, or lungs? It's interesting to wonder if they have a value, if there is anything more important than they are, and what could take their place? And what about your children, your closest relatives, or your best friend? Is there any form of wealth in the world that could be traded for one of these? It's very surprising that we often understand the value of some blessing only when we lose it. But it really shouldn't be that way.

"I remember my Grandfather Badr talking about when he and my grandmother had just gotten married and his friends came to visit them. Seeing that their home was so small, they asked with amazement, 'You're living in a one-bedroom apartment?' And my grandfather answered, 'For Hafiza and me, this is enough.' Then noticing their sofa: 'What a small couch!' And this time my grandfather answered confidently, 'Because of that little couch, Hafiza and I can sit closer to each other, which makes us feel cozier.'"

Willie used to bristle when he heard such edifying stories from Wisam, but now he listened in silence.

"Love will not grow in the presence of anger, rudeness, or insults. In such an atmosphere, even flowers in full bloom will wilt. Women aren't jealous because men pay attention to others but because they themselves get less attention and are forgotten. If women didn't feel forgotten, it's possible that they wouldn't get jealous."

"No, Wisam," Willie said. "Don't get started on this. You're not married, so those of us who are know more about this than you do."

"I won't argue. But it seems to me that women mostly covet a man's attention because they are afraid of losing him, afraid of being forgotten. Jealousy is actually an emotion that stems from a fear of loss."

"Wisam, if the man that you loved once is completely indifferent to you, and if your family doesn't appreciate your worth, then you don't want to share your love with that woman and that family. If nothing of a family remains but a dry husk, that family will eventually crumble. If the hearts of the members of a family are cold, then no matter how much they heat their house, you'll always be cold there."

"Willie, if you're distressed about Sarah and the children, that means they still matter to you. Sorrow indicates that love has not really left your heart—that it's still alive."

"You might be right. At first everything was good between Sarah and me. But then the attachment between us suddenly fizzled out, and now there's not a trace left of our former love."

"Love never vanishes suddenly all by itself. Nor, as a rule, does love die of old age. It's not possible to wake up one fine morning and realize that your love is gone, and now you have absolutely no feelings for someone you once loved. If so, that means you never truly loved them. Love dies gradually, because we don't know how to keep it alive. It is murdered by indifference, betrayal, mistakes, needless quarrels, harsh words, and rudeness. And unfulfilled, empty hopes can kill off love as well.

"It's true, however, that sometimes it can die unexpectedly. But that requires a real effort—by doing something truly reprehensible."

"How can a heart that has never known love understand it?" Willie was always surprised by what Wisam had to say about love and family.

"All you need is a heart in order to understand love." Wisam smiled.

> Don't ask me about love, don't ask anybody about it,
> Ask love itself about love!
> Love is like a glittering cloud, O my son.
> It does not need to be translated by me or thousands like me,
> Indeed, love expresses itself, O my son.
> Love is not a matter for the sleeping or weak,
> Love is a matter for the valiant and mighty, O my son!

"What was that, Wisam? Are you a poet as well?"

"No, that's not my poem. Many centuries ago there was a poet named Jalāl ad-Dīn Muhammad Rūmī who wrote poems based in Islamic Irfan mysticism. This is from one of his odes."

"You recited it beautifully."

"My translation might not be completely accurate. They say that when you read Rūmī in his native language, the meaning of the poem is clearer and deeper. The rhyming scheme is also very well chosen. Translations of Rūmī's poetry can't be compared with the originals."

"It's true what you said about love dying," Willie said. "While you were talking, I was thinking about my life with Sarah, and I realized that we did everything possible to kill our love for each other. My parents made the same mistake. It's a terrible shame that there's no way to go back in time."

"If misfortune befalls a family, and they are confronted with difficulties, there is no need to point fingers or say, 'This happened because of you.' At such times, they must say, 'Sweetheart, whatever happens, I'm here for you.'

"To rescue a family and rekindle love, you have to make an effort and fight. Never be ashamed of that fight! Human beings are obliged to share their love with someone. If not with you, then with someone else. Your children need a father. Don't deprive Sarah and the children of your love. If you have to give this love to someone anyway, why not to your own family?"

"My parents hoarded their love in their hearts," Willie said, "and as a result they deprived themselves as well as me of that love. They didn't understand that things can't go on that way for long. People want to share their love, it's true. My father went out and found another woman to share the love he had inside that had been bottled up for so many years. He wanted to give her and her children the love that belonged to my mother and me. And my mother also preferred to give away to another family the love that was mine and my father's." He shook his head. "That love belonged to me . . ."

"I don't think they were able to find someone else to take your place, Willie. Don't repeat their mistakes in your own family. You need to break this dysfunctional cycle. You're living out your parents' lives and making the same mistakes. Caitlin and Kevin will repeat this same pattern. And it won't end until someone musters the courage to stop this hurtful chain of events. Willie, you need to be that courageous person. Don't let your children share your fate. Even if they've hurt your feelings in the past, it doesn't matter; do it for yourself."

"It's too late; it's been this way for too long. Everything's too messed up to fix. Even if I wanted to, there's nothing I could do. I've already lost this hand. Life is really very strange; just when you decide you've got all the cards, life changes the game on you."

"Then don't play that game. None of us has to play the game life deals us. The one thing you need to remember is that, as long as you're still breathing, you still have a chance to fix what's been broken. Just do it! Don't think about it anymore; just do it! That's all there is to it." He fell silent for a while. "Now can I ask you to do something?"

Willie nodded.

"I want you to buy your wife some flowers today."

Willie burst out laughing.

"You know, Wisam, I've forgotten when was the last time I bought Sarah flowers. If I do that, Sarah's going to be really surprised. She'll probably laugh at me, or she'll take the flowers and stick them in a vase like it's no big deal."

"We made a deal—no objections. All I ask is that you do as I say. And another thing—when you get home, say hello to everyone using their names, and kiss them! That's when you'll be able to sense how happy you are. Once you start treating them this way, they'll feel happy too."

That evening Willie came home from work carrying a bouquet of flowers. He berated himself for it the whole way there. *Why have I done this? I'm letting a child tell me what to do.* But he periodically repeated the magic words Wisam had taught him.

"Willie, I'm going to teach you some words that His Lordship Ali once said. No woman can resist them—at the very sound of them they just instantly melt away."

Soon he was knocking at his own front door. As usual, it took a while for someone to open it. When Willie walked into his house, he kissed Caitlin on the cheek and said, "Hello, Caitlin. How's my sweetheart?"

"Hi, Dad!" she said. Caitlin stared at her father. Willie had never before come home with a bouquet of flowers. And it had been a long time since her father had greeted her so warmly.

Once again, Kevin was doing something in his room. Willie normally walked right past, but he took a deep breath and walked in. He kissed his son and greeted him by name. Immediately Kevin broke off his game and looked at him in bewilderment. Willie was never the first to greet anyone, usually only responding to others.

"Dad, you never do anything but glance into my room and keep going. Is everything okay? I never thought you'd do that." Only then did Willie realize that Kevin, although intent on his game, had been aware of his father's gaze upon him. That meant that Kevin had also been waiting for a long time to see some affection from Willie.

Sarah was in the kitchen. When Willie came in, her eyes widened, then she smiled. "Ah, but it's not my birthday yet! And you don't even bring me flowers when it's my birthday. What's the occasion?"

"Just because. You know, Sarah, a person feels helpless when no one loves him, and a person who loses the one who loves him feels even more helpless. Sarah, I don't want to lose you." Willie was so embarrassed he could barely speak the words Wisam had taught him. But he uttered those words with complete sincerity, appealing to her heart in a trembling voice. Sarah's eyes welled with tears.

"Willie . . . you haven't lost me. I'm still yours." As Sarah said this, the tears she could not restrain rolled down her cheeks. This was not at all the reaction Willie had expected. With his fingers, he wiped away her tears, then held her close.

The children stood watching, and Caitlin couldn't hold back her tears either. Willie's gesture had made an impression on the entire family.

Sarah bustled about, making Willie a nice dinner. Even though Caitlin and Kevin weren't hungry, they sat down to join them. Willie, who always arrived home in a distant, cold mood, had been an affectionate, attentive father from the moment he walked into the house that night. That one bouquet of flowers pleased Sarah so much that she even forgot to watch her favorite TV show. Nor did Sarah spend hours chatting with her friends that evening, as she usually did. Instead the whole family spent the evening together. Because they hadn't spent any quality time together in so long, it was a little difficult for them to talk. But every time the conversation faltered, Willie revived it again. He wasn't overly fond of talking, but that night, the desire to be with them came from deep within his heart. As he tried to remember what he needed to say and do, Willie kept an image of Wisam in his mind as a guide for how to speak and behave.

Seated at the table, Willie remembered what Wisam had said.

"Willie, why is it you think children are bad at making conversation? Spend time with them, treating them as individuals, like you would with an adult or a person whose thoughts are important to you, and then you'll understand how wrong you are. Then you'll see how those little men, whom we often overlook, actually think very interesting and meaningful thoughts. After all, they have their own world as well. And maybe that world is smaller than yours, but their company should make it more interesting for you. There are no creatures in this life that are closer to you than they are. You are of one flesh. Ali ibn Abi Talib said, 'Family and relatives are your wings, they help lift you up.' Don't cut yourself off from your wings."

Sitting at the table, Willie felt like the happiest husband and father in the world. As it turned out, Wisam was right. Willie's actions had made him and his entire family happy. Noticing the smile on Sarah's face, Willie felt he was witnessing the truth of Wisam's words:

"Sometimes, one affectionate word from a loved one can put a smile on your face for the whole day."

After the children had gone to bed, Willie and Sarah went out onto the porch. The weather had been beautiful that day. Willie brought a warm blanket out of the house and wrapped it around their shoulders. They hadn't sat alone together for many years, feeling like they had nothing more to talk about, and so they had avoided making conversation. The last attempt had ended in a great argument, and Willie had given up. Now they decided to give each other another chance.

"You know, Willie, having a husband doesn't necessarily mean a woman will be happy. There are so many married women who feel lonely."

"Sarah—"

Sarah put her finger on his lips. "Shh . . . Be quiet and hear me out. It's unbearable for a woman to be lonely. You have a husband right there with you, but you don't even want to touch him. Days turn into years. You live together like two strangers. You want to say something, but you don't know what . . ."

As Sarah spoke, Willie realized that she felt as he did. He wanted to open up to her in the same way, but he decided that this was not the time to try to make sense of their relationship. Willie remembered what Wisam had said: "If you want to start over, there's no need to point fingers. You might win the argument, but you'll end up losing someone you love."

Willie said softly, "Sarah, we need to forget the past if we're going to start over. Otherwise nothing's going to work out for us. We need to live for today. What difference does it make what happened in the past or what will happen in the future? We only get one life. If we're always thinking about past sorrows or future worries, we'll miss all the nice things happening today."

Sarah sat quietly. She was also worn out from the strain. She put her head on Willie's shoulder.

"We have this one patient at MD Anderson," Willie said. "You know him—Wisam. He always says, 'As long as you're alive and breathing, you can rebuild the wall and fix what's been broken.'"

"Maybe, but it won't be simple, Willie. To fix that wall, you need to forgive and start all over again. Otherwise . . ."

Willie decided to make a joke, because he didn't want the conversation to turn wistful again. "A woman can forgive a man anything. But she can't stop herself from always reminding that man of the mistakes she has forgiven him for." Willie laughed. "Actually, that patient said that as well."

Sarah chuckled along with him. "Yeah, well, he might be right about that too."

"Wisam once said to me, 'Willie, it's agonizing to have to act like you don't love someone when you actually do.'"

"Willie, if you only knew the agony I've been in all this time."

Willie realized that Sarah still nursed some love in her heart for him. That day marked a turning point in Willie and Sarah's life together.

♦   ♦   ♦

The next day, Willie entered Wisam's hospital room, their eyes met, and Willie began to laugh.

"Well? asked Wisam, smiling. "And? Did you do what I told you? What happened?"

"I think I've missed out on a lot in life because I assumed certain things were impossible and I was focused on how they might end badly. I've lost so many chances. I've been so stupid. Fate has always been conniving to outsmart and delude me," Willie replied thoughtfully.

"If fate had always outsmarted and deluded you, you would never have figured that out either. Which means that fate wasn't so smart after all." Wisam smiled again. "In my opinion, what you've said shows that things are going better than we thought."

All day Wisam wouldn't stop asking him what had happened at home. This was unlike Wisam, but he thought if he could share in Willie's family's happiness, that might ease his own burden. Wisam took great spiritual pleasure in Willie's contentment and in Sarah and the children's joy.

"Willie, when was the last time you called Sarah just to ask her how she was? Sometimes love is just asking 'How are you?' Sometimes emotions that have been bottled up in your heart and that you can't express can be hidden in questions like 'How are you?' and 'Is everything going okay?' This might sound odd or ridiculous, but it's true. You don't need thundering or poetic proclamations to show love and attention. Sometimes deep feelings can be expressed using ordinary words."

Never before in the years he'd worked there had Willie called his wife during his shift. The first thing Sarah asked was, "What happened? Is everything okay? Did something happen to the kids?" It never occurred to her that this call had been made at the insistence of an immigrant who was one of the "angels," that her husband was simply tired of being lonely and was taking an interest in her, wanting to share the great love for her he held in his heart.

Willie treated Wisam's pronouncements as if they were the valuable teachings of an elderly man with great experience. Despite the fact that Willie was much older, when he talked with Wisam, he realized that he did not understand anything about life. He was astonished at how an unmarried man could know so much about the female inner world.

"Willie, don't criticize your wife in front of other people! Be especially attentive to her on those days when she is ill or feels unwell. Don't forget to thank her when she does something for you, even something insignificant! When speaking to your wife, use the words of endearment that make her happy. Willie, if you can do this, you can hold your family together. Our Prophet said that 'the worst type of men are the ones who are stingy toward their families, speak to them rudely, force their wives to be dependent on others, raise their hands against them, quickly lose their temper, and are rarely satisfied.'"

Wisam's words were like a tonic for Willie. Even just a few quick statements inspired him. Despite Wisam's youth, his level-headed approach to everything, the attention he paid to others, the way he cared about what other people were going through, and his graciousness toward others' errors and shortcomings further elevated him in Willie's eyes. Wisam's years on this earth had been few, but he thought and acted like a wise elder. In his presence, Willie felt like he was standing before someone for whom his spirit had been searching for many years. Wisam gave him the spiritual strength that he had wanted but had been unable to obtain from his father. Willie realized that even Wisam's silences were intended to explain something to him. He also felt that Wisam was reading his heart and finding his way into his thoughts.

# LET US FORGIVE AND FREE OURSELVES
# OF THAT DISTRESS

*God commands people to forgive but requires society to punish.*
~ Louis Gabriel Ambroise de Bonald

"Willie, you came to Houston to forgive him."

"Who?" asked Willie in confusion. "I came here to forgive who?"

"Your father."

"No, that's just not true. Why would you think that? I came to Houston for work. I wasn't thinking of forgiving anyone. And I don't have any plans like that now either."

"Yet it seems to me like you're tired of being angry at your parents. It's really hard on you as well. This anger and hatred has almost ruined your life. I think it was actually your heart that led you here. It was no accident that this is where you chose to work."

"What are you trying to say now, Wisam?"

"It seems to me that by taking care of the terminally ill here, you're trying to win forgiveness from your father."

"What? Me? Forgiveness from my father? He ruined my whole life! He deserted me, abandoning me to a really tough situation. And now I want forgiveness from him?"

"I think you feel responsible for a lot of your family's problems. Even for the fact that your father deserted you and for the arguments with your mother and the scenes at your house. Willie, none of that was your fault."

"I know. I don't doubt that."

"That's right, Willie. What happened wasn't your fault."

As soon as Wisam repeated this, Willie began to weep. He wanted to empty himself of the anger he had stored up in his heart.

"I've cursed myself for years for even being born. I hate my birthday because it all started with me. No one in my life ever wanted me. I was just excess baggage in my family." Willie's hot tears seemed incongruous for someone of his age.

Wisam hugged him and whispered, "None of it was your fault." After Willie had calmed down, Wisam quietly said to him, "There's one thing you need to know. When we forgive someone who's treated us unfairly, we're actually doing something good for ourselves. You've been crushed by the heavy burden of the past for many years now. There's only one way to save yourself, and that's through forgiveness. Forgiving someone else for that person's mistakes might not exactly be the usual way to do things nowadays. But you have no choice. If you don't do it, you'll suffer instead of enjoying life. The discontent bottled up in your heart will turn into hatred later on, which will affect your relationships with the people around you. Sometimes a person finds himself behaving rudely, even toward the people he loves best, for no reason whatsoever, all because of his own negative emotions. More often than not, he doesn't even understand why he's acting that way. He doesn't know that rage, anger, envy, and the desire for revenge that have built up in his heart are affecting his thoughts and behavior, and that these feelings have taken control of him and are now calling the shots. Staying angry at people and hating them will affect you most of all and will worsen your own anxiety. Your heart will gradually be emptied of positive feelings and good thoughts, replaced by pessimistic thinking, hopelessness, and other negative emotions.

"In addition, don't forget that if you can't forgive others, you won't be able to forgive yourself. Willie, you're also judging yourself for your past. In truth, you need to forgive yourself as well as your parents. It's time to stop reproaching yourself for what others have done!"

"We should never be resentful toward anyone in our lives?" Willie sighed heavily, like a man facing a huge, difficult choice.

"We can never learn to forgive unless there's someone in our life whom we need to forgive for what he's done to us," Wisam said. "If the people around us have no faults, life becomes monotonous. Others won't even notice the greatness of all men who have reached perfection, and people will stop trying to grow and improve themselves.

"We notice others' mistakes and realize how bad those are. And thus we make an effort to rid ourselves of those kinds of bad qualities."

"It's very difficult for me to do what you're saying."

"Forgiving and being honest with yourself is a feat that can't be expected from low achievers. But you, Willie, truly do have a very big heart, and I expect such a feat from you." Hearing this from Wisam, Willie smiled.

"One evening Kevin and I were watching a movie," he said, "and suddenly he turned to me and said, 'Dad, this is cool. It's fun snuggling and watching movies with you.' Kevin had no idea how much his words meant to me. He doesn't play video games all day anymore like he used to. He waits for me to tell him what happened during the day. Probably he was suffering from loneliness before, just like me. He was looking for something to do, and when he couldn't find anything, he got sucked into those games. He didn't blame anyone but me for that loneliness. Just like I did with my parents."

"Willie, life is so short it's not worth wasting it on arguments, resentments, scenes, and meaningless stuff. If you're ever in a position like mine, you'll understand that very well. Healthy people think that life is like an infinite sea. But actually it's similar to a shadow, and at times, it's like a passing cloud. It's gone in an instant. In reality, people are granted very little time. Devote it to the ones you love. The day will come when you'll wake up and see that there's no one there."

"Yes, people are so stupid that they sabotage their own chances for happiness." Willie sighed. "We don't know how to get through a week of our lives, yet we dream of living forever."

# THE QUARTERBACK'S ELECTRIFYING TACKLE

The relationship between Dr. Stevens and the hospital personnel had grown tense lately. Stevens planted his nose squarely in their business, and his comments were pretty rude. This upset the staff. Sometime after the argument between Dr. Anna and Dr. Stevens in the movie theater, Dr. Anna was fired under mysterious circumstances, which prompted the employees to speculate that perhaps Stevens had a hand in that. Even Willie, who had always ignored Stevens in the past, was no longer willing to put up with his abuse.

It happened on a Saturday. When Willie got to work, he saw that Stevens was in his usual nasty temper. He had assembled the staff and was saying something peevish to them. Stevens had recently begun scolding them in this way quite often. Without uttering a word, Willie nonchalantly walked past them, heading for the locker room. Without turning to face Willie, Stevens asked, "Were you just born like that?"

"Meaning?" Willie said.

"Rude and crude."

"No, unlike you, I got that way later."

Turning to face Willie, Stevens took a step toward him. He was a tall man, so Willie had to look up to meet Stevens's eyes. Stevens was purple with rage. No one at the hospital had ever dared speak to him that way.

Willie said, "Dr. Stevens, why are you so disrespectful toward the staff? You try to demean them every chance you get."

"Because they don't deserve my respect and do nothing to earn it." Calming himself down a bit, as if mastering his anger, Stevens raised his chin and swallowed. "Willie Owen! I've done everything I could for you to feel at home at MD Anderson."

"No one should have to deal with such rudeness and mockery in his own house. So no, I don't feel at home."

A few patients came out into the hallway, attracted by the ruckus. Hearing Willie's voice sounding unusually heated, Wisam also stepped out of his room to see what was going on.

"I'm always struck by the fact that when you look at the patients, you seem to be thinking, 'They don't deserve to live' or 'They owe the hospital a lot of money, and the first chance they get, they'll try to get out of paying.'" Willie turned around to leave.

"Hold it right there, Willie! You listen to me—this isn't over yet! I'm not done with you!"

"Stevens, you're done with everyone! I figured that out long ago. You don't need anything but your lousy ambitions."

"Dr. Stevens . . ." Stevens pretended he didn't hear Wisam. "Dr. Stevens, Willie's a good worker. You two have had some kind of misunderstanding. Now, stop it! This noise is upsetting the patients."

It was clear how dismayed Stevens was to hear this. Ignoring Wisam, he said, "Willie, you pay too much attention to the words of people who are living out their final days. They occasionally come out with interesting statements that might even drag someone like you out of his depression. Gary Gilmore yelled, 'Just do it!' right before his execution, and Nike made it famous. But don't delude yourself, Willie. Any words you suddenly come out with right before you die have to be promoting something. Like once some guy who had been sentenced to death shouted before the assembled crowd, 'Drink Van Houten cocoa!' The next day the condemned man's last words were in all the newspapers. As a result, sales increased for the company that made that cocoa. But later, it was revealed that that company had paid the condemned man a lot of money to plug them. So Willie, don't pay too much attention to what they say. We don't know what's motivating them to come up with this stuff. And it might be better if you stayed away from him in particular." At this he pointed to Wisam and added, "You take this angel too seriously . . ." Stevens's long, philosophical sentences were full of irony. His words showed how very irritated he was of Willie's camaraderie with Wisam.

The last remark about Wisam drove Willie around the bend. "Stevens, I know you don't have a brain in your head, but you need to make an effort to understand other people." Realizing that reason was having no effect on Stevens, Willie began to mock him.

"You miserable loser, taking me to school?"

"Dr. Stevens, you couldn't be more wrong!" Wisam said. "A doctor shouldn't be so snippy with people."

"So now you're going to teach me medical ethics?" Then turning to face Willie, Stevens said, "You're a miserable, inhibited man with an inferiority complex. You and you," he said, pointing at Willie, then Wisam, "are the very last people in my life I could learn anything from."

"Shut your mouth!" Wisam shouted. "Don't you talk to him like that, you hear me? Who gave you the right to sneer at other people?"

None of the nurses in the vicinity or any of the patients wanted to get on Dr. Stevens's bad side, as he was very influential within the administration. They felt it was safest to stay out of their dispute and watched from a distance.

Nervously raising his hand, Stevens said, "Wisam, aren't you the grandson of the judge who killed his own son? You, of all people, should keep quiet! Your grandfather was a lot like George Stinney. Yeah, fourteen-year-old George Stinney who killed two white girls. Do you know what they had in common? George's destiny, just like your grandfather's, was altered by the holy book he believed in. He took a Bible into the death chamber with him, and they made him sit on it in the electric chair because he was so short. Just like those devout Christians, your religion is your undoing. What, the wise grandson of a stupid grandfather is teaching me now?"

Wisam was overwhelmed by what he heard. He didn't think that Dr. Stevens knew about his family, much less did he expect him to talk about it publicly. Hearing this, Willie — who had only just been managing to hold himself in check — completely lost control. He clenched his fists, extended his left leg back a bit, and crouched down, his weight over his right foot, as he had done over a thousand times preparing to tackle an opponent while carrying the ball. At that instant Willie felt more fired up than he had ever been at any football game. He gritted his teeth, and every muscle in his body tensed. With a burst of speed, he rushed Stevens, who had turned toward Wisam.

"Hey, you idiot linebacker!" At the sound of this cry, Stevens spun back around. But in fact it was not just a shout. It would be more accurate to call it an eruption of the pain, sadness, and despair that had been stored up in Willie's heart all these years, an outpouring of cruel memories. It was such an eerie and terrifying sound that every-one froze for an instant. Willie hadn't yelled like that in fifteen years. That had been an expression he used when running at a linebacker who tried to stop him. When Willie produced that powerful, furious cry, all the football fans would begin screaming at once:

"Atom! Go get him!"

"You're a beast!"

"Wipe him out, Atom! Rodeo, rodeo!"

Although Stevens was a tall man and weighed about two hun-dred pounds, his feet were suddenly swept from the floor as he was tossed in the air. A little higher and his feet would have touched the ceiling. Willie had sent Stevens flying by hitting him in the thigh with his shoulder at high speed. As Stevens's feet sailed as high as Willie's shoulders under the force of the blow, Willie punched Stevens as he rose up, sending Stevens even higher. Willie had resorted to his fa-mous rodeo play that he used to do during games. Stevens flipped over in midair and ended up landing on his left shoulder, right behind Willie.

There was a deathly silence. Only Stevens's moans could be heard from where he lay on the floor. Some nurses, recovering from their temporary shock, ran up to him and tried to help him back to his feet. After Stevens recovered a bit, he shoved the nurses aside and charged Willie like a wounded bear.

Stevens poured all his might into this attack. When he saw Ste-vens about to jump him, Willie remembered how the players from the opposing team had closed in on him during his last game. Back then, Willie had allowed them to throw him to the ground out of spite for his father. But he wasn't thinking that way this time. As soon as Stevens got near him, Willie leaned over, took a skillful step to the left, and grabbed Stevens around the waist from behind. Willie lifted Ste-vens above his head and then dropped him on his back. It was all over in an instant. This time, when he landed, Dr. Stevens did not attempt to stand up. The security guards arrived and hustled Willie into the hospital courtyard. Stevens was led into a patient room where nurses attempted to examine him. The other doctors rushed to help. His voice carried into the hallway. "Nothing happened to me. Leave me alone, I said. Go on, get off me!"

# THE MEETING BETWEEN BRUCE "THE STAR" AND WILLIE "THE ATOM"

The next morning, Willie was summoned to Bruce Cranston's office. He was the head of HR and handled hiring and firing, as well as overseeing job performance. He had held his position for less than a year. He was well-known as a strict one. When Willie entered the office, he found himself facing a tall, heavyset man in his mid-forties, with glasses and thinning hair. Cranston was looking at his computer. "May I?" Willie asked, indicating a chair in front of the desk.

"Have a seat!" Cranston said, in a voice that sounded like he was used to giving orders. "We haven't had a chance to meet yet, Mr. Owen."

"No, Mr. Cranston." Perhaps if Willie had met Mr. Cranston two months ago, he would not have spoken with such a confident tone.

"I've now watched your film precisely ten times. Precisely ten times . . ." Willie realized that he was talking about the footage from the security camera in the hallway. Cranston didn't take his eyes from the computer. Willie took advantage of the sudden silence to look around. His attention was drawn to something painfully familiar that had once been an intimate part of his life. In a cabinet lay a pair of footballs, the kind that are usually presented to game winners as a prize. The footballs were covered in autographs. A football uniform hung in the right side of the cabinet. There was a helmet hung on the wall with the familiar five-pointed star of the Cowboys. Willie was surprised to see all this in the manager's office. A variety of photos sat on the cabinet. Looking at the pictures, Willie recognized the faces. These were photos of the biggest, most legendary names in the history of football.

"There's something I'm very interested in," said Cranston, and his voice roused Willie from his memories.

"Yes, Mr. Cranston?"

"You're obviously a football player. And not only that, but on a professional level, with advanced training."

"Why do you think that, Mr. Cranston?"

"Why do I think that? Any true Texan who watched you tackle Dr. Stevens would see that instantly. I'm curious what a top-notch football player like you is doing here? Particularly working as an orderly. Are you punishing yourself by doing the kind of work where you don't score any touchdowns?" Willie was astounded by Cranston's words. Especially since he had assumed Cranston had summoned him for a reprimand before firing him and perhaps even calling the police. But now Cranston was saying all this with a smile.

"To be honest, at first I wanted to fire you. But after watching your 'game' with Stevens, I decided to ask around about you. The all-star quarterback, hero of the state championship in high school. College records for the longest pass and most touchdowns in a season. Lead your team to a NCAA championship. First round pick of the legendary Dallas Cowboys." Throwing his hands up, Cranston said, "The Atom!" No one had called Willie that in a long time.

"Son, you're a miracle! It's an honor for me to sit across from a professional player like you! My God, the legendary Atom works with me!" Cranston, of course, meant "works *for* us," but he phrased it differently out of respect for Willie.

"If I tell my friends at the club about this, no one will believe it." Cranston was so excited and emotional that he couldn't stop talking. Willie was elated to meet someone who thought so highly of him after so many years, especially under the current circumstances. He remembered his college days. He used to encounter a lot of fans back then who became emotional upon meeting him.

"Mr. Cranston, you're exaggerating just a bit. I didn't play professionally. I just won a lot of games as a student-athlete."

"And what is a 'student-athlete,' son? You played in the highest division of the NCAA. That's the same as playing for the NFL. Most NCAA players move up into the big leagues. You're very modest. Not every NFL player could reproduce the amazing moves you put on display during games. After all, you were a Dallas Cowboys draft pick. Why do you think that was? Why you? The Dallas Cowboys are the best, and if they drafted you, you're a top-notch professional. Son, you're amazing! You were so fast and agile, rushing right, then left—you would slide right through ten opponents as slippery as an eel. My God, the way you played! You could just touch an opposing player and knock him back two or three yards. You . . . You were like a big bear, swatting away attacking wolves using just one paw. Buddy, no one who hasn't seen you play could understand what I'm talking about. In one game, I saw you run toward these three massive giants who were right in front of you and hit them in the thigh, tossing them over your head. Good Lord, to take out three heavyweight players, one after the other . . . I don't know, I can't find the words to express my admiration. You're a football genius!"

Cranston's words sent Willie back to the past. For a second, he felt like he was still in college with his teammates Big Ben, Eddie, Richard, Small, Tony, Roughneck Chip. He wondered what they were doing. He hadn't even said good-bye to them when he left town, even though they were like his brothers. They were always together. Battling it out together in the games made them brothers. He hadn't heard anything about them in fifteen years now. He doubted that they were still playing. It could be that some of them weren't even alive anymore. He left without saying good-bye to them because he was afraid of questions, afraid that they might influence his decision. *I don't know, maybe there are other reasons deep down that I don't even know about.*

Cranston told Willie that he followed all the games but had a true passion for the Dallas Cowboys, and that his closest friends called him "Bruce Star" for the Dallas Cowboys' five-pointed star logo. Cranston often carried a football with him when he attended games. The higher-ups in the staff at the football stadium, as well as the police who provided the security there, knew him well since Cranston had helped many of them. He was given a green light everywhere he went and took advantage of this privilege to have his picture taken with the most famous players. He asked them all to sign his football. Cranston used this meeting to ask Willie for his autograph as well. At that, Willie's eyes filled with tears, but he kept his cool.

In the end, Cranston asked Willie to play at their club—where the players and fans meet—and to share some of his experiences with them. But Willie still retained a lot of emotional stress associated with football. He didn't even want to think about it.

"Mr. Cranston, with all due respect, please don't press me on this. I'm really through with football."

They sat talking for close to two hours. When Willie finally left, Cranston did something he did for very few of his guests—he rose from his desk and walked Willie right to the door.

# HOW TO CHANGE THE WORLD

The news about the "rodeo" play that Willie had used on Stevens spread quickly throughout the hospital. Many approved of what he had done, and although he had previously been fairly anonymous within the hospital, Willie suddenly found a degree of fame. He was now treated differently at work. Lately even total strangers there greeted the unassuming Willie with the words, "Hey, how's it going, Willie?" Willie wasn't used to people acting that way, and it made him uncomfortable.

Dr. Stevens's efforts to fire Willie had failed. He could not accept the loss of his authority, which he had formed over the years. For a while, he came to work with his tail between the legs, then he moved to another department.

Sarah was astonished when she heard about it all from her relative who had helped Willie get the job. Her husband — a calm, withdrawn man, not at all a fighter — decided to teach Dr. Stevens a lesson.

After that initial meeting, Mr. Cranston began inviting Willie to his office from time to time. He instructed his secretary to always let Willie Owen in before anyone else. As Willie was leaving the office once after a lengthy conversation, he saw the long line of people waiting to see Cranston, which made him feel awkward. Even outside of his office, whenever Cranston saw Willie — regardless of who else was nearby — he would immediately greet him in a very respectful way. From that point onward, everyone saw Willie as someone important.

Once Cranston spotted Willie at the entrance to MD Anderson. "Yes, this is our wonderful Mr. Willie Owen! Gentlemen, this is the man I was telling you about. I think he would make an excellent supervisor." Willie didn't understand what he was talking about and didn't know what to say. He merely greeted them and went inside.

The news spread throughout MD Anderson that Willie would soon be offered a supervisor's position. A week later, Cranston called Willie into his office and told him about it.

Willie first shared this joyful news with Wisam. He was as delighted as Willie. There was a big celebration at Willie's house that night. He would be earning more money, which meant there would be a new coat for Sarah, a jacket for Caitlin, the athletic shoes for Kevin that he had dreamed of for so long, and frequent family outings.

The atmosphere within the family had changed so much in such a short time. It was as if all the members of the family had been waiting for this for many years. Each of them was seeking someone to whom they could offer the love that they all nursed in their hearts. And it pleased them even more to give this love to someone who was worthy of it and to whom it belonged.

Wisam was pleased about the changes that had occurred too. Seeing Willie's family so happy, he pictured his own family feeling the same way — the way he wanted to see them. Wisam enjoyed seeing his own dashed hopes being resurrected in his friend's family. Willie sensed this, and as soon as anything good happened in his family, he told Wisam about it.

"Sarah and I are going shopping today."

"I picked up Kevin from school yesterday. He was so happy to see me."

"Caitlin has really grown up. To be honest, I'm only just now noticing it. She confessed to me that there's a boy who likes her. Wisam, do you know how great this is, the fact that she values my opinion and trusts me?"

Willie said to Wisam, "Recently I saw Davis, Sarah's older sister's first husband, at our house talking to Sarah. It was obvious he was once again filling her head with his stupid advice about domestic life. He always has unflattering things to say about me. Even from a distance I could tell that Sarah — who is usually pretty receptive to what he has to say — was speaking to him in a dismissive tone. I was so fed up that I walked over to him, squeezed his arm really tight, and said, 'Listen, you freak, you stay at least 120 yards away from my family, or I'll break your arm!' You should have seen that gasbag! He didn't know what to say. He just apologized, turned, and left, tripping over his own feet. Wisam, if only you had seen the expression on Sarah's face. She looked really gratified. As if she had been waiting for me to do that for a long time. Waiting for me to act like a man who's the head of his family. Wisam, I was blind for so long to the happiness that was always just right there, under my nose."

This conversation made Wisam as happy as if it was all happening to him. *I saved one family! One family has been given a new life!* Wisam felt like he had rescued his own family from ruin — the family that he had not been able to save back then. But now, having salvaged Willie's family, he wanted his own family's forgiveness, so to speak, to ease his own soul. He believed that he and Willie shared similar fates. It had not been possible to remedy anything in Wisam's own life. It was too late. In some ways, Wisam could see the parallels between Willie and his own father. Jafar had dug his own grave and then surrendered himself to it. Willie had been killing himself in just the same way, headed for the gallows that life so mercilessly erects for the weak who don't want to fight for their own happiness. Wisam had wanted to save Willie from those gallows. He wanted to do for him what he had been unable to do for his father.

And sometimes Wisam noted the similarities between himself and Willie's son. Kevin's life reminded him of his own, like that of a hamster running on a treadwheel. When Wisam had been a child doing all he could yet unable to save his father from the gallows and his family from collapse, he was not to blame for what happened, just as Kevin was completely innocent. Wisam did not want Kevin to live that life. Willie was very lucky. For him, it had not been too late to change things. Although it was true that, like Wisam, he had lost his childhood, he could now rescue his family and his children's lives. As Willie's family reclaimed their happiness, Wisam felt that he had reclaimed his past. He thought he had rectified the past by keeping his friend's family from falling apart the way his family and Willie's parents had. Wisam had been able to thwart this cycle of marred destinies. Every night as he thought of this, he forgot about the pain in his own heart. As he listened to Willie's stories about the happy, precious days spent with his family, Wisam was no longer even conscious of the fact that his own days were coming to an end.

# THE HERO OF DREAMS

Willie had been in turmoil when he met his "angel." Despite being younger, Wisam was someone who was able to cultivate Willie's spirit, helping it break free of its arrested state. Wisam could help Willie with all his emotional roadblocks. In Willie's eyes, Wisam seemed to offer all the care, attention, wisdom, and strength that Willie had so needed but never received from his father.

Willie had put his faith in his father, pinning all his hopes on him and offering him his love. Emotionally, all children feel weak and in need of protection. When a child doesn't get the love and care from his parents that are needed for normal emotional development, then that development will be handicapped, and he will live his life as someone who is, in some way, lacking and inadequate. Willie's emotional trauma was reflected in his thoughts and behavior. He felt himself to be under increasing strain. His inner tumult only grew as problems arose within his family and at work.

Now the feelings that Willie once had for his father, he now subconsciously addressed to another. In Wisam, he found someone he had needed for so many years, a friend close to his heart. Throughout his life, Willie had kept in his soul the love he wanted to give his father. He had missed fatherly care so badly! And now, his soul had looked into Wisam's eyes and seen tenderness. People miss maternal or paternal affection, care, love, many things . . . They can become strongly attached to a stranger in a short time. Orphans often have this feeling. Sometimes, such close relationships arise between a teacher and a student, a patient and a doctor, or between acquaintances who suddenly become friends. Age, race, skin color, and social status play no role here. Even a young child may assume the role of a father. For Willie, Wisam was a spiritual pillar, his savior. Psychologists call this transference, but for Willie, it was just an unexplained attachment.

# THE LAST MOMENTS OF THOMAS'S LIFE

*There is only life, and all that exists, exists only in the light of life.*

~ Sergei Bulgakov

Every day one of the "angels" ascended to heaven, so to speak. Each day they wondered who would be next. This morning, everyone sensed that someone in the ward was suffering. But they didn't know who.

"If only it were Dr. Stevens," joked one of the patients.

"Stevens is no angel; he's a real devil."

"All right, that's enough," said one of the nurses. "These jokes are inappropriate."

"What's going on in the next room, Nurse Theresa?" asked one of the patients, speaking to a nurse who had just walked in.

"Mr. Thomas has taken a turn for the worse. For the worse in the sense that . . . I'm sorry, we lost him. The doctors did everything they could."

All the patients in the room were very distressed by this news. Fifty-year-old Thomas had been a smiling, jocular presence. He had entertained everyone with his cheerful jokes, making the patients laugh and teasing the nurses and doctors. It wasn't only the patients who had been touched by his personality.

"We have been convicted and sentenced to die at MD Anderson for our crimes, in a prison cell for serious offenders," Thomas once said. "Dr. Stevens, do you know which criminal in a prison is considered the most dangerous and is feared even by the guards?"

"No, Thomas, I don't," Stevens said in a quiet and somewhat cautious voice.

"The one under a death sentence. Because he has nothing to lose in life. Get it? Nothing to lose." Thomas began to slowly lift the fruit knife he was holding, squinting with one eye. But then seeing Stevens's dismay, he quickly moved the knife toward the apple he held in his other hand and cut off a slice.

But for the patients, his jokes were like a balm for the soul. Thomas really liked Wisam. He called him "my Arab friend."

"Wisam, you're not related to bin Laden, are you? Because his name kind of sounds like yours. Osama bin Laden, and you're Wisam."

"No, Uncle Thomas, we're not related."

"Yeah, I don't know, but if you are, tell us beforehand so we know what to do. What if everything gets blown up here?"

Seeing how the nurses were paging through their textbooks every chance they got, Thomas said, "Studying, studying, always studying. You know why you need to study so much? Because you'll still never find a job. So keep studying!" This made the nurses laugh.

Trying to console Mrs. Stewart, who wanted to divorce her husband because he had an affair, Thomas said, "Why do you blame him? A man is so happy as soon as he finds his soul mate. 'My God, at last I've found my heart's desire. This is my soul mate.' But after a while, he notices other soul mates walking down the street or in the park, and it starts to eat away at the poor guy. He begins to doubt. 'My God, I wonder if I've truly found my soul mate.'"

"Thomas, that's not funny at all! Listen, this is not the place to make jokes like that!" Mrs. Stewart said.

Thomas was interested in horoscopes and zodiac signs. Sometimes he would ask one of the medical staff about his astrological sign and then tell him about that sign.

"Thomas, why are you constantly reading our horoscopes?" one of the staff said.

"I want to know more about you, so I know what to expect," Thomas said.

When he read about crime and the injustices that occurred in life, he'd often say, "A person only has rights until they conflict with the desires of someone stronger."

Thomas got along very well with Wisam. Despite the difference in their ages, Thomas treated him like a contemporary, and Wisam liked that.

Thomas had deteriorated in the last few days. Seeing him, Dr. Stevens asked, "Thomas, how are you today? It doesn't seem to me like you're doing too well."

"No, Dr. Stevens, if there's someone for whom things are going well, that person's definitely not me."

"Thomas, you have to be a little more realistic. This is the wing where the 'angels' live. And an angel's place is in heaven."

Thomas was not at all upset. "Would an angel stick around where there is devil? No, naturally he flies away!"

When Thomas saw that someone was upset about their illness and afraid of death, he would say, "Life is a disease that can't be treated and, inescapably, ends with death. Although before a person dies, he might think that his death will cause unbearable pain to his family and friends, but after death, it turns out that's not so. It was just a fuss that prompted a tear or two."

"Why should I be afraid of death? I broke my arm once, I broke my leg twice, I endured three serious operations, and now I have cancer. So I can be killed, but death can't frighten me at all."

Wisam was quite distraught over the news of Thomas's death. His eyes filled with tears, but he didn't cry. For a while, he stood silently. It was as if he were remembering something. And then he said quietly, *"Inna lillahi wa inna ilayhi raji'un."*

"What do those mysterious words mean, Wisam?" Betty said.

"They mean 'We belong to God, and to Him we shall return.' We say these words when someone leaves this world. This is how we comfort ourselves."

The night before, Thomas's condition had worsened, and Wisam had gone to his room and sat at the foot of Thomas's bed. He asked him if he wanted anything.

"Wisam, my soul isn't well today. During these last days of my life, I find myself wanting to do bad things. I feel resentful toward people. I always used to greet everyone with a joke. I always pretended to be so thick-skinned that I didn't notice the injustices and betrayals that were being done to me. So everyone thought that nothing bothered me, that I never took offense at anything, and that I didn't care about anything. But now I hate them. On the inside, I want to demean and wound all those who are crawling around me. What's so surprising is that these desires of mine don't bother me, and I don't feel guilty. I can't really figure out how I feel about people. I'm tired of living, and I've become disinterested in others. I told my children, 'Don't save a room for me in the new apartment. It doesn't matter; I'm dying.' But no one tried to convince me otherwise. They didn't say anything, not a word. Can you imagine, Wisam? My whole life I toiled away for them. My whole life I thought only about them. I even earned this illness working in heavy industry to support them. Yeah, I think I've earned it. When you're seen as expendable and unneeded, you want to quietly check out, without being a burden on anyone.

"I was awfully rude to the nurses today, and I offended my roommates. I've really lost my manners lately. I tried to always be cheerful to please others, even if I was crying inside my heart. Do you understand? Once you told me a prophet said, 'Say something nice or don't say anything at all.' You know, Wisam, sometimes words would come into my head that I wanted to speak, but I would stay quiet so I wouldn't offend anyone. I used to try to say kind things. But I no longer care. I want to pour out the words that are left inside me and causing me distress. So I fire away! I'll say them and let it ruffle everyone's feathers a little. I'm sick of worrying about the opinion of this person, that person.

"I want to be alone, far from everyone. This hospital is like a prison, and I want out. I know there's no escaping this illness. But I don't want to die here. Somewhere far from here, on the shores of the Mediterranean, sitting in a beach chair under some palm trees watching the sunset — that's where I want to close my eyes for the last time. I want the last thing I see to be an image of sea and sunset. Let the light in my life go out as the sun sets. It doesn't matter; let it go out, as long as I don't have to look at this hospital I'm stuck in that I hate so, plus all the medical staff I'm so sick of. I'm just worn out, Wisam.

"I wake up every morning, but I don't ever want to get out of bed. The first thing I think of is, 'Ah, it's morning again, and I have to live this disgusting life once more.' Every day I dream I have Aladdin's lamp. The first thing I would ask the genie in the lamp to do is to get me out of here."

"Where would you go?" Wisam said.

"Doesn't matter. Just away from here. The staff all think I'm a clown. They think I don't care about anything." Thomas took a deep breath and sighed.

"I really miss my kids lately. When I was young and healthy, I would never have believed that the time would come when I would need so much attention and care from them.

"Wisam, nowadays I feel like a baby who needs love, attention, and affection. And I don't expect that from the nurses or my roommates but from my family and my children. Is it really so hard to offer your own father a little love and care?" Thomas, always so cheerful and teasing, began to weep so much that Wisam's eyes also filled with tears.

"Wisam, I feel so lonely. I miss the past so much. Especially my sweet Emma. She's been gone five years now. She left me alone in this faithless world. I'm waiting to see her. I know she's waiting for me too. When I was with her, I felt calmer and more confident. I could tell her so much that I couldn't say to my children. My heart felt free to share my sorrows. And she always comforted me. More than anything, I wish she were with me now that I'm sick. Now . . . now when times are hardest, she's not at my side. We promised each other we'd grow old together. We swore to each other. And she broke her oath, Wisam." Thomas could not hold back his tears and Wisam heard him out without saying a word.

"I didn't use to joke around so much until I met Emma. I was a serious man, thinking about others' welfare. I only used to kid around like this with Emma. After she died, I started cracking jokes with other people to try to numb the pain and sadness I felt inside. I thought it would help drown my sorrows. Maybe I just use these jokes to remind myself of my sweet Emma. Every time I tease Dr. Stevens or banter with Mrs. Stewart, Dr. Anna, or Nels, it's like I'm kidding around with Emma. I want to use these jokes to disguise the pain and emptiness inside me. As soon as I open my eyes anymore, I see Emma. She's moving her lips and saying something to me. But I can't make it out. No matter how I try, I can't hear what she's saying. Maybe she's calling me. Maybe she wants to explain something to me. But probably she's asking for forgiveness.

"I can't take my eyes off the door. I wait for my family, the people I spent my whole life helping. But for some reason they don't come. I don't mean they never come at all. They come, but not as much as they should. My children come and my daughters-in-law and my grandchildren. Although they visit me, they always seem harassed. They try to talk to me as if they've really missed me and feel my pain. But in five or ten minutes, they've run out of things to talk about, and they're looking at the clock. They visit me because they feel obligated. It really annoys me to be treated like that. I'm not a child. I understand everything. After all, they're my children. I turn a deaf ear to their insincere words and just nod and try to keep a smile on my lips. And before they go, they put on a sad face, like people who don't want to say good-bye.

"I don't know . . . They also have busy lives. I try to understand them. But it doesn't seem like they try to understand me. I never used to allow myself to think about my children or loved ones in a negative way. But now I can't stop myself. Those thoughts just pop into my head of their own accord, and I can't do anything about them. As they leave, my children kiss me and say, 'Daddy, please, take care,' as though they'll really miss me. And I smile to their faces and act like nothing's wrong, forcing myself to play my role as an affectionate father.

"I've never been vindictive or borne a grudge. But now I find myself replaying in my mind everything they've done and said behind my back, and I want to punish them. I want to scream at the top of my lungs, 'Why have you done this to me? How have I wronged you?'

"Wisam, I am quite ready to leave this world. But not because I'm sick and have no choice but to live out my last days in the 'angel' wing at MD Anderson. No. Rather, it's because nothing in this world belongs to me, and nothing brings me joy. I've lost everything that ties me to this world.

"There was one thing that happened a few days ago. It severed the one thread that bound me to this world: my memories of the past. My life was in those memories. Beloved memories of Emma . . . Even during my most difficult moments, I would sift through them. And that gave me the strength and inspiration to fight my illness. You know, Wisam, I heard Emma's voice every day — it energized me. She set me on the right path. Now that's been taken from me. That was the only thing that gave me the strength to hold on and tethered me to life, but that's all fallen apart now. My God, why did I have to lose everything in my final years, lose my joy as I'm taking my last breaths? Why? Why should I leave this world filled with hatred and unhappiness? If only I could forget about it and wipe it from my memory."

Wisam didn't say a word as Thomas spoke. The last thing Thomas needed right then was advice about how to change his future or how to avoid making mistakes in life. He only needed someone's ear. Someone to listen and share his grief. Wisam was the one person available to Thomas who was suitable for this, yet Wisam felt he shouldn't have been the one acting as an ear for Thomas — that should have been his friends and loved ones.

The morning after Thomas's death, word got out that he had committed suicide. He had taken a large dose of sleeping pills and drifted off forever. No one knew the real reason why Thomas took such a step at the very end of his life. Many assumed that it was because he was sick. Only Wisam knew that was not the case. That very night, the nurse, seeing the patient's state of anxiety, gave Thomas a sedative. Wisam decided not to leave the old man alone and waited until he fell asleep. Thomas was half-awake, delirious. He held Wisam's hand tight with his bony fingers. He seemed to hover right between dreaming and reality, or even life and death. Emma was haunting him. "Why, oh why did this happen? You left this world . . . You left me alone. No, not even alone. You left me with this grief. What shall I do now, Emma? How am I supposed to live? How am I supposed to die? How could you deceive me? I wish I hadn't found out. Never!"

Wisam was confused. He wanted to leave, but his friend's fingers were squeezing his hand. Thomas's beloved Emma, whom he always cherished and remembered kindly, had cheated on him. He only found out after she died; he never said anything to anyone. It was as if he had forgotten this bitter truth. Strangely, now that he was dying, he remembered it as if it had happened yesterday. It was puzzling why he would experience such a mental shock and think of suicide now, after so much time had passed. *That's human psychology for you,* thought Wisam. *The pain isn't felt right away. You almost deliberately forget the worst news or a terrible event so that it does not kill you. You live on as if nothing had happened. Only later, when the self considers itself ready to face this event, the ice of memory begins to thaw, and it all comes back. This is what must have happened to poor Thomas.*

# A HEART THAT CAN LOVE CAN ALSO FORGIVE

Thomas's death made Wisam think about Willie's father again.

"Willie, when a heart can love, it can also forgive. You loved your father a great deal, maybe more than you loved your mother. Do not think that he is gone. You have a great chance: to do something that would have made him happy. Me, I'd love to fulfill my father's wish. He would have wanted me to take care of Havra, to support her. But I can't."

"What would have made my father happy? I don't know what you're trying to say."

"You have a brother. I think your father would have wanted you to find him. All fathers want their children to do what they couldn't."

"Well, I don't know . . ."

"You must find him, Willie. I'd have helped you myself if it weren't for this illness," Wisam said.

Willie was silent. After a long time of torment, he had destroyed all things that reminded him of his father and buried the memories deeply. But now his heart was slowly filling with warmth again. He wanted to see his father's grave, and he wanted to find that little boy.

He had to put a lot of effort into finding Brendan's address in Houston and finally, he found the firm where his father had worked. Brendan's colleagues knew his address, and they knew Willie as well. They had heard about Willie a lot and warmly welcomed him, which touched him greatly.

As Willie approached the given address, he could feel his heart racing. He stood for a while outside the door of his father's house, agonizing about whether to knock, but then the door opened. Before him appeared a woman who looked to be in her early fifties. Willie had not forgotten the face he had seen through the bus window. It was her. He didn't know what to say.

"Ah, uh . . . um . . . Is . . . is this . . . Brendan's house?"

She stared at him in amazement.

"Willie, you look so much like your father. You remind me of when Brendan was young . . ." She began to cry suddenly. "I . . . I'm Victoria. Please, come in, come."

She greeted Willie as if he were her own child and invited him in. He walked into the living room and saw family photos on the bookshelves, including pictures of Willie with his father. One picture of Willie by himself was propped up right next to their own family photos. Although Willie pretended not to have noticed his photo, he was very surprised.

Victoria brought him a cup of coffee. Willie had nursed anger against this woman for so many years, but now he felt quite at home in her house. It was strange. The malice that had seethed in Willie's heart for years had vanished. Perhaps this could be explained by Victoria's kindness and her motherly, affectionate demeanor. Victoria gave the impression of having found the dearest person who had been lost to her long ago and for whom her heart had been longing to see.

"Willie, Brendan really loved you very much. He always talked about you. He told me so much about what a great football player you were. That's why he got Ray into football. Yeah, your brother's a pretty good player himself." Victoria spoke the word "brother" hesitantly. "He's crazy about football, just like you . . .

"Your father really, really loved you. But all the stuff that happened between you . . . What can you do?" Willie listened to Victoria in silence.

"You know, Willie, I've felt really guilty about your relationship with your dad. Brendan worked at my dad's company. He was a real mess when I met him. He felt abandoned, lonely, and unwanted. But our relationship only got serious after he had made up his mind to divorce Helen. Afterward I worried that Brendan might go back to her. I was really scared. I thought I might be left on my own and Ray might be left without a father. So I insisted that he have no further contact with Helen, which meant that his connection with you was cut off as well. I thought that if Brendan's and Helen's relationship had fallen apart and he couldn't be happy with her, then it didn't make any sense for him to stay in touch with her. Helen couldn't give Brendan a happy family, but I was confident that I could.

"I tried to be a good wife to him, and I gave him a child. I wanted us to have a lot of children. But Brendan really struggled with his feelings after Ray was born. He felt so guilty that he didn't want to have any more children. Your father never stopped thinking about you. He worried about your life. For a while, I stopped him from getting in touch with you. We argued and fought over it all the time. My father also influenced him." Victoria took a sip of coffee, and Willie saw her hands were trembling.

"I figured that, after a while, Brendan would stop thinking about the past and forget about the family that was causing him pain. But that's not what happened, Willie. As things went on, it got worse. He seemed even more unhappy and started coming home late. And he was very moody when he was here. I realized things couldn't continue that way for long, with him feeling torn between the two of us. So one day, I sat down with him, and we really hashed it out. I saw how his conscience was tormenting him and how he was suffering. I realized that, although I had taken Brendan from Helen, I had no right to separate him from his son. That was wrong. On one hand, I had been focused on Ray and worried that he might lose his father, but on the other hand, I had separated a child I didn't know from his father. I felt really guilty.

"We agreed that Brendan needed to reestablish a relationship with you. We decided to bring you here and have you live with us for a little bit. You would have met Ray, and he would have gotten to know his older brother. We had hoped that the two of you might someday have each other to lean on once we were no longer around. Then something happened that completely altered the destinies of both our families. Brendan developed some pain in his chest and a bad cough. He seemed short of breath. He decided to go to the doctor. They spent a long time checking him out, and then they told us that he had lung cancer. Unfortunately, that type of cancer is very difficult to identify in its early stages. By the time he went to the doctor, the disease had spread to almost every part of his body, and it was too late to do anything.

"After Brendan came home, his condition worsened. I cried for a long time and didn't know what to do. I felt as if God was punishing me. I had separated Brendan from his son so as not to lose him, but in the end, God took him from me.

"We found a good specialist who put him in the hospital. They sent him to the MD Anderson Center . . ." Victoria didn't know that Willie worked there.

"After he underwent some procedures at MD Anderson, his condition improved somewhat. We brought him home. But we knew his days were numbered. That disease had robbed us of time.

"After all that happened, your father really wanted to go visit you, but he was afraid that so much time had passed since he had left you that you probably wouldn't agree to see him. Brendan also figured that if you found out about his illness, you would think that he was just looking for you to ask your forgiveness before he died. I pushed him to get in touch with you and told him that you would understand. I begged and begged him, and he finally agreed. He even bought a plane ticket. He was supposed to call you. But then he suddenly changed his mind. I didn't understand why he had done that. My pleas no longer had any effect. Later his condition deteriorated so much that we forgot about everything else. And pretty soon, he was gone . . ."

But Brendan had called. As Victoria talked and talked, Willie mentally filled in all the blank spaces in his understanding of what had happened. The call had made Willie very happy, although he had refused to show it. His ego wouldn't let him speak to his father affectionately. He had waited for his father to beg his forgiveness. He wanted his father to offer some persuasive reason why Willie should deign to forgive him. Willie had addressed Brendan scornfully and spoke rudely to him that day.

"Willie, please don't talk to me like this. You're breaking my heart. I already feel terrible," Brendan said, his voice sounding distressed.

"Let it break, just like my heart and my mother's heart have been broken for so many years."

"Willie, it hasn't exactly been easy for me either. Fate has given me the punishment I deserve. Now I'm asking your forgiveness for everything I did to you. Try to be more understanding."

"Brendan, don't you think it's more than a bit late for an apology?" It was the first time Willie had ever addressed his father by his first name.

"Willie, has it occurred to you that the person you're talking to on the phone right now might not have long to live? What do you think of that? Even then you won't forgive? You won't give me one more chance?"

These words touched Willie's heart, but the years of pain he had suffered kept him from giving in so quickly. He wanted to cry and tell his father how hard it was to be so far away from him. He was eager to say, "Dad I forgive you, but don't ever leave us again!" But the anger bottled up in his heart kept him from doing so.

"If you're about to die, that means you've called to say good-bye and ask for forgiveness. Just like a criminal who's spent his life committing crimes but who summons a priest when he's finally sentenced to death. If that's the case, you've dialed the wrong number. You don't need me; you need a priest!" As he said this, Willie understood that he was speaking too harshly. But he couldn't help himself.

Although his heart wanted to reconcile with his father, Willie could not take the first step. He waited for his father to say one more affectionate word or make yet another effort to persuade him, and then he would allow those words to induce him to open his heart. He would say that he had waited for him and missed him for many years, forlornly hoping for a phone call from him. But Brendan was silent. And saying nothing further, his father hung up the phone.

Willie didn't understand him. He didn't understand why he had done this and why he had given up so easily. At first Willie was very sorry that he had been so brusque with him. But afterward, he got really angry. "He'll never change! He only called to appease his conscience, and perhaps he has just gotten drunk and suddenly remembered that he has a son named Willie. And he then looked for an excuse to say good-bye to me in a dramatic fashion. Otherwise, the person who called to apologize wouldn't have hung up so quickly."

Willie hadn't understood his father's behavior back then. Only now did he realize the state his father had been in when he had called.

Victoria set the table for dinner as if Willie were a very dear guest. Just then, Ray arrived home after class. He recognized Willie as soon as he saw him. He hugged him like a real brother, as if they had known one another for years. Willie realized that everyone in this house knew and loved him, despite the fact that they had never met.

Ray had followed in his older brother's footsteps and was already playing for his college team. Right now he was playing for a school in Division II, but his coaches told him he had talent.

When Willie finally rose to leave, Victoria gave him a package his father had left for him. To get a package from his father after so many years surprised Willie. Although Victoria hinted at the idea of another visit as she walked Willie to the door, when she got no response, she let the subject drop. Ray was also silent.

The whole way home, Willie wondered about the contents of the package, but even once there, he waited until everyone else was asleep before opening it. It contained a football that had been purchased for Willie years ago, one letter, and an unused plane ticket. It was the ticket from Houston to Dallas that Brendan had bought to go visit Willie.

Willie opened the faded white sheet of paper with shaking hands.

# THE LAST LETTER

My dear son, Willie,

Perhaps it's insensitive to call you that because I was never in my life able to be a decent father to you.

I don't know where to begin, what to write, or how to ask for your forgiveness. I am writing this letter from MD Anderson Hospital, room number seventeen. I'm getting treatment here, but I don't think I'll be leaving. That's why I want to speak to you from my heart in this letter. I don't want to take these words with me. If this letter ever manages to find you, that will make me very happy.

Willie, how are you? What are you doing? Do you have children? If you do, how many? I'd like to ask you all these questions, plus some others. I've tried so hard to imagine your answers, but I'm not sure how accurate my guesses have been.

What should I say, Willie? What should I write? First of all, I'd like to thank you for the happy days you gave me. Yes, it was you who gave them to me. When I look back over the life I've lived, I can see that my happiest days were spent with you. When I was with you, I truly felt like a decent father. I can never forget the way you used to look at me, how respectful you were. My conscience always troubles me when I think of you. I tried to forget you so it wouldn't hurt so much, but I couldn't. That means I'm destined to live with this emotional pain for the rest of my days.

I'll soon be departing this life. They say there's a life after this one. I don't know, but I would very much like for it to be true, and I'd wait for you and your mother there. But I'm ready to vanish forever from this life. I'd like everyone to forget me and not leave even a memory behind. And to then be together with you in a new life. To start everything all over.

I don't think we'll ever be able to understand why everything happened the way it did. But in any case, I realize that I must accept a lot of the blame for the situation. At first I blamed Helen for everything. But eventually I was able to see my own missteps as well. Willie, I ask your forgiveness for everything I did wrong. I know that you really love me. Even during our last conversation, despite the harsh way you spoke to me, I could feel the love in your heart. Don't blame yourself for what you said. I have no right to forgive you, but if you believe that you have done me any wrong, please know that nothing that happened was your fault. And if you feel guilty, I forgive you for anything that you consider to be your fault. Please offer me this same forgiveness. I need it more than you.

I'm so flustered I'm jumping from one subject to the next. You know, Willie, I always dreamed about having a good family. About a family that included Helen and you. But things went wrong, Willie. I couldn't do it—it just didn't work out for me.

I dream of you every night. I remember every line of your face. I miss those small, round eyes of yours that used to look at me so sincerely and naively. I miss our conversations about life and football, sitting by the lake skimming stones on the water and looking at the reeds growing out of it. I long to see you play again, Willie. When I watched your amazing game moves, I felt like I was playing myself. I was prouder than I had ever been in my life. Willie, I'd like to confess something else to you. I was never a football fan. It was a sport I even sometimes looked down on. But I sensed that you really liked to play football. Your love and hunger for the game was what made me start coming to watch. And after a while, I fell in love with it too. It was all because of you, and only because of you. Now I find it interesting to watch football games, especially the Super Bowl—which I'd love to see you play in. Why aren't you competing, Willie? I signed Ray up for football as well. I wanted him to be like his older brother.

I always carry a picture of you with me. I find myself looking at it all the time lately. I love you very much, my dear son. I grew to hate myself after the last time we met. I really deserve to be raked over the coals for having deserted you. It's a terrible thing to have to live with such emotional pain, believe me. And it's even more agonizing to die with it.

I'm now fully aware that everything is finished. It's too late for anything. But I have one request for you. I know I have no right to ask, but I have faith in your big heart. Please look after Victoria and your brother, Ray. They're good people and have always been a tower of strength for me. Victoria has stayed by my side every second, and I know she will be with me to the end. She knows I don't love her — that my heart belongs to Helen — yet she's given me all her love and all that she has. She deserves a gold star for that. Ray is also a very kind and selfless child. But don't think that he was ever able to take your place in my heart. Not at all. Willie, I hope that you will grow to love them because they are the only thread that ties us together and reminds you of me.

Willie, have more pity on me than I ever had for you! Believe me, I know that this father who is doomed to die will never see his child again, yet I never take my eyes off the door of the hospital room in this city of "angels." I'm waiting for the day when you and Helen walk through that door. And although this hope is a very faint one, I long to see the two of you. I'm leaving, but deep in my heart, I'm taking you with me.

I called you for the last time and had so much I wanted to say, but you didn't want to talk to me. I died then, and life lost its meaning. But that wasn't your fault. I long ago lost the right to be your father, the right to hear kind words and receive warm glances from you. I would have acted just the same in your place. After our last conversation, I fell into a dark hole and lost my will to live. I've always loved you so much, Willie. I wanted to give you a wonderful life. But that didn't work out. I wanted you to have a storybook life, but everything turned out quite the opposite. I made your life a living hell.

Not a day goes by that I don't remember the last time we met. In your eyes, I could read everything that you wanted to tell me. I knew that you wanted me to stay and not abandon you. But believe me, I was just unable to summon up the strength. I pretended to be blind to your misery and heartache. I did exactly what I didn't want to do. There were a lot of reasons why. Sometimes you get to the point where you'd like to go back, but you can't; you don't have the strength to pull it off. You're so overwhelmed with anguish and doubt that you don't know what to do.

If you're reading this letter, that means you found Victoria. And that means you've forgiven me, a sick man in the last days of his life. Willie, I am grateful for your big heart. I'm grateful to you for having read this letter and thus giving me a chance to free my soul and say the things I wanted to say during our last conversation but couldn't.

Willie, my dear son! You're reading this letter, but I've already passed on. Perhaps you'll find it easier to forgive someone who's no longer in this world. I've been dreaming of Helen a lot recently. In my dream, she asks me for forgiveness. Apologizes for her mistakes. But she doesn't know that I already forgave her long ago. I don't blame anyone for what happened. Probably this was just our fate.

Willie, I ask God to give you all the wonderful things I couldn't give you. If you have children, tell them their disgraceful grandfather said hello. If you want, Victoria can tell you where I'm buried, and you can come visit me. I'd very much like to see you there. They say that the dead can see the people who come to visit them and talk to them. Although, of course, those visitors can't hear the voices of the departed. But I think you'll be able to hear me. Maybe we can speak together quietly, like father and son, if only after death.  But if you come to visit me, we won't talk about the past. Okay, Willie? Instead, why don't you tell me about your family, your plans, your work. Don't reproach me in my grave, Willie. I beg you. I won't be able to bear it.

If Helen is still alive, ask her for forgiveness on my behalf. Tell her that I love her very much as well. I always loved her. Even when things were very tense between us, even when I was very angry at her. If Helen has left this world . . . It's so hard for me to think these thoughts. No, in my mind she has always been beautiful, happy, and young. Let her remain that way for my sake!

Forgive me, son.

Living out my final days in need of your care, and always loving you,

Dad

# EVERYONE IS GIVEN A CHANCE
# TO REBUILD THEIR LIVES

The next day, Willie went to see Victoria once again. When she opened the door and saw him standing there, she just embraced him. Willie asked her where his father was buried. Victoria requested that he wait until noon. Ray came from the college, and they went to the cemetery together.

Ray pointed to his father's grave. Then he took a few steps away.

Willie sat down by the grave. In his hand, he had the football that his father had bought him. He didn't know where to start. "Thanks for the gift . . . Dad. I decided to give this ball to Kevin, my son. Anyway, I came, like you wanted me to. What shall we talk about? So much has happened. I've been working at MD Anderson for a year now. In your room, there's now . . ."

Willie told Brendan about his family, his work, his staff, the hospital's "angels," and Wisam and their friendship.

Willie stood up and put his hand on the tombstone. "I'll visit you often, Father. I don't need to make a deal with God. If anyone knows what it is to wait, it's me. Next time, I'll come with Sarah and the kids. I know you'd like to meet them. We've had things going on, you and me. But I told them all the good things about you that I remember. They know you the way I remember you from when I was little: gentle, attentive, selfless. If you only knew how much I loved you! You were everything to me . . . Well, anyway . . ."

Willie took a few steps away from the grave, but then he turned around. "A short while ago, mother died. Wisam says that loving hearts will be reunited in another world. I wonder if you are together now. I wasn't there for her in the last moments of her life. Don't ask me why. Our family must have been destined to live and die apart from each other. Maybe we'll be together some day. Okay, Dad, I'm going now. But I'll be back."

From that day onward, Willie began to think of Victoria as his mother and Ray as his brother. Willie often brought Sarah and his children to visit them. Soon they were in the habit of spending Sundays together. Ray was a very sincere and kind young man. He quickly became friends with Kevin and Caitlin. Sarah and Victoria also became friends. As Sarah had never met any of Willie's relatives, she was very pleased and surprised to have this opportunity to get to know Victoria.

# I WON'T BE ABLE TO SEE MY MOTHER

Willie noticed that Wisam had seemed quite agitated lately. Some uncharacteristic sadness was visible in the lines of his face. It didn't seem like he was sleeping at night at all. He spent most of the night sitting on his bed and praying. Willie worried about him.

Willie saw Wisam cry for the first time. The man who always had a smile on his face was crying like a baby — it was unprecedented. Willie was certain that this had nothing to do with physical pain or the fact that he was living out the final days of his life. Wisam was simply not the kind of person who would grieve over the physical world. Willie's throat tightened at the sight of Wisam's tears, and he could not speak. Wisam, the man who acted as a spiritual rock for Willie as well as everyone else, was now crying.

"Wisam, do you know what the hardest thing in life is?" Willie said. "It's watching someone cry who normally is a source of cheer and comfort to you. That's when you understand that—"

"Willie, we're all human beings. We're not made of stone. Anyone with a heart suffers and cries for some reason or another. Once, the Prophet Mohammed was seen crying over the death of one of his children. The people said to him, 'But you're the one who talks to us about life after death, saying that death is nothing but a bridge from one world to the next. So why are you crying now?' The Prophet answered them, 'I am also a man who mourns and weeps like everyone else. My eyes are crying, but I am not protesting God's will. I do not blame God for what has happened.'

"I often find myself thinking about my mother lately. I sense that my hour is near. I was left to live my life without a mother. We were separated by hardships, suffering, and death. I'm afraid that after death I won't be able to be with her in the next world. I'm very happy that once I die, I'll be able to see my father, Grandfather Badr, and Grandmother Hafiza. But I become quite anxious when I think about my mother.

"The soul of a person who has committed suicide is trapped between this world and the world to come. I am afraid that my mother cannot be saved." As he said this, tears poured down Wisam's cheeks and ran onto his pillow. Perfectly in keeping with his gentle personality, his weeping and grief were quiet and subdued. Willie felt as though Wisam were smiling even as he cried. The black shadow of the sadness in his heart could not entirely engulf his smiling face. Willie realized that Wisam was simply a man with a man's merits and weaknesses. At the same time, Willie felt that there was something different about him that made him stand out from most people. And now this amazing man, able to be Willie's entire world, was shedding tears. These tears reflected Wisam's sensitive soul more than any words could have.

His mother's act had been a bitter, crushing blow for Wisam. But a mother is still a mother, and it was agony for Wisam to think about his mother's torments in the afterlife. Willie was surprised, realizing the important role of faith in people's lives and how it affected the way they felt. He knew some people who had lost loved ones to suicide. But he couldn't say that any of them were as troubled over it as Wisam was about his mother. Wisam was viewing it from the perspective of his faith. The others were upset over the loss of the people they loved, but Wisam was also distressed by the prospect of his mother suffering in the next world. Wisam believed that his mother's suicide meant that he would be separated from her after he died.

Willie had heard about Wisam's mother's suicide from Aunt Bayan, but had never spoken to Wisam about it. With such a difficult subject, it was best to wait for the other person to bring it up. Now Wisam was ready to pour out his soul and talk about everything.

"My mother's suicide shook me to my core," he said. "I cried so much over it. I cried at night so no one would see. Suicide is a great sin. Those people are barred from entering paradise. I was stricken by the thought of my mother dying such a death. My poor mother's emotional suffering was so terrible. She faced so many setbacks on her path . . . The doctors claimed she was mentally ill. Perhaps that's why she took such a step—she was out of her head."

"Your God is merciful, Wisam. He will forgive your mother." Willie had now traded places with Wisam, the one who had always comforted him.

"Willie, my God is also your God. Suicide is a great sin. How do you think she could be forgiven?"

"You said she had psychological problems. She didn't know what she was doing."

"I wasn't the one who said that; it was the doctors. But maybe you're right. I console myself at times thinking about that. Probably, she was simply out of her head and under great mental stress at the moment she killed herself." Wisam, who had been staring at a picture on the wall opposite him, now turned toward Willie.

"Sometimes you just want to hear someone else repeat something that you already know. We're such weak creatures. Our emotions are so mercurial, Willie."

# THE HARBINGER OF SEPARATION

*When you entered this world, you cried, and the world laughed. Live in
such a way that as you are dying, you can laugh while the world cries.*

~ Indian proverb

It was mid-December. Snow was falling, a rare thing in Houston.
The children were excited about the snow, as were the adults. The
city's wide streets were ornamented with festive Christmas trees and
decorations. Willie's family had also decorated a tree at home. Victoria
and Ray were supposed to arrive a few days before Christmas and
spend the holiday with them. The whole family wanted to be together
for Christmas. Willie had already been very attentive to Victoria and
Ray, but his suggestion that they spend the holiday together had been
unexpected and moving. As soon as Willie had mentioned the idea to
Victoria, she began to cry. Ray could not contain his pleasure upon
hearing the news. Willie was like both an older brother as well as a
father to him.

There was a festive, decorated tree at the hospital as well. The
hospital organized an event for the patients on Christmas Day. The
families of the patients, doctors, and nurses were invited to attend.
Willie asked all the members of his family to come join this celebration.

And since Victoria and Ray were considered to be members of his
family, they were also invited to attend. Willie introduced them and
Sarah to Wisam's sister, Havra, and his aunt, Bayan.

Wisam's condition had greatly deteriorated by mid-December.
He now coughed up blood from time to time. All the doctors who had

come to love this smiling man were concerned. The physicians had truly taken Wisam under their wing and no longer saw him as just an ordinary patient.

That day, Wisam felt like breathing some fresh air. He asked Willie to help him up to the roof of the hospital. With a smile, he said to Willie, "This might be my last request." It was against the rules, but Willie didn't want to let him down. Taking him by the arm, he tried to lead him up there, but it wasn't possible. However, he remembered that at one end of that floor was a spacious balcony reserved for the doctors. Willie put Wisam in a wheelchair and pushed him there.

The balcony railing was covered in snow. Silence reigned, although the sounds of cars and the joyful shrieks of children could occasionally be heard from afar. The sparkling lights amid the darkness somehow seemed melancholy to Willie. As soon as Wisam came out on the balcony, he inhaled deeply. As he exhaled, Willie could feel his warm breath through the frosty air. Willie brought his friend some tea and sat down in a chair next to him. He wanted to talk to Wisam but didn't know where to start.

Wisam sensed that he was getting worse. He was physically extremely feeble, and the pain in his chest had grown sharper. He was spitting up bloody phlegm. Wisam knew this was all a sign that his ship of life was sailing into its last harbor. As often happened, it was Wisam who broke the silence.

"Here's to the first snowfall, Willie." Willie saw the smile that was always on Wisam's face. The moonlit, snowy weather made his wide eyes look even bigger and added to their sparkle. Willie felt the old yearning in his heart. The sensation felt very familiar, yet he couldn't remember when he'd felt it before. This feeling was so heavy and painful that he was unable to speak. Wisam, noticing this, answered for him.

"We're delighted by the snow that's fallen, but there are others who, despite seeing the snow, cannot enjoy it. May the Lord help them all!"

"Let the Almighty help them. Amen," Willie said in a small, quiet voice.

Wisam laughed. "Willie, that's the first time I've ever heard you say anything like that! Let the Almighty help you as well!"

Willie was thrown off balance, feeling as if he had been caught out, and said, "What do you mean? I often say that! I've always believed in God. I've always felt his warm presence."

Wisam smiled but didn't want to put him on the spot any further. "Willie, don't worry, it doesn't matter." He placed his skeletal hand with its bulging veins on Willie's arm. "No, Willie . . . It doesn't matter at all," he said, smiling.

"Wisam, what's your greatest fear in life?"

"I've always been afraid of something, but if you ask me specifically of what, I can't exactly say. But yeah, there's always been some kind of fear or worry inside of me and close at hand. You may find this hard to believe, but it was here at MD Anderson that I managed to escape those worries. This is a city of angels, Willie. That's probably why. And what are you afraid of?"

"I've had all sorts of different fears. As a kid I was afraid of not getting any presents on holidays; later, of fights between my parents and of them getting divorced. I was never frightened of the dark or of monsters, like other children were. Children are afraid that someone will take away their candy, but I never had time to be frightened of such things. I was either afraid of being punished by my mother or of hearing an argument between my parents over the fact that he didn't earn very much or of being separated from my family. I was afraid that some strange event would happen in my family, and I would be left alone."

"Children aren't like adults," Wisam said. "They can find happiness in the smallest, most insignificant things. They're delighted by a single piece of candy. Girls are in a hurry to grow up and wear their mothers' dresses and high heels, and boys yearn for stubbly chins like their fathers. If only adults could be content with so little, Willie, and enjoy what they already have yet do not value."

"We're all human beings, but our lives and fates are so different," Willie said.

"I feel like a candle that melts a bit each day, but I believe that it's only my body that's melting. My soul is the light that's released from the melting candle, and it will live forever."

"Wisam, I can't believe that that's how it all ends," Willie said. "That's not possible. Life must continue after death. Some sort of place must exist. A place where those who couldn't freely enjoy the beauty of this world or breathe this clean air deep into their lungs can live without hardship. A place where you will see Judge Badr, as well as your father, Jafar, and your mother. Yes, even your mother. A place without illness, where everything is wonderful. There is no need there for MD Anderson or for doctors . . ."

The balcony gradually became covered with snow. They were both freezing but didn't want to interrupt their conversation. Wisam reached his hand out, and the snowflakes that landed on it melted in the warmth of his fingers.

"My Grandmother Hafiza said every snowflake is brought down by an angel," Wisam said. "And as these snowflakes fall to earth, they bring God's mercy down from heaven with them. At that moment, the doors to God's mercy are opened, and every prayer is welcomed in." Wisam was smiling, speaking half seriously, half jokingly, and gazing at the lights burning in the houses opposite the hospital as he vividly recalled his Grandmother Hafiza.

"When you see them, tell them I said hello!" Only then did Willie realize the meaning of the words that had come out of his mouth. When Wisam heard his friend's unexpected wish, he looked at him without concealing his surprise. Seeing how embarrassed Willie became, he began to laugh.

"All right, Willie. I'll be sure to tell them." Hearing Wisam's laughter, Willie could not hold back his own.

"Willie, when faced with death, you see things differently. You see life as it is, unvarnished and completely transparent. That just doesn't happen under normal circumstances.

"Life is very, very surprising. That's the opinion I now hold, at least. And it seems to me that man is even more surprising than life. After all, life is made up of people like us. There was a psychiatrist by the name of Viktor Frankl who spent five years in a German concentration camp. He saw his own family and parents murdered. In the end, he was the only member of his family to survive. After he was freed, he wrote a book titled *Man's Search for Meaning*. It's intriguing why someone who had seen such horror in his life would give his book such a title. I often remember words by Frankl, which reflect the contradictions of what it means to be human:

If I am asked, "What was the most important thing you learned in the concentration camp?" I will answer that there we saw man at his most naked, as no generation has ever before seen or beheld him. And to the question, "And the man you beheld there, who is he really?" I will answer that this man is a being with free will, who makes decisions every moment. That man retains the ability to make the final decision in any situation — the final decision is always up to him. Up to him and no one else. And if you ask, "And what decisions does that man make?" I will say that this is a being who creates gas chambers in order to kill people of his own species. However, at the same time, this is also a being who goes off to take a friend's place in those gas chambers, entering them upright, with a prayer to God on his lips and unafraid of death!

"I've read about him. He's a very interesting person."

"Willie, I've come to understand one important thing during my illness. I've realized that a human being has unusual abilities. When he is busy doing something useful and beneficial to others, he doesn't get tired. When he is near someone he loves, even in his dreams, his pain and suffering are reduced.

"We are human beings, and we want to love and be loved. All my pain recedes when I contemplate the fact that my closest family members, and even God, love me, and when I am mindful that they are waiting for me and that God has an eternal life in store for me. When I see a purpose for my life and I think about good deeds, even small ones, I completely forget that I can't leave my room or even rise from my bed. I'm not complaining about my life. In general, it is difficult to fathom what lies beyond the veil of life.

"We claim that so much is unfair. But justice, in that sense, is a concept we have created ourselves. The universe is unlike life in that it operates in accordance with completely different laws. Under those laws, justice has a different meaning. Under the system of justice in this universe, no one will be in the least mistreated. This is the truth. There is good in everything and sense in everything. This is something that's hard for us to grasp. But it's wrong to examine our fate for examples of injustice or get angry over our lot in life. I don't mind that I'm sick and have very little time left. If I hadn't fallen ill, it might have been someone else, and so let it be me." Wisam gave a weak smile. "I'm alone, with no one. No one will suffer from my absence.

"I'm always scrutinizing my life, especially the period during which I've been sick. And each time, I am persuaded that I needed this disease. That might sound strange, but it's true. Because of my illness, I've learned to view life very differently and have discerned the meaning of life. I've begun to see the world around me in its true colors. I've made sense of things that I would have never understood if I'd lived a different life. Truth, which was something I understood theoretically before, I now comprehend on a more visceral level.

"Willie, I've never dreamed about my mother since her suicide. I've dreamed about my father and had conversations with him. But I've never dreamed about my mother. In my dreams, I would ask my father how she was and why she never came to see me. But he never answered. While waking up, I thought that my mother wasn't in paradise with my father. That's why he didn't know anything about her . . . That's why he didn't say anything. This always bothered me. But something strange happened in my dream last night. This time my father wasn't alone. He said, 'Look who I brought with me!' He took my mother's hand and began ascending. It was as if my mother were climbing up a staircase from the cellar. I froze as soon as I saw her. That was the first time I had dreamed of her since she departed this world.

"I had always wondered what I would say to her, what I would ask, if she appeared in one of my dreams. But when I saw her, I was at a loss for words. I felt an emptiness inside because she was not near me. I wanted to cry but couldn't. The tears froze in my eyes. She came closer to me and stroked my hair. How I needed that. I looked at her. There were no signs of her former illness—she was beautiful, young, and smiling. Her eyes were smiling and filled with joy. As if she had not endured all those misfortunes. We didn't talk but nonetheless understood one another. Then I gave her a hug and fell deeper asleep. It was the first time in my life I had ever slept so tranquilly, without being startled or frightened.

"I likely don't have much time left, huh! My mom came for me. They're waiting for me. I'm happy, Willie. Everything has ended well. I saw them all together: my father, mother, Grandfather Badr, and Grandmother Hafiza. My mother was standing right next to my grandfather. She bent her head and answered him respectfully, just like she used to, back when times were good. The family was on friendly terms once again. Clearly God has forgiven my mother. She has been plucked from the fire. Now I also need to go—"

The doctor on duty unexpectedly came out onto the balcony, inhibiting their conversation.

"Willie, are you here? Mr. Cranston was looking for you. He asked me to remind you that you're going to a football game today."

Willie didn't feel like doing that at all. This conversation with Wisam was more enjoyable.

"Go, Willie. Don't worry! We'll continue our conversation later. I'd like to stay here a little longer, alone."

Wisam was so insistent that Willie had no choice but to agree. He said, "I'll tell the nurse to come take you back to the room in a little bit. Don't stay out here too long; you'll freeze."

Willie had a strange, leaden feeling as he left Wisam, a foreboding that he would never hear his voice again, as if he were leaving him forever. As he walked away, he felt an urge to rush back and hug Wisam and thank him for being a presence in his life and for restoring his family and loved ones to him.

Wisam had taught him how to live like a human being. He taught him a lesson about life. At a time when Willie had lost faith in people, Wisam came and restored that faith to him. Just when Willie's emotions had died, Wisam resurrected them. *Wisam brought me back to life again.*

But Willie didn't go back. He was too timid. He didn't understand what made him uncomfortable. For an instant, he thought that such an opportunity might still present itself. Willie had still not thanked Wisam for everything that he had done for him. He was always grateful to Wisam in his heart. Always. But Willie never said it out loud. He thought that if Wisam had been in Willie's place, he would never have let those loving words remain in his heart. He would have repeated them every chance he got.

Wisam once said, "Willie, the Prophet said that if you love someone, then say it. If you say 'I love you' to someone dear to you, those words will remain in his heart forever."

Willie left there in doubt, with anxiety and grief in his heart. He didn't get to see the game with Mr. Cranston. Something urgent came up that Cranston had to attend to, and Willie didn't want to go to the game alone. Halfway there he turned around and went home. All night he lay awake. He thought about his life, about the people he loved, and about the people who meant a lot to him. He thought about the strangeness of life, about the differences between people, and about death.

Why were people like himself so difficult to understand? Why did they come into this world? Why must they be faced with so many difficulties and diseases, only to then cease to exist after such sound and fury?

They either disappear or else there is a mystery here they don't know about. Sometimes it was impossible to even understand himself. Was he created this way? Maybe he was created more simply, but he complicated his own affairs and, as a result, his life.

Human beings were like an extraordinary bit of handiwork by an engineer. If death is the destruction of that achievement, then he didn't understand anything. Why paint a human being using such a palette of colors and then destroy him? Why cut everything short? His thoughts were a muddle over these questions he hadn't previously considered. Why hadn't he paid attention? Was there really anything more important than these questions? *We complicate our lives in the same way that we complicate simple answers to life's most essential questions.*

Willie tried to remember the last time he had felt the way he did that evening as he parted from Wisam. Eventually, it finally came back to him. He questioned the memory at first but was later thoroughly convinced he was right. *I felt exactly this way the last time I said good-bye to my father.* Willie would always remember that heavy feeling in his heart as the harbinger of separation.

# ON THE PATH TO ETERNITY

*The span between the first and last days of life is inconstant and unknown. Measured by its hardships, that path is long even for a child, measured by its speed – it is short, even for an old man.*

~ Lucius Annaeus Seneca

When Willie arrived at MD Anderson the next morning, he discovered that he would never again hear Wisam's sweet, wise voice with its Arabic accent. He was told that his friend was living out his final days on artificial respiration. He had been transferred to the intensive care unit. Willie missed Wisam's sweet, gentle words, but his eyes seemed to express all his feelings and thoughts. His eyes, as always, were smiling, and he looked directly at Willie. Wisam smiled. He wanted to say something but failed. His gaze made Willie quite anxious. Their discussion from the day before flashed instantly into Willie's mind. He broke out in a cold sweat. He felt a pain in his heart and, realizing that it was all over, knitted his brows to keep from crying.

Wisam wore an expression that Willie knew quite well. He understood that it was meant to convey something to him that Wisam often said: "Who better than me can feel death breathing down the back of his neck? And yet you're seemingly in a more dire predicament than I am." Willie always smiled when Wisam said that. But this time it was a sad smile.

"Everything turned out all right in the end, Willie. Don't worry about me! They're waiting for me there, and one day you, too, will join me. But for now, you need to live. And I will wait patiently for you, my dear friend." Willie knew Wisam would certainly have said that to him if his friend could speak. Willie took Wisam's hand and squeezed it gently. He saw the gratitude in Wisam's eyes.

"Do you need anything?"

Wisam shook his head. It was hard for Willie to see the shadow of death on this dear face, to see Wisam's face becoming sallower day after day. His temples were sunken because of his emaciated state, and his veins bulged. Willie wanted to burst into hot tears and pour out his heart. *Wisam, I beg you, don't leave me all alone!* At that instant, he imagined Wisam consoling him.

"Willie, I'll always be with you. In your heart . . . I'll be watching over you from afar. Like the light from a candle, I'll stay with you through any darkness. My dear friend, please don't forget what I've told you. I'm going to miss you. And I know that you will also miss me, but what can we do? Such is life . . . And life is still life, along with all its hardships, illnesses, misfortunes, and death. Life is about more than just being healthy and happy. Life is the sum of both day and night, beginning and end."

*Wisam, why didn't the holy Khidr give you life, why didn't he help you?* Willie very much wished that Khidr would touch Wisam with his resuscitating breath.

Probably if Wisam could speak, he would have said, "It is fate. And this is what is best for me. Like the child killed by Khidr, it is better that I go. And you too should acquiesce and not resist it, Willie. Under no circumstances should you protest matters when you are not wise to their inherent mystery. We create divisions when we oppose our fate."

That day, Willie remained at work long after his shift had ended, sitting at Wisam's bed. He didn't want to leave him alone. Wisam was asleep. Willie just stood there next to him, watching him. He contemplated that the events from the lives of the holy Khidr and the Prophet Musa were actually true. And those who examined this kind of truth carefully would be able to see it in their own lives. Wisam could certainly be called the Khidr of Willie's life. He entered Willie's life as it was petering out and revived him, revealing to him the true meaning of the events that happened to him. Wisam had explained that one should not resist life, but live it. *I wonder, why did Khidr help that malevolent city?* Willie could not understand the possible wisdom of his final act. Years later, when he asked a couple of Muslims this question, he realized that they didn't know either.

Midnight had long passed. The man on duty called Willie. "Your wife has phoned several times. She's worried that you're late. I didn't know you were here."

Willie called home, but to no avail. Apparently, Sarah was out looking for him. Immersed in his thoughts, he went home.

*Naturally, Khidrs did not die. And in that sense, Wisam could also never die. He was the source of Willie's rebirth. It is not possible that someone who gives life to another could cease to exist.*

# ONE MORE ANGEL

*A man must have grown old and lived
long in order to see how short life is.*

~ Arthur Schopenhauer

This is Saida. Judge Badr's house . . . A knock at the door. Jafar opens it. Uncle Said walks in, smiling. He and Jafar share a laugh and walk into the living room together. It is the eve of the holiday of Kurban. The whole family is at home, including Judge Badr. He has not gone to work. As usual, he is reading the newspapers that cover politics. The civil war in Lebanon has ended, and the Muslims have made peace with the Christians.

Havra is watching television. And Grandmother Hafiza and Asma are in the kitchen making dinner. Badr is very pleased to see Said alongside Jafar. He offers Said the chair right beside his own. When Grandmother Hafiza spots this favorite guest, she comes to greet him. How wonderful that the whole family can be together in this springtime weather. Standing to one side and observing it all, Wisam says, "Yes, everything's all right!" The family is all together and on good terms, as they always have been.

Wisam smiled with joy and felt great relief in his heart. He moved his tongue to utter the words he always used to say: *"Inna lillahi wa inna ilayhi raji'un . . ."* Surely we belong to God and to Him we shall return. After which he closed his eyes and reunited with eternity. At that instant, the equipment attached to him made the terrifying sound that indicates cardiac arrest.

That night Willie lay awake until morning. By the time dawn broke, he was already back at the hospital. Filled with apprehension, he went to the intensive care unit to see his friend. When he approached, he didn't want to believe his eyes. Wisam's bed was empty. As if no such person had ever been there. Looking at the empty bed, he felt a terrible emptiness in his heart. All of Willie's feelings and thoughts had frozen. He felt he was in a dream and couldn't understand what was happening. He hurried down to room seventeen. Wisam's bed was empty there, too.

The nurse touched his arm gently and pointed to the table by the bed. A scrap of paper and a drawing with Willie's name on it lay on the table. Wisam had given this letter to a nurse who had taken him to his room from the balcony that snowy night. He had asked her to give the letter, after his death, to Willie. The letter consisted of a single sentence: "Willie, you only need ten seconds to feel happy in life."

Feeling utterly drained, Willie sat down on his friend's empty bed. He sat, frozen, with the letter in his hand. Tears flowed from his eyes. He glanced at the letter once again and kept rereading that sentence with eyes hazy from tears, as if he were searching for the invisible words written behind it. He found and read them. These were, in fact, the words that Willie wanted to hear from his friend. Wisam lived in Willie's heart. His wide eyes, smiling face, and amiable conversations would remain with him forever. *Yes, that is just how I remember you.*

Willie asked the nurse about Wisam's final moments.

"You wouldn't believe it; his face had a smile, as usual."

These words made Willie even more emotional. Wiping away his tears, he said, "He was reunited with the ones he loved. He's finally together with them."

Willie thought life had been merciless to Wisam, although Wisam had had quite a different view of all that. Willie acknowledged that there were some happy moments in Wisam's life, but there were even more hardships. Naturally, Wisam wanted to live a longer, healthier life. He had wanted to spend time with Willie far from this city of angels. Wisam always dreamed that he and Willie might drink tea together in some beautiful, peaceful place. Willie had long wanted to show him his house, built with his own hands. He wanted Wisam to get to know his family better. *My family had a lot to learn from such a wise man, who had seen so much in life.*

Wisam was not destined to see his sister Havra's wedding. He had promised Havra that he would never abandon her the way their father and mother had. He always thought about that promise and about the fact that Havra would be alone in this foreign country, and he wondered what would happen to her after their aunt departed this world. Willie had promised his friend that, should Aunt Bayan die, he would care for Havra and not leave her on her own but would do everything possible to ensure her happiness. Willie saw this as his final duty to the friend who had restored his life to him, and he would keep that promise.

*Yes, Wisam died before he could grow old . . . Nor did he have time to create a family . . . He died early in the morning, at four o'clock this morning. His aunt said that he had also been born early in the morning. MD Anderson has witnessed the ascent of many angels to heaven. Each angel had his own destiny, his own life story. But Wisam's life was quite different.*

Willie was unable to work that day and left the hospital early. As he walked by the park to the right of the road, without thinking, he started down the steps he knew so well. The park on the right, the green bench, the sadness, the helplessness, the loneliness. All this was very familiar to Willie. Halfway down the stairs, he stopped. On the bench in front of him, he saw Wisam. He gestured to Willie and said, "Go back; don't come in here!"

Wisam's final words rang in his ears: "I've made sense of things that I would have never understood if I'd lived a different life . . . I'm happy, Willie. Everything turned out all right in the end."

*You'll always be with me, and your light will always live in my heart, Wisam.* After all that had happened, Willie knew he would never go back to his former life again. He wouldn't shut himself off. *No, if only for your sake, Wisam, I won't let what you did for me be in vain.* Willie could no longer go down to the park or sit on the green bench. He turned around and went home to his family. Once he got home, he embraced Sarah and cried.

◆  ◆  ◆

By that evening Willie couldn't take his eyes off Wisam's drawing. The drawing showed a patient, with an IV in his arm, holding a rose. The patient's arm was made by lead pencil, but the rose he was holding was a vivid red. To Willie, the drawing seemed to depict a patient living out the last days of his life and presenting someone else with a new life as a parting gift. There was an implication that beauty can be found in every sadness. Willie would never know the true meaning of that drawing because its real meaning was only known to the one who drew it. And he was an "angel" who had ascended to heaven.

There were two labels at the bottom of the picture. On one was written "From Wisam, to his friend, Willie" and on the other, "Is this city empty of people?"

Sometimes people asked Willie, "What were Wisam's last days like? How did he pass on?"

And he answered them, "Let me tell you how he lived!"

# THE RETURN

It was pouring rain in Houston the next morning. The stadium was soaking wet. The football players were all set to practice. But to avoid the rain, some players were standing under a shelter on one side of the stadium, and from there they looked out at the field. They were waiting for instructions from their coaches. There were only two coaches and a couple of players in the center of the field.

At that moment, a man with big, confident strides was heading for the football field despite the rain. It was impossible to recognize him since he was wearing a hood over his cap. Mr. Cranston, who was standing with the players and looking at the stranger's pace, was reminded of someone he knew. The man had the long arms of a basketball player but the big quad and calf muscles of a football player. He stopped before reaching the center of the field, as if remembering something, then he raised his head and looked up at the sky. His small eyes radiated confidence and hope for the future. It was destined for him after his long, difficult road in life. This was clear from the loss and sadness mixed with joy that was reflected in his eyes.

He smiled at someone. *Wisam, thank you, my dear friend. Thanks for everything! I'll never forget you!*

"Willie, you're looking for me in heaven, but I'm right here with you!" He looked in the direction of that dear voice. Wisam was sitting in the bleachers. He waved to him from afar. Nor was he alone. Beside him were Brendan and Helen. Little Thea sat in Helen's lap. Helen pointed out Thea's brother to her and smiled at Willie. Brendan also looked happy. From his expression and posture, it was quite clear that he was proud of his son. They had come to watch his game.

Cranston's voice boomed out. "Oh, my dear, Willie! You've finally accepted my offer. We're honored that you've joined our team!" Cranston, who seemed very pleased with the situation, was standing with his hands in his pockets and smiling at Willie. Then, turning to the people standing next to him, he said with a note of victory in his voice, "Gentlemen, this is the famous quarterback, Willie "Atom", whom I've told you about. It's time to put all the other teams in their place."

Willie threw one last glance at his loved ones. He smiled and waved at them. And then he ran with big, confident strides to the center of the field.

◆     ◆     ◆

"O Lord! Exalted are You; we have no knowledge except what You have taught us. Indeed, it is You who is the Knowledgeable, the Wise," said the angels, admitting their error.[11]

At that moment, an angel who had just arrived indicated the man running across the ground and asked, "How is he living?"

Another angel was about to make some answer when God Himself cried out, "Don't ask how he is living now. Ask instead how he will live and how he will ultimately leave this world."

---

[11] Al-Bagarah, 32, The Quran

So we came to the end of the trip. It was nice to visit with a companion like you. Your impression is very important to me. If my story turned out to be interesting and useful for you, please leave a review on Amazon – it will guide other readers to find and read the book. See you in the next books!